Rasmus Björn Anderson, Snorri Sturluson

The Younger Edda

also called Snorre's Edda, or the Prose Edda. An English version of the foreword -

The fooling of Gylfe, the afterword - Brage's talk, the afterword to Brage's talk, and

the important passages in the Poetical diction - Skáldskaparmál

Rasmus Björn Anderson, Snorri Sturluson

The Younger Edda
also called Snorre's Edda, or the Prose Edda. An English version of the foreword - The fooling of Gylfe, the afterword - Brage's talk, the afterword to Brage's talk, and the important passages in the Poetical diction - Skáldskaparmál

ISBN/EAN: 9783337370428

Printed in Europe, USA, Canada, Australia, Japan

Cover: Foto ©Andreas Hilbeck / pixelio.de

More available books at **www.hansebooks.com**

THE YOUNGER EDDA:

ALSO CALLED

SNORRE'S EDDA, OR THE PROSE EDDA.

AN ENGLISH VERSION OF THE FOREWORD; THE FOOLING OF
GYLFE, THE AFTERWORD; BRAGE'S TALK, THE AFTER-
WORD TO BRAGE'S TALK, AND THE IMPORTANT
PASSAGES IN THE POETICAL DICTION
(SKALDSKAPARMAL),

WITH AN

INTRODUCTION, NOTES, VOCABULARY, AND INDEX.

By RASMUS B. ANDERSON,

PROFESSOR OF THE SCANDINAVIAN LANGUAGES IN THE UNIVERSITY OF WIS-
CONSIN, AUTHOR OF "AMERICA NOT DISCOVERED BY COLUMBUS,"
"NORSE MYTHOLOGY," "DEN NORSKE MAALSAG,"
"VIKING TALES OF THE NORTH," ETC.

CHICAGO:
S. C. GRIGGS AND COMPANY.
LONDON: TRÜBNER & CO.
1880.

DONOHUE & HENNEBERRY, BINDERS, CHICAGO.

TO

HJALMAR HJORTH BOYESEN.

PREFACE.

—

In the beginning, before the heaven and the earth and the sea were created, the great abyss Ginungagap was without form and void, and the spirit of Fimbultyr moved upon the face of the deep, until the ice-cold rivers, the Elivogs, flowing from Niflheim, came in contact with the dazzling flames from Muspelheim. This was before Chaos.

And Fimbultyr said: Let the melted drops of vapor quicken into life, and the giant Ymer was born in the midst of Ginungagap. He was not a god, but the father of all the race of evil giants. This was Chaos.

And Fimbultyr said: Let Ymer be slain and let order be established. And straightway Odin and his brothers — the bright sons of Bure — gave Ymer a mortal wound, and from his body made they the universe; from his flesh, the earth; from his blood, the sea; from his bones, the rocks; from his hair, the trees; from his skull, the vaulted heavens; from his eye-brows, the bulwark called Midgard. And the gods formed man and woman in their own image of two trees, and breathed into them the breath of life. Ask and Embla became living souls, and they received a garden in Midgard as a dwelling-place for themselves and their children until the end of time. This was Cosmos.

The gods themselves dwelt in Asgard. Some of them were of the mighty Asa-race: Valfather Odin, and Frigg his Queen; Thor, the master of Mjolner; Balder, the good; the one-handed Tyr; Brage, the song-smith. Idun having the youth-giving apples, and Heimdal, the watcher of Asgard. Others were mild and gentle vans: Njord, Frey, and Freyja, the goddess of love; but in the midst of Asgard in daily intercourse with the gods, the serpent Loke, the friend of the giants, winded his slimy coils.

To these gods our Teutonic ancestors offered sacrifices, to them prayers ascended, and from them came such blessings as each god found it proper to bestow. Most of all were these gods worshiped on the battle-field, for *there* was the home of the Teuton. There he lived and there he hoped some day to die; for if the norns, the weavers of fate, permitted him to fall sword in hand, then would he not descend to the shades of Hel, but be carried in valkyrian arms up to Valhal, where a new life would be granted unto him, or better, where he would continue his earthly life in intercourse with the gods.

Happy gatherings at the banquet, where the flowing mead-horn was passed freely round, and where words of wisdom and wit abounded, or martial games with sharp swords and spears, were the delight of the asas. Under the ash Ygdrasil they met in council, and if they ever appeared outside of the walls of Asgard, it was to go on errands of love, or to make war on the giants, their enemies from the beginning. Especially did Thor seldom sit still when he heard rumors of giants; with his heavy hammer, Mjolner, he slew Hrungner and the Midgard-serpent, gave Thrym and all that race of giants bloody bridal-gifts in Freyja's garments, and frightened the juggler Loke, of Utgard, who had to resort to his black art for safety. Thus lived the gods in heaven very much like their worshipers on earth, excepting that Idun's apples ever preserved them fresh and youthful.

But Loke, the serpent, was in the midst of them. Frigg's heart was filled with gloomy forebodings in regard to Balder, her beloved son, and her mind could not find rest until all things that could harm him had sworn not to injure Balder. Now they had nothing to fear for the best god, and with perfect abandon and security they themselves made him serve as a mark, and hurled darts, stones and other weapons at him, whom nothing could scathe. But the serpent Loke was more subtle than any one within or without Asgard, whom Fimbultyr had made; and he came to Hoder, the blind god, put the tender mistletoe in his hand and directed his arm, so that Balder sank from the joys of Valhal down into the abodes of pale Hel, and did not return. Loke is bound and tortured, but innocence has departed from Asgard; among men there are bloody wars; brothers slay brothers; sensual sins grow huge; perjury has taken the place of truth. The elements themselves become discordant, and then comes the great Fimbul-winter, with its howling storms and terrible snow, that darkens the air and takes all gladness from the sun.

The world's last day approaches. All bonds and fetters that bound the forces of heaven and earth together are severed, and the powers of good and of evil are brought together in an internecine feud. Loke advances with the Fenris-wolf and the Midgard-serpent, his own children, with all the hosts of the giants, and with Surt, who flings fire and flame over the world. Odin advances with all the asas and all the blessed einherjes. They meet, contend, and fall. The wolf swallows Odin, but Vidar, the Silent, sets his foot upon the monster's lower jaw, he seizes the other with his hand, and thus rends him till he dies. Frey encounters Surt, and terrible blows are given ere Frey falls. Heimdal and Loke fight and kill each other, and so do Tyr and the dog Garm from the Gnipa Cave. Asa-Thor fells the Midgard-serpent with his Mjolner, but he retreats only nine paces when he himself falls dead, suffocated by the serpent's venom. Then smoke wreathes up around the ash Ygdrasil, the high flames play against the heavens, the graves of the gods, of the giants and of men are swallowed up by the sea, and the end has come. This is Ragnarok, the twilight of the gods.

But the radiant dawn follows the night. The earth, completely green, rises again from the sea, and where the mews have but just been rocking on restless waves, rich fields unplowed and unsown, now wave their golden harvests before the gentle breezes. The asas awake to a new life, Balder is with them again. Then comes the mighty Fimbultyr, the god who is from everlasting to everlasting; the god whom the Edda skald dared not name. The god of gods comes to the asas. He comes to the great judgment and gathers all the good into Gimle to dwell there forever, and evermore delights enjoy; but the perjurers and murderers and adulterers he sends to Nastrand, that terrible hall, to be torn by Nidhug until they are purged from their wickedness. This is Regeneration.

These are the outlines of the Teutonic religion. Such were the doctrines established by Odin among our ancestors. Thus do we find it recorded in the Eddas of Iceland.

The present volume contains all of the Younger Edda that can possibly be of any importance to English readers. In fact, it gives more than has ever before been presented in any translation into English, German or any of the modern Scandinavian tongues.

We would recommend our readers to omit the Forewords and Afterwords until they have perused the Fooling of Gylfe and Brage's Speech. The Forewords and Afterwords, it will readily be seen, are written by a later and less skillful hand, and we should be sorry to have anyone lay the book aside and lose the pleasure of reading Snorre's and Olaf's charming work, because he became disgusted with what seemed to him mere silly twaddle. And yet these Forewords and Afterwords become interesting enough when taken up in connection with a study of the historical anthropomorphized Odin. With a view of giving a pretty complete outline of the founder of the Teutonic race we have in our notes given all the Heimskringla sketch of the Black Sea Odin. We have done this, not only on account of the material it furnishes as the groundwork of a Teutonic epic, which we trust the muses will ere long direct some one to write, but also on account of the vivid picture it gives of Teutonic life as shaped and controlled by the Odinic faith.

All the poems quoted in the Younger Edda have in this edition been traced back to their sources in the Elder Edda and elsewhere.

Where the notes seem to the reader insufficient, we must refer him to our Norse Mythology, where he will, we trust, find much of the additional information he may desire.

Well aware that our work has many imperfections, and begging our readers to deal generously with our shortcomings, we send the book out into the world with the hope that it may aid some young son or daughter of Odin to find his way to the fountains of Urd and Mimer and to Idun's rejuvenating apples. The son must not squander, but husband wisely, what his father has accumulated. The race must cherish and hold fast and add to the thought that the past has bequeathed to it. Thus does it grow greater and richer with each new generation. The past is the mirror that reflects the future.

R. B. ANDERSON.

University of Wisconsin,
Madison, Wis., *September, 1879.*

CONTENTS.

THE FOOLING OF GYLFE.

CHAPTER I.

CHAPTER II.

CHAPTER III.

CHAPTER IV.

CHAPTER V.

CHAPTER VI.

CHAPTER VII.

CHAPTER VIII.

CHAPTER IX.

CHAPTER X.

CHAPTER XI.

CHAPTER XII.

CHAPTER XIII.

CHAPTER XIV.

CHAPTER XV.

CHAPTER XVI.

CHAPTER XVII.

BRAGE'S TALK.

CHAPTER I.

CHAPTER II.

CHAPTER III.

CHAPTER IV.

EXTRACTS FROM THE POETICAL DICTION.

CONTENTS.

NOTES.

THE YOUNGER EDDA.

INTRODUCTION.

THE records of our Teutonic past have hitherto received but slight attention from the English-speaking branch of the great world-ash Ygdrasil. This indifference is the more deplorable, since a knowledge of our heroic forefathers would naturally operate as a most powerful means of keeping alive among us, and our posterity, that spirit of courage, enterprise and independence for which the old Teutons were so distinguished.

The religion of our ancestors forms an important chapter in the history of the childhood of our race, and this fact has induced us to offer the public an English translation of the Eddas. The purely mythological portion of the Elder Edda was translated and published by A. S. Cottle, in Bristol, in 1797, and the whole work was translated by Benjamin Thorpe, and published in London in 1866. Both these works are now out of print. Of the Younger Edda we have likewise had two translations into English,—the first by Dasent in 1842, the second by Blackwell, in his edition of Mallet's Northern Antiquities, in 1847. The former has long been out of print, the latter is a poor imitation of Dasent's. Both of them are very incomplete. These four books constitute all the Edda literature we have had in the English language, excepting, of course, single lays and chapters translated by Gray, Henderson, W. Taylor, Herbert, Jamieson, Pigott, William and Mary Howitt, and others.

The Younger Edda (also called Snorre's Edda, or the Prose Edda), of which we now have the pleasure of presenting our readers an English version, contains, as usually published in the original, the following divisions:

1. The Foreword.
2. Gylfaginning (The Fooling of Gylfe).
3. The Afterword to Gylfaginning.
4. Brage's Speech.
5. The Afterword.
6. Skaldskaparmal (a collection of poetic paraphrases, and denominations in Skaldic language without paraphrases).
7. Hattatal (an enumeration of metres; a sort of Clavis Metrica).

In some editions there are also found six additional chapters on the alphabet, grammar, figures of speech, etc.

There are three important parchment manuscripts of the Younger Edda, viz:

1. *Codex Regius*, the so-called King's Book. This was presented to the Royal Library in Copenhagen, by Bishop Brynjulf Sveinsson, in the year 1640, where it is still kept.

2. *Codex Wormianus.* This is found in the University Library in Copenhagen, in the Arne Magnæan collection. It takes its name from Professor Ole Worm [died 1654], to whom it was presented by the learned Arngrim Jonsson. Christian Worm, the grandson of Ole Worm, and Bishop of Seeland [died 1737], afterward presented it to Arne Magnusson.

3. *Codex Upsaliensis.* This is preserved in the Upsala University Library. Like the other two, it was found in Iceland, where it was given to Jon Rugmann. Later it fell into the hands of Count Magnus Gabriel de la Gardie, who in the year 1669 presented it to the Upsala University. Besides these three chief documents, there exist four fragmentary parchments, and a large number of paper manuscripts.

The first printed edition of the Younger Edda, in the original, is the celebrated "Edda Islandorum," published by Peter Johannes Resen, in Copenhagen, in the year 1665. It contains a translation into Latin, made partly by Resen himself, and partly also by Magnus Olafsson, Stephan Olafsson and Thormod Torfason.

Not until eighty years later, that is in 1746, did

the second edition of the Younger Edda appear in Upsala under the auspices of Johannes Goransson. This was printed from the Codex Upsaliensis.

In the present century we find a third edition by Rasmus Rask, published in Stockholm in 1818. This is very complete and critical. The fourth edition was issued by Sveinbjorn Egilsson, in Reykjavik, 1849; the fifth by the Arne-Magnæan Commission in Copenhagen, 1852.* All these five editions have long been out of print, and in place of them we have a sixth edition by Thorleif Jonsson (Copenhagen, 1875), and a seventh by Ernst Wilkin (Paderborn, 1877). Both of these, and especially the latter, are thoroughly critical and reliable.

Of translations, we must mention in addition to those into English by Dasent and Blackwell, R. Nyerup's translation into Danish (Copenhagen, 1808); Karl Simrock's into German (Stuttgart and Tübingen, 1851); and Fr. Bergmann's into French (Paris, 1871). Among the chief authorities to be consulted in the study of the Younger Edda may be named, in addition to those already mentioned, Fr. Dietrich, Th. Mobius, Fr. Pfeiffer, Ludw. Ettmuller, K. Hildebrand, Ludw. Uhland, P E. Muller, Adolf Holzmann, Sophus Bugge, P. A. Munch and Rudolph Keyser. For the material in our introduction and notes, we are chiefly

* The third volume of this work has not yet appeared.

indebted to Simrock, Wilkin and Keyser. While we have had no opportunity of making original researches, the published works have been carefully studied, and all we claim for our work is, that it shall contain the results of the latest and most thorough investigations by scholars who live nearer the fountains of Urd and Mimer than do we. Our translations are made from Egilsson's, Jonsson's and Wilkins' editions of the original. We have not translated any of the Hattatal, and only the narrative part of Skaldskaparmal, and yet our version contains more of the Younger Edda than any English, German, French or Danish translation that has hitherto been published. The parts omitted cannot possibly be of any interest to any one who cannot read them in the original. All the paraphrases of the asas and asynjes, of the world, the earth, the sea, the sun, the wind, fire, summer, man, woman, gold, of war, arms, of a ship, emperor, king, ruler, etc., are of interest only as they help to explain passages of Old Norse poems. The same is true of the enumeration of metres, which contains a number of epithets and metaphors used by the scalds, illustrated by specimens of their poetry, and also by a poem of Snorre Sturleson, written in one hundred different metres.

There has been a great deal of learned discussion in regard to the authorship of the Younger

Edda. Readers specially interested in this knotty subject we must refer to Wilkins' elaborate treatise, Untersuchungen zur Snorra Edda (Paderborn, 1878), and to P. E. Muller's, Die Æchtheit der Asalehre (Copenhagen, 1811).

Two celebrated names that without doubt are intimately connected with the work are Snorre Sturleson and Olaf Thordsson Hvitaskald. Both of these are conspicuous, not only in the literary, but also in the political history of Iceland.

Snorre Sturleson* was born in Iceland in the year 1178. Three years old, he came to the house of the distinguished chief, Jon Loptsson, at Odde, a grandson of Sæmund the Wise, the reputed collector of the Elder Edda, where he appears to have remained until Jon Loptsson's death, in the year 1197. Soon afterward Snorre married into a wealthy family, and in a short time he became one of the most distinguished leaders in Iceland. He was several times elected chief magistrate, and no man in the land was his equal in riches and prominence. He and his two elder brothers, Thord and Sighvat, who were but little inferior to him in wealth and power, were at one time well-nigh supreme in Iceland, and Snorre sometimes appeared at the Althing at Thingvols accompanied by from eight hundred to nine hundred armed men.

* Keyser.

Snorre and his brothers did not only have bitter feuds with other families, but a deadly hatred also arose between themselves, making their lives a perpetual warfare. Snorre was shrewd as a politician and magistrate, and eminent as an orator and skald, but his passions were mean, and many of his ways were crooked. He was both ambitious and avaricious. He is said to have been the first Icelander who laid plans to subjugate his fatherland to Norway, and in this connection is supposed to have expected to become a jarl under the king of Norway. In this effort he found himself outwitted by his brother's son, Sturle Thordsson, and thus he came into hostile relations with the latter. In this feud Snorre was defeated, but when Sturle shortly after fell in a battle against his foes, Snorre's star of hope rose again, and he began to occupy himself with far-reaching, ambitious plans. He had been for the first time in Norway during the years 1218-1220, and had been well received by King Hakon, and especially by Jarl Skule, who was then the most influential man in the country. In the year 1237 Snorre visited Norway again, and entered, as it is believed. into treasonable conspiracies with Jarl Skule. In 1239 he left Norway against the wishes of King Hakon, whom he owed obedience, and thereby incurred the king's greatest displeasure. When King Hakon, in

1240, had crushed Skule's rebellion and annihilated this dangerous opponent, it became Snorre's turn to feel the effects of the king's wrath. At the instigation of King Hakon, several chiefs of Iceland united themselves against Snorre and murdered him at Reykholt, where ruins of his splendid mansion are still to be seen. This event took place on the 22d of September, 1241, and Snorre Sturleson was then sixty-three years old. Snorre was Iceland's most distinguished skald and sagaman. As a writer of history he deserves to be compared with Herodotos or Thukydides. His Heimskringla, embracing an elaborate history of the kings of Norway, is famous throughout the civilized world, and Emerson calls it the Iliad and Odyssey of our race. An English translation of this work was published by Samuel Laing, in London, in 1844. Carlyle's Early Kings of Norway (London, 1875) was inspired by the Heimskringla.

Olaf Thordsson, surnamed Hvitaskald,* to distinguish him from his contemporary, Olaf Svartaskald,† was a son of Snorre's brother. Though not as prominent and influential as his uncle, he took an active part in all the troubles of his native island during the first half of the thirteenth century. He visited Norway in 1236, whence he went to Denmark, where he was a guest at the

* White Skald.   † Black Skald.

court of King Valdemar, and is said to have enjoyed great esteem. In 1240 we find him again in Norway, where he espoused the cause of King Hakon against Skule. On his return to Iceland he served four years as chief magistrate of the island. His death occurred in the year 1259, and he is numbered among the great skalds of Iceland.

Snorre Sturleson and Olaf Hvitaskald are the two names to whom the authorship of the Younger Edda has generally been attributed, and the work is by many, even to this day, called Snorra Edda — that is, Snorre's Edda. We do not propose to enter into any elaborate discussion of this complicated subject, but we will state briefly the reasons given by Keyser and others for believing that these men had a hand in preparing the Prose Edda. In the first place, we find that the writer of the grammatical and rhetorical part of the Younger Edda distinctly mentions Snorre as author of Hattatal (the Clavis Metrica), and not only of the poem itself, but also of the treatise in prose. In the second place, the Arne Magnæan parchment manuscript, which dates back to the close of the thirteenth or beginning of the fourteenth century, has the following note prefaced to the Skaldskaparmal. "Here ends that part of the book which Olaf Thordsson put together, and now begins Skaldskaparmal and the Kenningar,

according to that which has been found in the
lays of the chief skalds, and which Snorre afterward suffered to be brought together." In the
third place, the Upsala manuscript of the Younger
Edda, which is known with certainty to have
been written in the beginning of the fourteenth
century, contains this preface, written with the
same hand as the body of the work: "This book
hight Edda. Snorre has compiled it in the manner in which it is arranged: first, in regard to
the asas and Ymer, then Skaldskaparmal and the
denominations of many things, and finally that
Hattatal, which Snorre composed about King Hakon and Duke Skule." In the fourth place, there
is a passage in the so-called Annales Breviores,
supposed to have been written about the year
1400. The passage relates to the year 1241, and
reads thus: "Snorre Sturleson died at Reykholt.
He was a wise and very learned man, a great
chief and shrewd. He was the first man in this
land who brought property into the hands of the
king (the king of Norway). He compiled Edda
and many other learned historical works and
Icelandic sagas. He was murdered at Reykholt
by Jarl Gissur's men."

It seems, then, that there is no room for any
doubt that these two men have had a share in
the authorship of the Younger Edda. How great
a share each has had is another and more difficult

problem to solve.   Rudolf Keyser's opinion is (and we know no higher authority on the subject), that Snorre is the author, though not in so strict a sense as we now use the word, of Gyl-faginning, Brage's Speech, Skaldskaparmal and Hattatal. This part of the Younger Edda may thus be said to date back to the year 1230, though the material out of which the mythological system is constructed is of course much older. We find it in the ancient Vala's Prophecy, of the Elder Edda, a poem that breathes in every line the purest asa-faith, and is, without the least doubt, much older than the introduction of christianity in the north, or the discovery and settlement of Iceland. It is not improbable that the religious system of the Odinic religion had assumed a permanent prose form in the memories of the people long before the time of Snorre, and that he merely was the means of having it committed to writing almost without verbal change.

Olaf Thordsson is unmistakably the author of the grammatical and rhetorical portion of the Younger Edda, and its date can therefore safely be put at about 1250. The author of the treatise on the alphabet is not known, but Professor Keyser thinks it must have been written, its first chapter, about the year 1150, and its second chapter about the year 1200. The forewords and afterwords are evidently also from another pen.

Their author is unknown, but they are thought to have been written about the year 1300. To sum up, then, we arrive at this conclusion: The mythological material of the Younger Edda is as old as the Teutonic race. Parts of it are written by authors unknown to fame. A small portion is the work of Olaf Thordsson. The most important portion is written, or perhaps better, compiled, by Snorre Sturleson, and the whole is finally edited and furnished with forewords and afterwords, early in the fourteenth century,— according to Keyser, about 1320–1330.

About the name Edda there has also been much learned discussion. Some have suggested that it may be a mutilated form of the word Odde, the home of Sæmund the Wise, who was long supposed to be the compiler of the Elder Edda. In this connection, it has been argued that possibly Sæmund had begun the writing of the Younger Edda, too. Others derive the word from *óðr* (mind, soul), which in poetical usage also means song, poetry. Others, again, connect Edda with the Sanscrit word Veda, which is supposed to mean knowledge. Finally, others adopt the meaning which the word has where it is actually used in the Elder Edda, and where it means great-grandmother. Vigfusson adopts this definition, and it is certainly both scientific and poetical. What can be more beautiful than the idea that our great ancestress teaches her descendants the sacred traditions, the concentrated wisdom, of the race? To sum up, then, we say the Younger, or Prose, or Snorre's Edda has been produced at different times by various hands, and the object of its authors has been to produce a manual for the skalds. In addition to the forewords and afterwords, it contains two books, one greater (Gyl-faginning) and one lesser (Brage's Speech), giving a tolerably full account of Norse mythology. Then follows Skaldskaparmal, wherein is an analysis of the various circumlocutions practiced by the skalds, all illustrated by copious quotations from the poets. How much of these three parts is written by Snorre is not certain, but on the other hand, there is no doubt that he is the author of Hattatal (Clavis Metrica), which gives an enumeration of metres. To these four treatises are added four chapters on grammar and rhetoric. The writer of the oldest grammatical treatise is thought to be one Thorodd Runemaster, who lived in the middle of the twelfth century; and the third treatise is evidently written by Olaf Thordsson Hvitaskald, the nephew of Snorre, a scholar who spent some time at the court of the Danish king, Valdemar the Victorious. The Younger Edda contains the systematized theogony and cosmogony of our forefathers, while the Elder Edda presents the Odinic faith in a series of lays or rhapsodies. The Elder Edda is poetry, while the Younger Edda is mainly prose. The Younger Edda may in one sense be regarded as the sequel or commentary of the Elder Edda. Both complement each other, and both must be studied in connection with the sagas and all the Teutonic traditions and folk-lore in order to get a comprehensive idea of the asa-faith. The two Eddas constitute, as it were, the Odinic Bible. The Elder Edda is the Old Testament, the Younger Edda the New. Like the Old Testament, the Elder Edda is in poetry. It is prophetic and enigmatical. Like the New Testament, the Younger Edda is in prose; it is lucid, and gives a clue to the obscure passages in the Elder Edda. Nay, in many respects do the two Eddas correspond with the two Testaments of the Christian Bible.

It is a deplorable fact that the religion of our forefathers seems to be but little cared for in this country. The mythologies of other nations every student manifests an interest for. He reads with the greatest zeal all the legends of Rome and Greece, of India and China. He is familiar with every room in the labyrinth of Crete, while when he is introduced to the shining halls of Valhal and Gladsheim he gropes his way like a blind man. He does not know that Idun, with her beautiful apples, might, if applied to, render even greater services than Ariadne with her wonderful thread. When we inquire whom Tuesday and Wednesday and Thursday and Friday are named after, and press questions in reference to Tyr, Odin, Thor and Freyja, we get at best but a wise and knowing look. Are we, then, as a nation, like the ancient Jews, and do we bend the knee before the gods of foreign nations and forsake the altars of our own gods? What if we then should suffer the fate of that unhappy people — be scattered over all the world and lose our fatherland? In these Eddas our fathers have bequeathed unto us all their profoundest, all their sublimest, all their best thought. They are the concentrated result of their greatest intellectual and spiritual effort, and it behooves us to cherish this treasure and make it the fountain at which the whole American branch of the Ygdrasil ash may imbibe a united national sentiment. It is not enough to brush the dust off these gods and goddesses of our ancestors and put them up on pedestals as ornaments in our museums and libraries. These coins of the past are not to be laid away in numismatic collections. The grandson must use what he has inherited from his grandfather. If the coin is not intelligible, then it will have to be sent to the mint and stamped anew, in order that it may circulate freely. Our ancestral deities want a place in our hearts and in our songs.

On the European continent and in England the zeal of the priests in propagating christianity was so great that they sought to root out every trace of the asa-faith. They left but unintelligible fragments of the heathen religious structure. Our gods and goddesses and heroes were consigned to oblivion, and all knowledge of the Odinic religion and of the Niblung-story would have been well nigh totally obliterated had not a more lucky star hovered over the destinies of Iceland. In this remotest corner of the world the ancestral spirit was preserved like the glowing embers of Hekla beneath the snow and ice of the glacier. From the farthest Thule the spirit of our fathers rises and shines like an aurora over all Teutondom. It was in the year 860 that Iceland was discovered. In 874 the Teutonic spirit fled thither for refuge from tyranny. Here a government based on the principles of old Teutonic liberty was established. From here went forth daring vikings, who discovered Greenland and Vinland, and showed Columbus the way to America. From here the courts of Norway, Sweden, Denmark, England and Germany were supplied with skalds to sing their praises. Here was put in writing the laws and sagas that give us a clue to the form of old Teutonic institutions. Here was preserved the Old Norse language, and in it a record of the customs, the institutions and the religion of our fathers. Its literature does not belong to that island alone,—it belongs to the whole Teutonic race! Iceland is for the Teutons what Greece and Rome are for the south of Europe, and she accomplished her mission with no less efficiency and success. Cato the Elder used to end all his speeches with these words: "*Præterea censeo Carthaginem esse delendam.*" In these days, when so many worship at the shrine of Romanism, we think it perfectly just to adopt Cato's sentence in this form: *Præterea censeo Romam esse delendam.*

FOREWORD.

1. In the beginning Almighty God created heaven and earth, and all things that belong to them, and last he made two human beings, from whom the races are descended (Adam and Eve), and their children multiplied and spread over all the world. But in the course of time men became unequal; some were good and right-believing, but many more turned them after the lusts of the world and heeded not God's laws; and for this reason God drowned the world in the flood, and all that was quick in the world, except those who were in the ark with Noah. After the flood of Noah there lived eight men, who inhabited the world, and from them the races are descended; and now, as before, they increased and filled the world, and there were very many men who loved to covet wealth and power, but turned away from obedience to God, and so much did they do this that they would not name God. And who could then tell their sons of the wonderful works of God? So it came to pass that they lost God's name; and in the wide world the man was not to be found who could tell of his

Maker. But, nevertheless, God gave them earthly gifts, wealth and happiness, that should be with them in the world; he also shared wisdom among them, so that they understood all earthly things, and all kinds that might be seen in the air and on the earth. This they thought upon, and wondered at, how it could come to pass that the earth and the beasts and the birds had the same nature in some things but still were unlike in manners.

One evidence of this nature was that the earth might be dug into upon high mountain-peaks and water would spring up there, and it was not necessary to dig deeper for water there than in deep dales; thus, also, in beasts and birds it is no farther to the blood in the head than in the feet. Another proof of this nature is, that every year there grow on the earth grass and flowers, and the same year it falls and withers; thus, also, on beasts and birds do hair and feathers grow and fall off each year. The third nature of the earth is, that when it is opened and dug into, then grass grows on the mould which is uppermost on the earth. Rocks and stones they explained to correspond to the teeth and bones of living things. From these things they judged that the earth must be quick and must have life in some way, and they knew that it was of a wonderfully great age and of a mighty nature. It nourished all that was quick and took to itself all that died. On this account they gave it a name, and numbered their ancestors back to it. This they also learned from their old kinsmen, that when many hundred winters were numbered, the course of the heavenly bodies was uneven; some had a longer course than others. From such things they suspected that some one must be the ruler of the heavenly bodies who could stay their course at his own will, and he must be strong and mighty; and of him they thought that, if he ruled the prime elements, he must also have been before the heavenly bodies, and they saw that, if he ruled the course of the heavenly bodies, he must rule the sunshine, and the dew of the heavens, and the products of the earth that follow them; and thus, also, the winds of the air and therewith the storms of the sea. They knew not where his realm was, but they believed that he ruled over all things on the earth and in the air, over the heavens and the heavenly bodies, the seas and the weather. But in order that these things might be better told and remembered, they gave him the same name with themselves, and this belief has been changed in many ways, as the peoples have been separated and the tongues have been divided.

2. In his old age Noah shared the world with his sons: for Ham he intended the western region, for Japheth the northern region, but for

Shem the southern region, with those parts which
will hereafter be marked out in the division of
the earth into three parts. In the time that the
sons of these men were in the world, then increased forthwith the desire for riches and power,
from the fact that they knew many crafts that
had not been discovered before, and each one
was exalted with his own handiwork; and so far
did they carry their pride, that the Africans,
descended from Ham, harried in that part of the
world which the offspring of Shem, their kinsman, inhabited. And when they had conquered
them, the world seemed to them too small, and
they smithied a tower with tile and stone, which
they meant should reach to heaven, on the plain
called Sennar. And when this building was so
far advanced that it extended above the air, and
they were no less eager to continue the work,
and when God saw how their pride waxed high,
then he sees that he will have to strike it down
in some way. And the same God, who is almighty, and who might have struck down all
their work in the twinkling of an eye, and made
themselves turn into dust, still preferred to frus-
trate their purpose by making them realize their
own littleness, in that none of them should understand what the other talked; and thus no one
knew what the other commanded, and one broke
what the other wished to build up, until they came

to strife among themselves, and therewith was frus-
trated, in the beginning, their purpose of building
a tower. And he who was foremost, hight Zoroaster, he laughed before he wept when he came
into the world; but the master-smiths were seventy-two, and so many tongues have spread over
the world since the giants were dispersed over
the land, and the nations became numerous. In
this same place was built the most famous city,
which took its name from the tower, and was
called Babylon. And when the confusion of
tongues had taken place, then increased the names
of men and of other things, and this same Zoroaster had many names; and although he understood that his pride was laid low by the said
building, still he worked his way unto worldly
power, and had himself chosen king over many
peoples of the Assyrians. From him arose the
error of idolatry; and when he was worshiped
he was called Baal; we call him Bel; he also
had many other names. But as the names increased in number, so was truth lost; and from
this first error every following man worshiped
his head-master, beasts or birds, the air and the
heavenly bodies, and various lifeless things, until
the error at length spread over the whole world;
and so carefully did they lose the truth that no
one knew his maker, excepting those men alone
who spoke the Hebrew tongue, — that which

flourished before the building of the tower,— and still they did not lose the bodily endowments that were given them, and therefore they judged of all things with earthly understanding, for spiritual wisdom was not given unto them. They deemed that all things were smithied of some one material.

3. The world was divided into three parts, one from the south, westward to the Mediterranean Sea, which part was called Africa; but the southern portion of this part is hot and scorched by the sun. The second part, from the west and to the north and to the sea, is that called Europe, or Enea. The northern portion of this is cold, so that grass grows not, nor can anyone dwell there. From the north around the east region, and all to the south, that is called Asia. In that part of the world is all beauty and pomp, and wealth of the earth's products, gold and precious stones. There is also the mid-world, and as the earth there is fairer and of a better quality than elsewhere, so are also the people there most richly endowed with all gifts, with wisdom and strength, with beauty and with all knowledge.

4. Near the middle of the world was built the house and inn, the most famous that has been made, which was called Troy, in the land which we call Turkey. This city was built much larger than others, with more skill in many ways, at

great expense, and with such means as were at hand. There were twelve kingdoms and one over-king, and many lands and nations belonged to each kingdom; there were in the city twelve chief languages.* Their chiefs have surpassed all men who have been in the world in all heroic things. No scholar who has ever told of these things has ever disputed this fact, and for this reason, that all rulers of the north region trace their ancestors back thither, and place in the number of the gods all who were rulers of the city. Especially do they place Priamos himself in the stead of Odin; nor must that be called wonderful, for Priamos was sprung from Saturn, him whom the north region for a long time believed to be God him-self.

5. This Saturn grew up in that island in Greece which hight Crete. He was greater and stronger and fairer than other men. As in other natural endowments, so he excelled all men in wisdom. He invented many crafts which had not before been discovered. He was also so great in the art of magic that he was certain about things that had not yet come to pass. He found, too, that red thing in the earth from which he smelted gold, and from such things he soon became very mighty. He also foretold har-

* Dasent translates "hövuðtungur" (chief or head tongues) with "lords," which is certainly an error.

vests and many other secret things, and for such,
and many other deeds, he was chosen chief of the
island.　And when he had ruled it a short time,
then there speedily enough became a great abundance of all things.　No money circulated excepting gold coins, so plentiful was this metal; and
though there was famine in other lands, the crops
never failed in Crete, so that people might seek
there all the things which they needed to have.
And from this and many other secret gifts of
power that he had, men believed him to be God,
and from him arose another error among the
Cretans and Macedonians like the one before
mentioned among the Assyrians and Chaldeans
from Zoroaster.　And when Saturn finds how
great strength the people think they have in
him, he calls himself God, and says that he rules
heaven and earth and all things.

6. Once he went to Greece in a ship, for there
was a king's daughter on whom he had set his
heart.　He won her love in this way, that one
day when she was out with her maid-servants, he
took upon himself the likeness of a bull, and lay
before her in the wood, and so fair was he that
the hue of gold was on every hair; and when
the king's daughter saw him she patted his lips.
He sprang up and threw off the bull's likeness
and took her into his arms and bore her to the
ship and took her to Crete.　But his wife, Juno,

found this out, so he turned her (the king's daughter) into the likeness of a heifer and sent her east to the arms of the great river (that is, of the Nile, to the Nile country), and let the thrall, who hight Argulos, take care of her. She was there twelve months before he changed her shape again. Many things did he do like this, or even more wonderful. He had three sons: one hight Jupiter, another Neptune, the third Pluto. They were all men of the greatest accomplishments, and Jupiter was by far the greatest; he was a warrior and won many kingdoms; he was also crafty like his father, and took upon himself the likeness of many animals, and thus he accom·plished many things which are impossible for mankind; and on account of this, and other things, he was held in awe by all nations. Therefore Jupiter is put in the place of Thor, since all evil wights fear him.

7. Saturn had built in Crete seventy-two burgs, and when he thought himself firmly established in his kingdom, he shared it with his sons, whom he set up with himself as gods; and to Jupiter he gave the realm of heaven; to Neptune, the realm of the earth, and to Pluto, hell; and this last seemed to him the worst to manage, and there·fore he gave to him his dog, the one whom he called Cerberos, to guard hell. This Cerberos, the Greeks say, Herakles dragged out of hell and

upon earth. And although Saturn had given the realm of heaven to Jupiter, the latter nevertheless desired to possess the realm of the earth, and so he harried his father's kingdom, and it is said that he had him taken and emasculated, and for such great achievements he declared himself to be god, and the Macedonians say that he had the members taken and cast into the sea, and therefore they believed for ages that therefrom had come a woman; her they called Venus, and numbered among the gods, and she has in all ages since been called goddess of love, for they believed she was able to turn the hearts of all men and women to love. When Saturn was emasculated by Jupiter, his son, he fled from the east out of Crete and west into Italy. There dwelt at that time such people as did not work, and lived on acorns and grass, and lay in caves or holes in the earth. And when Saturn came there he changed his name and called himself Njord, for the reason that he thought that Jupiter, his son, might afterward seek him out. He was the first there to teach men to plow and plant vineyards. There the soil was good and fresh, and it soon produced heavy crops. He was made chief and thus he got possession of all the realms there and built many burgs.

8. Jupiter, his son, had many sons, from whom races have descended; his son was Dardanos, his

son Herikon, his son Tros, his son Ilos, his son Laomedon, the father of the chief king Priamos. Priamos had many sons; one of them was Hektor, who was the most famous of all men in the world for strength, and stature and accomplishments, and for all manly deeds of a knightly kind; and it is found written that when the Greeks and all the strength of the north and east regions fought with the Trojans, they would never have become victors had not the Greeks invoked the gods; and it is also stated that no human strength would conquer them unless they were betrayed by their own men, which afterward was done. And from their fame men that came after gave themselves titles, and especially was this done by the Romans, who were the most famous in many things after their days; and it is said that, when Rome was built, the Romans adapted their customs and laws as nearly as possible to those of the Trojans, their forefathers. And so much power accompanied these men for many ages after, that when Pompey, a Roman chieftain, harried in the east region, Odin fled out of Asia and hither to the north country, and then he gave to himself and his men their names, and said that Priamos had hight Odin and his queen Frigg, and from this the realm afterward took its name and was called Frigia where the burg stood. And whether Odin said this of himself out of pride, or that it was wrought by the changing of tongues; nevertheless many wise men have regarded it a true saying, and for a long time after every man who was a great chieftain followed his example.

9. A king in Troy hight Munon or Mennon, his wife was a daughter of the head-king Priamos and hight Troan; they had a son who hight Tror, him we call Thor. He was fostered in Thrace by the duke, who is called Loricos. But when he was ten winters old he took his father's weapons. So fair of face was he, when he stood by other men, as when ivory is set in oak; his hair was fairer than gold. When he was twelve winters old he had full strength; then he lifted from the ground ten bear skins all at once, and then he slew Loricos, the duke, his foster-father and his wife, Lora or Glora, and took possession of Thrace; this we call Thrud-heim. Then he visited many lands and knew the countries of the world, and conquered single-handed all the berserks and all the giants, and one very big dragon and many beasts. In the north region he found that prophetess who hight Sibyl, whom we call Sif, and married her. None can tell the genealogy of Sif; she was the fairest of all women, her hair was like gold. Their son was Loride (Hloride), who was like his father; his son was Henrede; his son Vingethor (Ving-

thor); his son Vingener (Vingner); his son Moda (Mode); his son Magi (Magne); his son Kesfet; his son Bedvig; his son Atra, whom we call Annan; his son Itrman; his son Heremod (Hermod); his son Skjaldun, whom we call Skjold; his son Bjaf, whom we call Bjar; his son Jat; his son Gudolf, his son Fjarlaf, whom we call Fridleif; he had the son who is called Vodin, whom we call Odin; he was a famous man for wisdom and all accomplishments. His wife hight Frigida, whom we call Frigg.

10. Odin had the power of divination, and so had his wife, and from this knowledge he found out that his name would be held high in the north part of the world, and honored beyond that of all kings. For this reason he was eager to begin his journey from Turkey, and he had with him very many people, young and old, men and women, and he had with him many costly things. But wherever they fared over the lands great fame was spoken of them, and they were said to be more like gods than men. And they stopped not on their journey before they came north into that land which is now called Saxland; there Odin remained a long time, and subjugated the country far and wide. There Odin established his three sons as a defense of the land. One is named Veggdegg; he was a strong king and ruled over East Saxland. His son was

Vitrgils, and his sons were Ritta, the father of Heingest (Hengist), and Sigar, the father of Svebdegg, whom we call Svipdag. Another son of Odin hight Beldegg, whom we call Balder; he possessed the land which now hight Vestfal; his son was Brander, and his son Frjodigar, whom we call Froda (Frode). His son was Freovit, his son Yvigg, his son Gevis, whom we call Gave. The third son of Odin is named Sigge, his son Verer. These forefathers ruled the land which is now called Frankland, and from them is come the race that is called the Volsungs. From all of these many and great races are descended.

11. Then Odin continued his journey north-ward and came into the country which was called Reidgotaland, and in that land he conquered all that he desired. He established there his son, who hight Skjold; his son hight Fridleif; from him is descended the race which hight Skjoldungs; these are the Dane kings, and that land hight now Jutland, which then was called Reidgotaland.

12. Thereupon he fared north to what is now called Svithjod (Sweden), there was the king who is called Gylfe. But when he heard of the coming of those Asiamen, who were called asas, he went to meet them, and offered Odin such things in his kingdom as he himself might desire.

And such good luck followed their path, that wherever they stopped in the lands, there were bountiful crops and good peace; and all believed that they were the cause thereof. The mighty men of the kingdom saw that they were unlike other men whom they had seen, both in respect to beauty and understanding. The land there seemed good to Odin, and he chose there for himself a place for a burg, which is now called Sigtuna.* He there established chiefs, like unto what had formerly existed in Troy; he appointed twelve men in the burg to be judges of the law of the land, and made all rights to correspond with what had before been in Troy, and to what the Turks had been accustomed.

13. Thereupon he fared north until he reached the sea, which they thought surrounded all lands, and there he established his son in the kingdom, which is now called Norway; he is hight Saming, and the kings of Norway count their ancestors back to him, and so do the jarls and other mighty men, as it is stated in the Haleygjatal.† But Odin had with him that son who is called Yngve, who was king in Sweden, and from him is descended the families called Ynglings (Yngvelings). The asas took to themselves wives there within the land. But some took

---

* Near Upsala.
† A heroic poem, giving the pedigree (tal) of Norse kings.

wives for their sons, and these families became so numerous that they spread over Saxland, and thence over the whole north region, and the tongue of these Asiamen became the native tongue of all these lands. And men think they can understand from the way in which the names of their forefathers is written, that these names have belonged to this tongue, and that the asas have brought this tongue hither to the north, to Norway, to Sweden and to Saxland. But in England are old names of places and towns which can be seen to have been given in another tongue than this.

THE FOOLING OF GYLFE.

CHAPTER I.

GEFJUN'S PLOWING.

1. KING GYLFE ruled the lands that are now called Svithjod (Sweden). Of him it is said that he gave to a wayfaring woman, as a reward for the entertainment she had afforded him by her story-telling, a plow-land in his realm, as large as four oxen could plow it in a day and a night. But this woman was of the asa-race; her name was Gefjun. She took from the north, from Jotunheim, four oxen, which were the sons of a giant and her, and set them before the plow. Then went the plow so hard and deep that it tore up the land, and the oxen drew it westward into the sea, until it stood still in a sound. There Gefjun set the land, gave it a name and called it Seeland. And where the land had been taken away became afterward a sea, which in Sweden is now called Logrinn (the Lake, the Malar Lake in Sweden). And in the Malar Lake the bays cor-

respond to the capes in Seeland.   Thus says
Brage, the old skald:

> Gefjun glad
> Drew from Gylfe
> The excellent land,
> Denmark's increase,
> So that it reeked
> From the running beasts.
> Four heads and eight eyes
> Bore the oxen
> As they went before the wide
> Robbed land of the grassy isle.*

* Heimskringla: Ynglinga Saga, ch. v.

CHAPTER II.

2. King Gylfe was a wise man and skilled in the black art. He wondered much that the asa-folk was so mighty in knowledge, that all things went after their will. He thought to himself whether this could come from their own nature, or whether the cause must be sought for among the gods whom they worshiped. He therefore undertook a journey to Asgard. He went secretly, having assumed the likeness of an old man, and striving thus to disguise himself. But the asas were wiser, for they see into the future, and, foreseeing his journey before he came, they received him with an eye-deceit. So when he came into the burg he saw there a hall so high that he could hardly look over it. Its roof was thatched with golden shields as with shingles. Thus says Thjodolf of Hvin, that Valhal was thatched with shields:

> Thinking thatchers
> Thatched the roof;
> The beams of the burg
> Beamed with gold.*

* Heimskringla: Harald Harfager's Saga, ch. xix.

In the door of the hall Gylfe saw a man who played with swords so dexterously that seven were in the air at one time. That man asked him what his name was. Gylfe answered that his name was Ganglere;* that he had come a long way, and that he sought lodgings for the night. He also asked who owned the burg. The other answered that it belonged to their king: I will go with you to see him and then you may ask him for his name yourself. Then the man turned and led the way into the hall. Ganglere followed, and suddenly the doors closed behind him. There he saw many rooms and a large number of people, of whom some were playing, others were drinking, and some were fighting with weapons. He looked around him, and much of what he saw seemed to him incredible. Then quoth he:

> Gates all,
> Before in you go,
> You must examine well;
> For you cannot know
> Where enemies sit
> In the house before you.†

He saw three high-seats, one above the other, and in each sat a man. He asked what the names of these chiefs were. He, who had conducted him in, answered that the one who sat

*The walker.   †Elder Edda: Havamal.

in the lowest high-seat was king, and hight Har;
the one next above him, Jafnhar; but the one
who sat on the highest throne, Thride.   Har
asked the comer what more his errand was, and
added that food and drink was there at his ser·
vice, as for all in Har's hall.   Ganglere answered
that he first would like to ask whether there was
any wise man.   Answered Har: You will not
come out from here hale unless you are wiser.

> And stand now forth
> While you ask;
> He who answers shall sit.

CHAPTER III.

OF THE HIGHEST GOD.

3. Ganglere then made the following question: Who is the highest and oldest of all the gods? Made answer Har: Alfather he is called in our tongue, but in Asgard of old he had twelve names. The first is Alfather, the second is Herran or Herjan, the third Nikar or Hnikar, the fourth Nikuz or Hnikud, the fifth Fjolner, the sixth Oske, the seventh Ome, the eighth Biflide or Biflinde, the ninth Svidar, the tenth Svidrer, the eleventh Vidrer, the twelfth Jalg or Jalk. Ganglere asks again: Where is this god? What can he do? What mighty works has he accomplished? Answered Har: He lives from everlasting to everlasting, rules over all his realm, and governs all things, great and small. Then remarked Jafnhar: He made heaven and earth, the air and all things in them. Thride added: What is most important, he made man and gave him a spirit, which shall live, and never perish, though the body may turn to dust or burn to ashes. All who live a life of virtue shall dwell with him in Gimle or Vingolf. The wicked,

on the other hand, go to Hel, and from her to Niflhel, that is, down into the ninth world. Then asked Ganglere: What was he doing before heaven and earth were made? Har gave answer: Then was he with the frost-giants.

CHAPTER IV.

THE CREATION OF THE WORLD.

4. Said Ganglere: How came the world into existence, or how did it rise? What was before? Made answer to him Har: Thus is it said in the Vala's Prophecy:

> It was Time's morning,
> When there nothing was;
> Nor sand, nor sea,
> Nor cooling billows.
> Earth there was not,
> Nor heaven above.
> The Ginungagap was,
> But grass nowhere.*

Jafnhar remarked: Many ages before the earth was made, Niflheim had existed, in the midst of which is the well called Hvergelmer, whence flow the following streams: Svol, Gunnthro, Form, Fimbul, Thul, Slid and Hrid, Sylg and Ylg, Vid, Leipt and Gjoll, the last of which is nearest the gate of Hel. Then added Thride: Still there was before a world to the south which hight Muspelheim. It is light and hot, and so bright and dazzling that no stranger, who is not a

* Elder Edda: The Vala's Prophecy, 6.

native there, can stand it. Surt is the name of
him who stands on its border guarding it. He
has a flaming sword in his hand, and at the end
of the world he will come and harry, conquer
all the gods, and burn up the whole world with
fire. Thus it is said in the Vala's Prophecy:

> Surt from the south fares
> With blazing flames;
> From the sword shines
> The sun of the war-god.
> Rocks dash together
> And witches collapse,
> Men go the way to Hel
> And the heavens are cleft.*

5. Said Ganglere: What took place before the
races came into existence, and men increased and
multiplied? Replied Har, explaining, that as
soon as the streams, that are called the Elivogs,
had come so far from their source that the ven-
omous yeast which flowed with them hardened,
as does dross that runs from the fire, then it
turned into ice. And when this ice stopped and
flowed no more, then gathered over it the drizzling rain that arose from the venom and froze
into rime, and one layer of ice was laid upon the
other clear into Ginungagap. Then said Jafnhar: All that part of Ginungagap that turns
toward the north was filled with thick and
heavy ice and rime, and everywhere within were

* Elder Edda: The Vala's Prophecy, 56.

drizzling rains and gusts. But the south part of Ginungagap was lighted up by the glowing sparks that flew out of Muspelheim. Added Thride: As cold and all things grim proceeded from Niflheim, so that which bordered on Muspelheim was hot and bright, and Ginungagap was as warm and mild as windless air. And when the heated blasts from Muspelheim met the rime, so that it melted into drops, then, by the might of him who sent the heat, the drops quickened into life and took the likeness of a man, who got the name Ymer. But the Frost giants call him Aurgelmer. Thus it is said in the short Prophecy of the Vala (the Lay of Hyndla):

<blockquote>
All the valas are
From Vidolf descended;
All wizards are
Of Vilmeide's race;
All enchanters
Are sons of Svarthofde;
All giants have
Come from Ymer.*
</blockquote>

And on this point, when Vafthrudner, the giant, was asked by Gangrad:

<blockquote>
Whence came Aurgelmer
Originally to the sons
Of the giants?—thou wise giant! †
</blockquote>

* Elder Edda: Hyndla's Lay, 34.
† Elder Edda: Vafthrudner's Lay, 30.

he said

> From the Elivogs
> Sprang drops of venom,
> And grew till a giant was made.
> Thence our race
> Are all descended,
> Therefore are we all so fierce.*

Then asked Ganglere: How were the races developed from him? Or what was done so that more men were made? Or do you believe him to be god of whom you now spake? Made answer Har: By no means do we believe him to be god; evil was he and all his offspring, them we call frost-giants. It is said that when he slept he fell into a sweat, and then there grew under his left arm a man and a woman, and one of his feet begat with the other a son. From these come the races that are called frost-giants. The old frost-giant we call Ymer.

6. Then said Ganglere: Where did Ymer dwell, and on what did he live? Answered Har: The next thing was that when the rime melted into drops, there was made thereof a cow, which hight Audhumbla. Four milk-streams ran from her teats, and she fed Ymer. Thereupon asked Ganglere: On what did the cow subsist? Answered Har: She licked the salt-stones that were covered with rime, and the first day that she

* Elder Edda: Vafthrudner's Lay, 31.

licked the stones there came out of them in the evening a man's hair, the second day a man's head, and the third day the whole man was there. This man's name was Bure; he was fair of face, great and mighty, and he begat a son whose name was Bor. This Bor married a woman whose name was Bestla, the daughter of the giant Bolthorn; they had three sons,— the one hight Odin, the other Vile, and the third Ve. And it is my belief that this Odin and his brothers are the rulers of heaven and earth. We think that he must be so called. That is the name of the man whom we know to be the greatest and most famous, and well may men call him by that name.

7. Ganglere asked: How could these keep peace with Ymer, or who was the stronger? Then answered Har: The sons of Bor slew the giant Ymer, but when he fell, there flowed so much blood from his wounds that they drowned therein the whole race of frost-giants; excepting one, who escaped with his household. Him the giants call Bergelmer. He and his wife went on board his ark and saved themselves in it. From them are come new races of frost-giants, as is here said:

> Countless winters
> Ere the earth was made,
> Was born Bergelmer.

> This first I call to mind
> How that crafty giant
> Safe in his ark lay.*

8. Then said Ganglere: What was done then by the sons of Bor, since you believe that they were gods? Answered Har: About that there is not a little to be said. They took the body of Ymer, carried it into the midst of Ginungagap and made of him the earth. Of his blood they-made the seas and lakes; of his flesh the earth was made, but of his bones the rocks; of his teeth and jaws, and of the bones that were broken, they made stones and pebbles. Jafnhar remarked: Of the blood that flowed from the wounds, and was free, they made the ocean; they fastened the earth together and around it they laid this ocean in a ring without, and it must seem to most men impossible to cross it. Thride added: They took his skull and made thereof the sky, and raised it over the earth with four sides. Under each corner they set a dwarf, and the four dwarfs were called Austre (east), Vestre (West), Nordre (North), Sudre (South). Then they took glowing sparks, that were loose and had been cast out from Muspelheim, and placed them in the midst of the boundless heaven, both above and below, to light up heaven and earth. They gave resting-places to all fires, and set some in heaven;

---

*Elder Edda: Vafthrudner's Lay, 35.

some were made to go free under heaven, but they gave them a place and shaped their course. In old songs it is said that from that time days and years were reckoned. Thus in the Prophecy of the Vala:

> The sun knew not
> Where her hall she had;
> The moon knew not
> What might he had;
> The stars knew not
> Their resting-places.*

Thus it was before these things were made. Then said Ganglere: Wonderful tidings are these I now hear; a wondrous great building is this, and deftly constructed. How was the earth fashioned? Made answer Har: The earth is round, and without it round about lies the deep ocean, and along the outer strand of that sea they gave lands for the giant races to dwell in; and against the attack of restless giants they built a burg within the sea and around the earth. For this purpose they used the giant Ymer's eyebrows, and they called the burg Mid-gard. They also took his brains and cast them into the air, and made therefrom the clouds, as is here said:

* Elder Edda: The Vala's Prophecy, 8. In Old Norse the sun is feminine, and the moon masculine. See below, sections 11 and 12.

Of Ymer's flesh
The earth was made,
And of his sweat the seas;
Rocks of his bones,
Trees of his hair,
And the sky of his skull;
But of his eyebrows
The blithe powers
Made Midgard for the sons of men.
Of his brains
All the melancholy
Clouds were made.*

* Elder Edda: Grimner's Lay, 40, 41. Comp. Vafthrudner's Lay, 21.

CHAPTER V.

THE CREATION — (CONTINUED.)

9. Then said Ganglere: Much had been done, it seemed to me, when heaven and earth were made, when sun and moon were set in their places, and when days were marked out; but whence came the people who inhabit the world? Har answered as follows: As Bor's sons went along the sea-strand, they found two trees. These trees they took up and made men of them. The first gave them spirit and life; the second endowed them with reason and power of motion; and the third gave them form, speech, hearing and eyesight. They gave them clothes and names; the man they called Ask, and the woman Embla. From them all mankind is descended, and a dwelling-place was given them under Midgard. In the next place, the sons of Bor made for themselves in the middle of the world a burg, which is called Asgard, There dwelt the gods and their race, and thence were wrought many tidings and adventures, both on earth and in the sky. In Asgard is a place called Hlidskjalf, and when

Odin seated himself there in the high-seat, he
saw over the whole world, and what every man
was doing, and he knew all things that he saw.
His wife hight Frigg, and she was the daughter
of Fjorgvin, and from their offspring are descended the race that we call asas, who inhabited Asgard the old and the realms that lie about
it, and all that race are known to be gods. And
for this reason Odin is called Alfather, that he is
the father of all gods and men, and of all things
that were made by him and by his might. Jord
(earth) was his daughter and his wife; with her
he begat his first son, and that is Asa-Thor. To
him was given force and strength, whereby he
conquers all things quick.

10. Norfe, or Narfe, hight a giant, who dwelt in
Jotunheim. He had a daughter by name Night.
She was swarthy and dark like the race she belonged to. She was first married to a man who
hight Naglfare. Their son was Aud. Afterward
she was married to Annar. Jord hight their
daughter. Her last husband was Delling (Daybreak), who was of asa-race. Their son was Day,
who was light and fair after his father. Then
took Alfather Night and her son Day, gave them
two horses and two cars, and set them up in heaven
to drive around the earth, each in twelve hours
by turns. Night rides first on the horse which is
called Hrimfaxe, and every morning he bedews

the earth with the foam from his bit. The horse on which Day rides is called Skinfaxe, and with his mane he lights up all the sky and the earth.

11. Then said Ganglere: How does he steer the course of the sun and the moon? Answered Har: Mundilfare hight the man who had two children. They were so fair and beautiful that he called his son Moon, and his daughter, whom he gave in marriage to a man by name Glener, he called Sun. But the gods became wroth at this arrogance, took both the brother and the sister, set them up in heaven, and made Sun drive the horses that draw the car of the sun, which the gods had made to light up the world from sparks that flew out of Muspelheim. These horses hight Arvak and Alsvid. Under their withers the gods placed two wind-bags to cool them, but in some songs it is called ironcold (ísarnkol). Moon guides the course of the moon, and rules its wax-ing and waning. He took from the earth two children, who hight Bil and Hjuke, as they were going from the well called Byrger, and were carrying on their shoulders the bucket called Sager and the pole Simul. Their father's name is Vidfin. These children always accompany Moon, as can be seen from the earth.

12. Then said Ganglere: Swift fares Sun, almost as if she were afraid, and she could make no more haste in her course if she feared her destroyer.

Then answered Har: Nor is it wonderful that she speeds with all her might. Near is he who pursues her, and there is no escape for her but to run before him. Then asked Ganglere: Who causes her this toil? Answered Har: It is two wolves. The one hight Skol, he runs after her; she fears him and he will one day overtake her. The other hight Hate, Hrodvitner's son; he bounds before her and wants to catch the moon, and so he will at last.* Then asked Ganglere: Whose offspring are these wolves? Said Har: A hag dwells east of Midgard, in the forest called Jarnved (Ironwood), where reside the witches called Jarnvidjes. The old hag gives birth to many giant sons, and all in wolf's likeness. Thence come these two wolves. It is said that of this wolf-race one is the mightiest, and is called Moongarm. He is filled with the life-blood of all dead men. He will devour the moon, and stain the heavens and all the sky with blood. Thereby the sun will be darkened, the winds will grow wild, and roar hither and thither, as it is said in the Prophecy of the Vala:

> In the east dwells the old hag,
> In the Jarnved forest;
> And brings forth there
> Fenrer's offspring.
> There comes of them all
> One the worst,

* That wolves follow the sun and moon, is a wide-spread popular superstition. In Sweden, a parhelion is called Solvarg (sun-wolf).

> The moon's devourer
> In a troll's disguise.
>
> He is filled with the life-blood
> Of men doomed to die;
> The seats of the gods
> He stains with red gore;
> Sunshine grows black
> The summer thereafter,
> All weather gets fickle.
> Know you yet or not?*

13. Then asked Ganglere: What is the path from earth to heaven? Har answered, laughing: Foolishly do you now ask. Have you not been told that the gods made a bridge from earth to heaven, which is called Bifrost? You must have seen it. It may be that you call it the rainbow. It has three colors, is very strong, and is made with more craft and skill than other structures. Still, however strong it is, it will break when the sons of Muspel come to ride over it, and then they will have to swim their horses over great rivers in order to get on. Then said Ganglere: The gods did not, it seems to me, build that bridge honestly, if it shall be able to break to pieces, since they could have done so, had they desired. Then made answer Har: The gods are worthy of no blame for this structure. Bifrost is indeed a good bridge, but there is no thing in the world that is able to stand when the sons of Muspel come to the fight.

*Elder Edda: The Vala's Prophecy, 43, 44.

14. Then said Ganglere: What did Alfather do when Asgard had been built? Said Har: In the beginning he appointed rulers in a place in the middle of the burg which is called Idavold, who were to judge with him the disputes of men and decide the affairs of the burg. Their first work was to erect a court, where there were seats for all the twelve, and, besides, a high-seat for Alfather. That is the best and largest house ever built on earth, and is within and without like solid gold. This place is called Gladsheim. Then they built another hall as a home for the goddesses, which also is a very beautiful mansion, and is called Vingolf. Thereupon they built a forge; made hammer, tongs, anvil, and with these all other tools. Afterward they worked in iron, stone and wood, and especially in that metal which is called gold. All their household wares were of gold. That age was called the golden age, until it was lost by the coming of those women from Jotunheim. Then the gods set themselves in their high-seats and held counsel.

They remembered how the dwarfs had quickened in the mould of the earth like maggots in flesh. The dwarfs had first been created and had quickened in Ymer's flesh, and were then maggots; but now, by the decision of the gods, they got the understanding and likeness of men, but still had to dwell in the earth and in rocks. Modsogner was one dwarf and Durin another. So it is said in the Vala's Prophecy:

> Then went all the gods,
> The all-holy gods,
> On their judgment seats,
> And thereon took counsel
> Who should the race
> Of dwarfs create
> From the bloody sea
> And from Blain's bones.
> In the likeness of men
> Made they many
> Dwarfs in the earth,
> As Durin said.

And these, says the Vala, are the names of the dwarfs:

> Nye, Nide,
> Nordre, Sudre,
> Austre, Vestre,
> Althjof, Dvalin,
> Na, Nain,
> Niping, Dain,
> Bifur, Bafur,
> Bombor, Nore,
> Ore, Onar,
> Oin, Mjodvitner,
> Vig, Gandalf,
> Vindalf, Thorin.

> File, Kile,
> Fundin, Vale,
> Thro, Throin,
> Thek, Lit, Vit,
> Ny, Nyrad,
> Rek, Radsvid.

But the following are also dwarfs and dwell in the rocks, while the above-named dwell in the mould:

> Draupner, Dolgthvare,
> Hor, Hugstare,
> Hledjolf, Gloin,
> Dore, Ore,
> Duf, Andvare,
> Hepte, File,
> Har, Siar.

But the following come from Svarin's How to Aurvang on Joruvold, and from them is sprung Lovar. Their names are:

> Skirfer, Virfir,
> Skafid, Ae,
> Alf, Inge,
> Eikinskjalde,
> Fal, Froste,
> Fid, Ginnar.*

* Elder Edda: The Vala's Prophecy, 12, 14–16, 18, 19.

CHAPTER VII.

ON THE WONDERFUL THINGS IN HEAVEN.

15. Then said Ganglere: Where is the chief or most holy place of the gods? Har answered: That is by the ash Ygdrasil. There the gods meet in council every day. Said Ganglere: What is said about this place? Answered Jafnhar: This ash is the best and greatest of all trees; its branches spread over all the world, and reach up above heaven. Three roots sustain the tree and stand wide apart; one root is with the asas and another with the frost-giants, where Gin-ungagap formerly was; the third reaches into Niflheim; under it is Hvergelmer, where Nidhug gnaws the root from below. But under the second root, which extends to the frost-giants, is the well of Mimer, wherein knowledge and wisdom are concealed. The owner of the well hight Mimer. He is full of wisdom, for he drinks from the well with the Gjallar-horn. Alfather once came there and asked for a drink from the well, but he did not get it before he left one of his eyes as a pledge. So it is said in the Vala's Prophecy:

> Well know I, Odin,
> Where you hid your eye:
> In the crystal-clear
> Well of Mimer.
> Mead drinks Mimer
> Every morning
> From Valfather's pledge.
> Know you yet or not?*

The third root of the ash is in heaven, and beneath it is the most sacred fountain of Urd. Here the gods have their doomstead. The asas ride hither every day over Bifrost, which is also called Asa-bridge. The following are the names of the horses of the gods: Sleipner is the best one; he belongs to Odin, and he has eight feet. The second is Glad, the third Gyller, the fourth Gler, the fifth Skeidbrimer, the sixth Silfertop, the seventh Siner, the eighth Gisl, the ninth Falhofner, the tenth Gulltop, the eleventh Letfet. Balder's horse was burned with him. Thor goes on foot to the doomstead, and wades the following rivers:

> Kormt and Ormt
> And the two Kerlaugs;
> These shall Thor wade
> Every day
> When he goes to judge
> Near the Ygdrasil ash;
> For the Asa-bridge
> Burns all ablaze,—
> The holy waters roar.†

---

* Elder Edda: The Vala's Prophecy, 24.
† Elder Edda: Grimner's Lay, 29.

4

Then asked Ganglere: Does fire burn over Bifrost? Har answered: The red which you see in the rainbow is burning fire. The frost-giants and the mountain-giants would go up to heaven if Bifrost were passable for all who desired to go there. Many fair places there are in heaven, and they are all protected by a divine defense. There stands a beautiful hall near the fountain beneath the ash. Out of it come three maids, whose names are Urd, Verdande and Skuld. These maids shape the lives of men, and we call them norns. There are yet more norns, namely those who come to every man when he is born, to shape his life, and these are known to be of the race of gods; others, on the other hand, are of the race of elves, and yet others are of the race of dwarfs. As is here said:

> Far asunder, I think,
> The norns are born,
> They are not of the same race.
> Some are of the asas,
> Some are of the elves,
> Some are daughters of Dvalin.*

Then said Ganglere: If the norns rule the fortunes of men, then they deal them out exceedingly unevenly. Some live a good life and are rich; some get neither wealth nor praise. Some have a long, others a short life. Har answered:

* Elder Edda: Fafner's Lay, 13.

Good norns and of good descent shape good lives,
and when some men are weighed down with
misfortune, the evil norns are the cause of it.

16. Then said Ganglere: What other remarkable things are there to be said about the ash?
Har answered: Much is to be said about it. On
one of the boughs of the ash sits an eagle, who
knows many things. Between his eyes sits a
hawk that is called Vedfolner. A squirrel, by
name Ratatosk, springs up and down the tree,
and carries words of envy between the eagle and
Nidhug. Four stags leap about in the branches
of the ash and bite the leaves.* Their names are:
Dain, Dvalin, Duney and Durathro. In Hvergelmer with Nidhug are more serpents than tongue
can tell. As is here said:

> The ash Ygdrasil
> Bears distress
> Greater than men know.
> Stags bite it above,
> At the side it rots,
> Nidhug gnaws it below.

And so again it is said:

> More serpents lie
> 'Neath the Ygdrasil ash
> Than is thought of
> By every foolish ape.
> Goin and Moin
> (They are sons of Grafvitner),

* The Icelandic barr. See Vigfusson, *sub voce.*

> Grabak and Grafvollud,
> Ofner and Svafner
> Must for aye, methinks,
> Gnaw the roots of that tree.*

Again, it is said that the norns, that dwell in the fountain of Urd, every day take water from the fountain and take the clay that lies around the fountain and sprinkle therewith the ash, in order that its branches may not wither or decay. This water is so holy that all things that are put into the fountain become as white as the film of an egg-shell. As is here said:

> An ash 1 know
> Hight Ygdrasil;
> A high, holy tree
> With white clay sprinkled.
> Thence come the dews
> That fall in the dales.
> Green forever it stands
> Over Urd's fountain.†

The dew which falls on the earth from this tree men call honey-fall, and it is the food of bees. Two birds are fed in Urd's fountain; they are called swans, and they are the parents of the race of swans.

17. Then said Ganglere: Great tidings you are able to tell of the heavens. Are there other remarkable places than the one by Urd's fountain? Answered Har: There are many magnifi-

* Elder Edda: Grimner's Lay, 35, 34.
† Elder Edda: The Vala's Prophecy, 22.

cent dwellings. One is there called Alf'heim. There dwell the folk that are called light-elves; but the dark-elves dwell down in the earth, and they are unlike the light-elves in appearance, but much more so in deeds. The light-elves are fairer than the sun to look upon, but the dark-elves are blacker than pitch. Another place is called Breidablik, and no place is fairer. There is also a mansion called Glitner, of which the walls and pillars and posts are of red gold, and the roof is of silver. Furthermore, there is a dwelling, by name Himinbjorg, which stands at the end of heaven, where the Bifrost-bridge is united with heaven. And there is a great dwelling called Valaskjalf, which belongs to Odin. The gods made it and thatched it with sheer silver. In this hall is the high-seat, which is called Hlid-skjalf, and when Alfather sits in this seat, he sees over all the world. In the southern end of the world is the palace, which is the fairest of all, and brighter than the sun; its name is Gimle. It shall stand when both heaven and earth shall have passed away. In this hall the good and the righteous shall dwell through all ages. Thus says the Prophecy of the Vala:

> A hall I know, standing
> Than the sun fairer,
> Than gold better,
> Gimle by name.

> There shall good
> People dwell,
> And forever
> Delights enjoy.*

Then said Ganglere: Who guards this palace when Surt's fire burns up heaven and earth? Har answered: It is said that to the south and above this heaven is another heaven, which is called Andlang. But there is a third, which is above these, and is called Vidblain, and in this heaven we believe this mansion (Gimle) to be situated; but we deem that the light-elves alone dwell in it now.

* Elder Edda: The Vala's Prophecy, 70.

CHAPTER VIII.

THE ASAS.

18. Then said Ganglere: Whence comes the wind? It is so strong that it moves great seas, and fans fires to flame, and yet, strong as it is, it cannot be seen. Therefore it is wonderfully made. Then answered Har: That I can tell you well. At the northern end of heaven sits a giant, who hight Hrasvelg. He is clad in eagles' plumes, and when he spreads his wings for flight, the winds arise from under them. Thus is it here said:

> Hrasvelg hight he
> Who sits at the end of heaven,
> A giant in eagle's disguise.
> From his wings, they say,
> The wind does come
> Over all mankind.*

19. Then said Ganglere: How comes it that summer is so hot, but the winter so cold? Har answered: A wise man would not ask such a question, for all are able to tell this; but if you alone have become so stupid that you have not heard of it, then I would rather forgive you for

* Elder Edda: Vafthrudner's Lay, 37.

asking unwisely once than that you should go any longer in ignorance of what you ought to know. Svasud is the name of him who is father of summer, and he lives such a life of enjoyment, that everything that is mild is from him called sweet (svasligt). But the father of winter has two names, Vindlone and Vindsval. He is the son of Vasad, and all that race are grim and of icy breath, and winter is like them.

20. Then asked Ganglere: Which are the asas, in whom men are bound to believe? Har answered him: Twelve are the divine asas. Jafnhar said: No less holy are the asynjes (goddesses), nor is their power less. Then added Thride: Odin is the highest and oldest of the asas. He rules all things, but the other gods, each according to his might, serve him as children a father. Frigg is his wife, and she knows the fate of men, although she tells not thereof, as it is related that Odin himself said to Asa-Loke:

> Mad are you, Loke!
> And out of your senses;
> Why do you not stop?
> Fortunes all,
> Methinks, Frigg knows,
> Though she tells them not herself.*

Odin is called Alfather, for he is the father of all the gods; he is also called Valfather, for all

* Elder Edda. Loke's Quarrel, 29. 47.

who fall in fight are his chosen sons. For them
he prepares Valhal and Vingolf, where they are
called einherjes (heroes). He is also called
Hangagod, Haptagod, Farmagod; and he gave
himself still more names when he came to King
Geirrod:

Grim is my name,
And Ganglare,
Herjan, Hjalmbore,
Thek, Thride,
Thud, Ud,
Helblinde, Har,
Sad, Svipal,
Sangetal,
Herteit, Hnikar,
Bileyg, Baleyg,
Bolverk, Fjolner,
Grimner, Glapsvid, Fjolsvid,
Sidhot, Sidskeg,
Sigfather, Hnikud,
Alfather, Atrid, Farmatyr,
Oske, Ome,
Jafnhar, Biflinde,
Gondler, Harbard,
Svidur, Svidrir,
Jalk, Kjalar, Vidur,
Thro, Yg, Thund,
Vak, Skilfing,
Vafud, Hroptatyr,
Gaut, Veratyr.*

Then said Ganglere: A very great number of
names you have given him; and this I know, forsooth, that he must be a very wise man who is
able to understand and decide what chances are

* Elder Edda: Grimner's Lay, 46-50.

the causes of all these names. Har answered:
Much knowledge is needed to explain it all
rightly, but still it is shortest to tell you that
most of these names have been given him for the
reason that, as there are many tongues in the
world, so all peoples thought they ought to turn
his name into their tongue, in order that they
might be able to worship him and pray to him
each in its own language. Other causes of
these names must be sought in his journeys,
which are told of in old sagas; and you can lay
no claim to being called a wise man if you are
not able to tell of these wonderful adventures.

21. Then said Ganglere: What are the names
of the other asas? What is their occupation, and
what works have they wrought? Har answered:
Thor is the foremost of them. He is called Asa-
Thor, or Oku-Thor.* He is the strongest of all
gods and men, and rules over the realm which
is called Thrudvang. His hall is called Bilskirner.
Therein are five hundred and forty floors, and it
is the largest house that men have made. Thus
it is said in Grimner's Lay:

> Five hundred floors
> And forty more,
> Methinks, has bowed Bilskirner.
> Of houses all
> That I know roofed
> I know my son's is the largest.†

* Oku is derived from the Finnish thunder-god, Ukko.
† Elder Edda: Grimner's Lay, 24.

Thor has two goats, by name Tangnjost and Tangrisner, and a chariot, wherein he drives. The goats draw the chariot; wherefore he is called Oku-Thor.* He possesses three valuable treasures. One of them is the hammer Mjolner, which the frost-giants and mountain-giants well know when it is raised; and this is not to be wondered at, for with it he has split many a skull of their fathers or friends. The second treasure he possesses is Megingjarder (belt of strength); when he girds himself with it his strength is doubled. His third treasure that is of so great value is his iron gloves; these he cannot do without when he lays hold of the hammer's haft. No one is so wise that he can tell all his great works; but I can tell you so many tidings of him that it will grow late before all is told that I know.

22. Thereupon said Ganglere: I wish to ask tidings of more of the asas. Har gave him answer: Odin's second son is Balder, and of him good things are to be told. He is the best, and all praise him. He is so fair of face and so bright that rays of light issue from him; and there is a plant so white that it is likened unto Balder's brow, and it is the whitest of all plants. From this you can judge of the beauty both of his hair and of his body. He is the wisest, mildest and

---

*The author of the Younger Edda is here mistaken. See note on page 82.

most eloquent of all the asas; and such is his nature that none can alter the judgment he has pronounced. He inhabits the place in heaven called Breidablik, and there nothing unclean can enter. As is here said:

> Breidablik it is called,
> Where Balder has
> Built for himself a hall
> In the land
> Where I know is found
> The least of evil.*

23. The third asa is he who is called Njord. He dwells in Noatun, which is in heaven. He rules the course of the wind and checks the fury of the sea and of fire. He is invoked by seafarers and by fishermen. He is so rich and wealthy that he can give broad lands and abundance to those who call on him for them. He was fostered in Vanaheim, but the vans † gave him as a hostage to the gods, and received in his stead as an asa-hostage the god whose name is Honer. He established peace between the gods and vans. Njord took to wife Skade, a daughter of the giant Thjasse. She wished to live where her father had dwelt, that is, on the mountains in Thrymheim; Njord, on the other hand, preferred to be near the sea. They therefore agreed to pass nine

---

* Elder Edda: Grimner's Lay, 12.

† Compare Vainamoinen, the son of Ukko, in the Finnish epic Kalevala.

nights in Thrymheim and three in Noatun. But when Njord came back from the mountains to Noatun he sang this:

> Weary am I of the mountains,
> Not long was I there,
> Only nine nights.
> The howl of the wolves
> Methought sounded ill
> To the song of the swans.

Skade then sang this:

> Sleep I could not
> On my sea-strand couch,
> For the scream of the sea-fowl.
> *There* wakes me,
> As he comes from the sea,
> Every morning the mew.

Then went Skade up on the mountain, and dwelt in Thrymheim. She often goes on skees (snow-shoes), with her bow, and shoots wild beasts. She is called skee-goddess or skee-dis. Thus it is said:

> Thrymheim it is called
> Where Thjasse dwelt,
> That mightiest giant.
> But now dwells Skade,
> Pure bride of the gods,
> In her father's old homestead.*

24. Njord, in Noatun, afterward begat two children: a son, by name Frey, and a daughter, by name Freyja. They were fair of face, and

* Elder Edda: Grimner's Lay, 11.

mighty. Frey is the most famous of the asas. He rules over rain and sunshine, and over the fruits of the earth. It is good to call on him for harvests and peace. He also sways the wealth of men. Freyja is the most famous of the goddesses. She has in heaven a dwelling which is called Folkvang, and when she rides to the battle, one half of the slain belong to her, and the other half to Odin. As is here said:

> Folkvang it is called,
> And there rules Freyja.
> For the seats in the hall
> Half of the slain
> She chooses each day;
> The other half is Odin's.*

Her hall is Sesrymner, and it is large and beautiful. When she goes abroad, she drives in a car drawn by two cats. She lends a favorable ear to men who call upon her, and it is from her name the title has come that women of birth and wealth are called frur.† She is fond of love ditties, and it is good to call on her in love affairs.

25. Then said Ganglere: Of great importance these asas seem to me to be, and it is not wonderful that you have great power, since you have such excellent knowledge of the gods, and know to which of them to address your prayers on each

---

*Elder Edda: Grimner's Lay, 14.

† Icel. *frú* (Ger. *frau;* Dan. *frue*), pl. *frúr*, means a lady. It is used of the wives of men of rank or title. It is derived from Freyja.

occasion. But what other gods are there? Har answered: There is yet an asa, whose name is Tyr. He is very daring and stout-hearted. He sways victory in war, wherefore warriors should call on him. There is a saw, that he who surpasses others in bravery, and never yields, is Tyr-strong. He is also so wise, that it is said of anyone who is specially intelligent, that he is Tyr-learned. A proof of his daring is, that when the asas induced the wolf Fenrer to let himself be bound with the chain Gleipner, he would not believe that they would loose him again until Tyr put his hand in his mouth as a pledge. But when the asas would not loose the Fenris-wolf, he bit Tyr's hand off at the place of the wolf's joint (the wrist; Icel. *úlfliðr**). From that time Tyr is one-handed, and he is now called a peacemaker among men.

26. Brage is the name of another of the asas. He is famous for his wisdom, eloquence and flowing speech. He is a master-skald, and from him song-craft is called brag (poetry), and such men or women as distinguish themselves by their eloquence are called brag-men † and brag-women. His wife is Idun. She keeps in a box those

---

*This etymology is, however, erroneous, for the word is derived from *oln* or *öln*, and the true form of the word is *ölnliðr* = the ell-joint (wrist); thus we have *ölnboge* = the elbow; *öln* = *alin* (Gr. ὠδίνη; Lat. *ulna;* cp. A.-S. *el-boga;* Eng. *elbow*) is the arm from the elbow to the end of the middle finger, hence an ell in long measure.

† Compare the Anglo-Saxon *brego* = princeps, chief.

apples of which the gods eat when they grow old, and then they become young again, and so it will be until Ragnarok (the twilight of the gods). Then said Ganglere: Of great importance to the gods it must be, it seems to me, that Idun preserves these apples with care and honesty. Har answered, and laughed: They ran a great risk on one occasion, whereof I might tell you more, but you shall first hear the names of more asas.

27. Heimdal is the name of one. He is also called the white-asa. He is great and holy; born of nine maidens, all of whom were sisters. He hight also Hallinskide and Gullintanne, for his teeth were of gold. His horse hight Gulltop (Gold-top). He dwells in a place called Himin-bjorg, near Bifrost. He is the ward of the gods, and sits at the end of heaven, guarding the bridge against the mountain-giants. He needs less sleep than a bird; sees an hundred miles around him, and as well by night as by day. He hears the grass grow and the wool on the backs of the sheep, and of course all things that sound louder than these. He has a trumpet called the Gjallarhorn, and when he blows it it can be heard in all the worlds. The head is called Heimdal's sword. Thus it is here said:

> Himinbjorg it is called,
> Where Heimdal rules
> Over his holy halls;
> There drinks the ward of the gods
> In his delightful dwelling
> Glad the good mead.*

And again, in Heimdal's Song, he says himself:

> Son I am of maidens nine,
> Born I am of sisters nine.

28. Hoder hight one of the asas, who is blind, but exceedingly strong; and the gods would wish that this asa never needed to be named, for the work of his hand will long be kept in memory both by gods and men.

29. Vidar is the name of the silent asa. He has a very thick shoe, and he is the strongest next after Thor. From him the gods have much help in all hard tasks.

30. Ale, or Vale, is the son of Odin and Rind. He is daring in combat, and a good shot.

31. Uller is the name of one, who is a son of Sif, and a step-son of Thor. He is so good an archer, and so fast on his skees, that no one can contend with him. He is fair of face, and possesses every quality of a warrior. Men should invoke him in single combat.

32. Forsete is a son of Balder and Nanna, Nep's daughter. He has in heaven the hall which hight

* Elder Edda: Grimner's Lay, 13.

Glitner. All who come to him with disputes go away perfectly reconciled. No better tribunal is to be found among gods and men. Thus it is here said:

> Glitner hight the hall,
> On gold pillars standing,
> And roofed with silver.
> There dwells Forsete
> Throughout all time,
> And settles all disputes.*

* Elder Edda: Grimner's Lay, 15.

CHAPTER IX.

LOKE AND HIS OFFSPRING.

33. There is yet one who is numbered among the asas, but whom some call the backbiter of the asas. He is the originator of deceit, and the disgrace of all gods and men. His name is Loke, or Lopt. His father is the giant Farbaute, but his mother's name is Laufey, or Nal. His brothers are Byleist and Helblinde. Loke is fair and beautiful of face, but evil in disposition, and very fickleminded. He surpasses other men in the craft called cunning, and cheats in all things. He has often brought the asas into great trouble, and often helped them out again, with his cunning contrivances. His wife hight Sygin, and their son, Nare, or Narfe.

34. Loke had yet more children. A giantess in Jotunheim, hight Angerboda. With her he begat three children. The first was the Fenris-wolf; the second, Jormungand, that is, the Midgardserpent, and the third, Hel. When the gods knew that these three children were being fostered in Jotunheim, and were aware of the prophecies that much woe and misfortune would thence come to

them, and considering that much evil might be looked for from them on their mother's side, and still more on their father's, Alfather sent some of the gods to take the children and bring them to him. When they came to him he threw the serpent into the deep sea which surrounds all lands. There waxed the serpent so that he lies in the midst of the ocean, surrounds all the earth, and bites his own tail. Hel he cast into Niflheim, and gave her power over nine worlds,* that she should appoint abodes to them that are sent to her, namely, those who die from sickness or old age. She has there a great mansion, and the walls around it are of strange height, and the gates are huge. Eljudner is the name of her hall. Her table hight famine; her knife, starvation. Her man-servant's name is Ganglate; her maid-servant's, Ganglot.† Her threshold is called stumbling-block; her bed, care; the precious hangings of her bed, gleaming bale. One-half of her is blue, and the other half is of the hue of flesh; hence she is easily known. Her looks are very stern and grim.

35. The wolf was fostered by the asas at home, and Tyr was the only one who had the courage to go to him and give him food. When the gods

---

* Possibly this ought to read the ninth world, which would correspond with what we read on page 72, and in the Vala's Prophecy. See also notes. It may be a mistake of the transcriber.

† Both these words mean sloth.

saw how much he grew every day, and all prophecies declared that he was predestined to become
fatal to them, they resolved to make a very strong
fetter, which they called Lading. They brought
it to the wolf, and bade him try his strength on
the fetter. The wolf, who did not think it would
be too strong for him, let them do therewith as
they pleased. But as soon as he spurned against
it the fetter burst asunder, and he was free from
Lading. Then the asas made another fetter, by
one-half stronger, and this they called Drome.
They wanted the wolf to try this also, saying to
him that he would become very famous for his
strength, if so strong a chain was not able to
hold him. The wolf thought that this fetter was
indeed very strong, but also that his strength
had increased since he broke Lading. He also
took into consideration that it was necessary to
expose one's self to some danger if he desired to
become famous; so he let them put the fetter
on him. When the asas said they were ready,
the wolf shook himself, spurned against and
dashed the fetter on the ground, so that the
broken pieces flew a long distance. Thus he
broke loose out of Drome. Since then it has been
held as a proverb, "to get loose out of Lading"
or "to dash out of Drome," whenever anything
is extraordinarily hard. The asas now began to
fear that they would not get the wolf bound.

So Alfather sent the youth, who is called Skirner, and is Frey's messenger, to some dwarfs in Svartalfaheim, and had them make the fetter which is called Gleipner. It was made of six things: of the footfall of cats, of the beard of woman, of the roots of the mountain, of the sinews of the bear, of the breath of the fish, and of the spittle of the birds. If you have not known this before, you can easily find out that it is true and that there is no lie about it, since you must have observed that a woman has no beard, that a cat's footfall cannot be heard, and that mountains have no roots; and I know, forsooth, that what I have told you is perfectly true, although there are some things that you do not understand. Then said Ganglere: This I must surely understand to be true. I can see these things which you have taken as proof. But how was the fetter smithied? Answered Har: That I can well explain to you. It was smooth and soft as a silken string. How strong and trusty it was you shall now hear. When the fetter was brought to the asas, they thanked the messenger for doing his errand so well. Then they went out into the lake called Amsvartner, to the holm (rocky island) called Lyngve, and called the wolf to go with them. They showed him the silken band and bade him break it, saying that it was somewhat stronger than its thinness would lead one to suppose.

Then they handed it from one to the other and tried its strength with their hands, but it did not break. Still they said the wolf would be able to snap it. The wolf answered: It seems to me that I will get no fame though I break asunder so slender a thread as this is. But if it is made with craft and guile, then, little though it may look, that band will never come on my feet. Then said the asas that he would easily be able to break a slim silken band, since he had already burst large iron fetters asunder. But even if you are unable to break this band, you have nothing to fear from the gods, for we will immediately loose you again. The wolf answered: If you get me bound so fast that I am not able to loose myself again, you will skulk away, and it will be long before I get any help from you, wherefore I am loth to let this band be laid on me; but in order that you may not accuse me of cowardice, let some one of you lay his hand in my mouth as a pledge that this is done without deceit. The one asa looked at the other, and thought there now was a choice of two evils, and no one would offer his hand, before Tyr held out his right hand and laid it in the wolf's mouth. But when the wolf now began to spurn against it the band grew stiffer, and the more he strained the tighter it got. They all laughed except Tyr; he lost his hand. When the asas saw that the wolf was sufficiently well bound, they took the chain which was fixed to the fetter, and which was called Gelgja, and drew it through a large rock which is called Gjol, and fastened this rock deep down in the earth. Then they took a large stone, which is called Tvite, and drove it still deeper into the ground, and used this stone for a fastening-pin. The wolf opened his mouth terribly wide, raged and twisted himself with all his might, and wanted to bite them; but they put a sword in his mouth, in such a manner that the hilt stood in his lower jaw and the point in the upper, that is his gag. He howls terribly, and the saliva which runs from his mouth forms a river called Von. There he will lie until Ragnarok. Then said Ganglere: Very bad are these children of Loke, but they are strong and mighty. But why did not the asas kill the wolf when they have evil to expect from him? Har answered: So great respect have the gods for their holiness and peace-stead, that they would not stain them with the blood of the wolf, though prophecies foretell that he must become the bane of Odin.

CHAPTER X.

36. Ganglere asked: Which are the goddesses?
Har answered: Frigg is the first; she possesses
the right lordly dwelling which is called Fensaler. The second is Saga, who dwells in Sokvabek, and this is a large dwelling. The third is
Eir, who is the best leech. The fourth is Gefjun,
who is a may, and those who die maids become
her hand-maidens. The fifth is Fulla, who is also
a may, she wears her hair flowing and has a
golden ribbon about her head; she carries Frigg's
chest, takes care of her shoes and knows her
secrets. The sixth is Freyja, who is ranked with
Frigg. She is wedded to the man whose name is
Oder; their daughter's name is Hnos, and she is
so fair that all things fair and precious are called,
from her name, Hnos. Oder went far away. Freyja
weeps for him, but her tears are red gold. Freyja
has many names, and the reason therefor is that
she changed her name among the various nations
to which she came in search of Oder. She is called
Mardol, Horn, Gefn, and Syr. She has the necklace Brising, and she is called Vanadis. The

seventh is Sjofn, who is fond of turning men's and women's hearts to love, and it is from her name that love is called Sjafne. The eighth is Lofn, who is kind and good to those who call upon her, and she has permission from Alfather or Frigg to bring together men and women, no matter what difficulties may stand in the way; therefore "love" is so called from her name, and also that which is much loved by men. The ninth is Var. She hears the oaths and troths that men and women plight to each other. Hence such vows are called vars, and she takes vengeance on those who break their promises. The tenth is Vor, who is so wise and searching that nothing can be concealed from her. It is a saying that a woman becomes vor (ware) of what she becomes wise. The eleventh is Syn, who guards the door of the hall, and closes it against those who are not to enter. In trials she guards those suits in which anyone tries to make use of falsehood. Hence is the saying that "syn is set against it," when anyone tries to deny ought. The twelfth is Hlin, who guards those men whom Frigg wants to protect from any danger. Hence is the saying that he hlins who is forewarned. The thirteenth is Snotra, who is wise and courtly. After her, men and women who are wise are called Snotras. The fourteenth is Gna, whom Frigg sends on her errands into various worlds. She rides upon a horse called Hǫfvarpner, that runs through the air and over the sea. Once, when she was riding, some vans saw her faring through the air. Then said one of them:

> What flies there?
> What fares there?
> What glides in the air?

She answered

> I fly not,
> Though I fare
> And glide through the air
> On Hofvarpner,
> That Hamskerper,
> Begat with Gardrofa.*

From Gna's name it is said that anything that fares high in the air gnas. Sol and Bil are numbered among the goddesses, but their nature has already been described.†

37. There are still others who are to serve in Valhal, bear the drink around, wait upon the table and pass the ale-horns. Thus they are named in Grimner's Lay:

> Hrist and Mist
> I want my horn to bring to me;
> Skeggold and Skogul,
> Hild and Thrud,
> Hlok and Herfjoter,
> Gol and Geirahod,
> Randgrid and Radgrid,
> And Reginleif;
> These bear ale to the einherjes.‡

* Elder Edda: Grimner's Lay, 36.
† See page 66.
‡ Elder Edda: Grimner's Lay, 36.

These are called valkyries. Odin sends them to all battles, where they choose those who are to be slain, and rule over the victory. Gud and Rosta, and the youngest norn, Skuld, always ride to sway the battle and choose the slain. Jord, the mother of Thor, and Rind, Vale's mother, are numbered among the goddesses.

CHAPTER XI.

38. Gymer hight a man whose wife was Orboda, of the race of the mountain giants. Their daughter was Gerd, the fairest of all women. One day when Frey had gone into Hlidskjalf, and was looking out upon all the worlds, he saw toward the north a hamlet wherein was a large and beautiful house. To this house went a woman, and when she raised her hands to open the door, both the sky and the sea glistened therefrom, and she made all the world bright. As a punishment for his audacity in seating himself in that holy seat, Frey went away full of grief. When he came home, he neither spake, slept, nor drank, and no one dared speak to him. Then Njord sent for Skirner, Frey's servant, bade him go to Frey and ask him with whom he was so angry, since he would speak to nobody. Skirner said that he would go, though he was loth to do so, as it was probable that he would get evil words in reply. When he came to Frey and asked him why he was so sad that he would not

*This is the Niblung story in a nut-shell.

talk, Frey answered that he had seen a beautiful woman, and for her sake he had become so filled with grief, that he could not live any longer if he could not get her. And now you must go, he added, and ask her hand for me and bring her home to me, whether it be with or without the consent of her father. I will reward you well for your trouble. Skirner answered saying that he would go on this errand, but Frey must give him his sword, that was so excellent that it wielded itself in fight. Frey made no objection to this and gave him the sword. Skirner went on his journey, courted Gerd for him, and got the promise of her that she nine nights there-after should come to Bar-Isle and there have her wedding with Frey. When Skirner came back and gave an account of his journey, Frey said:

> Long is one night,
> Long are two nights,
> How can I hold out three?
> Oft to me one month
> Seemed less
> Than this half night of love.*

This is the reason why Frey was unarmed when he fought with Bele, and slew him with a hart's horn. Then said Ganglere: It is a great wonder that such a lord as Frey would give away his sword, when he did not have another as good.

---

* Elder Edda: Skirner's Journey, 42.

A great loss it was to him when he fought with
Bele; and this I know, forsooth, that he must
have repented of that gift. Har answered: Of
no great account was his meeting with Bele.
Frey could have slain him with his hand. But
the time will come when he will find himself in
a worse plight for not having his sword, and that
will be when the sons of Muspel sally forth to
the fight.

CHAPTER XII.

LIFE IN VALHAL.

39. Then said Ganglere: You say that all men who since the beginning of the world have fallen in battle have come to Odin in Valhal. What does he have to give them to eat? It seems to me there must be a great throng of people. Har answered: It is true, as you remark, that there is a great throng; many more are yet to come there, and still they will be thought too few when the wolf* comes. But however great may be the throng in Valhal, they will get plenty of flesh of the boar Sahrimner. He is boiled every day and is whole again in the evening. But as to the question you just asked, it seems to me there are but few men so wise that they are able to answer it correctly. The cook's name is Andhrimner, and the kettle is called Eldhrimner. as is here said:

> Andhrimner cooks
> In Eldhrimner
> Sahrimner.
> 'Tis the best of flesh.
> There are few who know
> What the einherjes eat.†

* The Fenris-wolf in Ragnarok.
† Elder Edda: Grimner's Lay, 18.

Ganglere asked: Does Odin have the same kind of food as the einherjes? Har answered: The food that is placed on his table he gives to his two wolves, which hight Gere and Freke. He needs no food himself. Wine is to him both food and drink, as is here said:

Gere and Freke
Sates the warfaring,
Famous father of hosts;
But on wine alone
Odin in arms renowned
Forever lives.*

Two ravens sit on Odin's shoulders, and bring to his ears all that they hear and see. Their names are Hugin and Munin. At dawn he sends them out to fly over the whole world, and they come back at breakfast time. Thus he gets information about many things, and hence he is called Rafnagud (raven-god). As is here said:

Hugin and Munin
Fly every day
Over the great earth.
I fear for Hugin
That he may not return,
Yet more am I anxious for Munin.†

40. Then asked Ganglere: What do the einherjes have to drink that is furnished them as bountifully as the food? Or do they drink water? Har answered: That is a wonderful question.

____
* Elder Edda: Grimner's Lay, 19.
† Elder Edda: Grimner's Lay, 20.

Do you suppose that Alfather invites kings, jarls, or other great men, and gives them water to drink? This I know, forsooth, that many a one comes to Valhal who would think he was paying a big price for his water-drink, if there were no better reception to be found there,— persons, namely, who have died from wounds and pain. But I can tell you other tidings. A she-goat, by name Heidrun, stands up in Valhal and bites the leaves off the branches of that famous tree called Lerad. From her teats runs so much mead that she fills every day a vessel in the hall from which the horns are filled, and which is so large that all the einherjes get all the drink they want out of it. Then said Ganglere: That is a most useful goat, and a right excellent tree that must be that she feeds upon. Then said Har: Still more re-markable is the hart Eikthyrner, which stands over Valhal and bites the branches of the same tree. From his horns fall so many drops down into Hvergelmer, that thence flow the rivers that are called Sid, Vid, Sekin, Ekin, Svol, Gunthro, Fjorm, Fimbulthul, Gipul, Gopul, Gomul and Geirvimul, all of which fall about the abodes of the asas. The following are also named: Thyn, Vin, Thol, Bol, Grad, Gunthrain, Nyt, Not, Non, Hron, Vina, Vegsvin, Thjodnuma.

41. Then said Ganglere: That was a wonder-ful tiding that you now told me. A mighty

house must Valhal be, and a great crowd there must often be at the door. Then answered Har: Why do you not ask how many doors there are in Valhal, and how large they are? When you find that out, you will confess that it would rather be wonderful if everybody could not easily go in and out. It is also a fact that it is no more difficult to find room within than to get in. Of this you may hear what the Lay of Grimner says:

> Five hundred doors
> And forty more,
> I trow, there are in Valhal.
> Eight hundred einherjes
> Go at a time through one door
> When they fare to fight with the wolf.*

42. Then said Ganglere: A mighty band of men there is in Valhal, and, forsooth, I know that Odin is a very great chief, since he commands so mighty a host. But what is the pastime of the einherjes when they do not drink? Har answered: Every morning, when they have dressed themselves, they take their weapons and go out into the court and fight and slay each other. That is their play. Toward breakfast-time they ride home to Valhal and sit down to drink. As is here said:

> All the einherjes
> In Odin's court
> Hew daily each other.

* Elder Edda: Grimner's Lay, 23.

They choose the slain
And ride from the battle-field,
Then sit they in peace together.*

But true it is, as you said, that Odin is a great chief. There are many proofs of that. Thus it is said in the very words of the asas themselves:

The Ygdrasil ash
Is the foremost of trees,
But Skidbladner of ships,
Odin of asas,
Sleipner of steeds,
Bifrost of bridges,
Brage of Skalds,
Habrok of hows,
But Garm of dogs.†

* Elder Edda: Vafthrudner's Lay, 41.
† Elder Edda: Grimner's Lay, 44.

CHAPTER XIII.

43. Ganglere asked: Whose is that horse Sleipner, and what is there to say about it? Har answered: You have no knowledge of Sleipner, nor do you know the circumstances attending his birth; but it must seem to you worth the telling. In the beginning, when the town of the gods was building, when the gods had established Midgard and made Valhal, there came a certain builder and offered to make them a burg, in three half years, so excellent that it should be perfectly safe against the mountain-giants and frost-giants, even though they should get within Midgard. But he demanded as his reward, that he should have Freyja, and he wanted the sun and moon besides. Then the asas came together and held counsel, and the bargain was made with the builder that he should get what he demanded if he could get the burg done in one winter; but if on the first day of summer any part of the burg was unfinished, then the contract should be void. It was also agreed that no man should help him with the work. When they told him these terms, he re-

quested that they should allow him to have the help of his horse, called Svadilfare, and at the suggestion of Loke this was granted him.

On the first day of winter he began to build the burg, but by night he hauled stone for it with his horse. But it seemed a great wonder to the asas what great rocks that horse drew, and the horse did one half more of the mighty task than the builder. The bargain was firmly established with witnesses and oaths, for the giant did not deem it safe to be among the asas without truce if Thor should come home, who now was on a journey to the east fighting trolls. Toward the end of winter the burg was far built, and it was so high and strong that it could in nowise be taken. When there were three days left before summer, the work was all completed excepting the burg gate. Then went the gods to their judgment-seats and held counsel, and asked each other who could have advised to give Freyja in marriage in Jotunheim, or to plunge the air and the heavens in darkness by taking away the sun and the moon and giving them to the giant; and all agreed that this must have been advised by him who gives the most bad counsels, namely, Loke, son of Laufey, and they threatened him with a cruel death if he could not contrive some way of preventing the builder from fulfilling his part of the bargain, and they pro-

ceeded to lay hands on Loke. He in his fright
then promised with an oath that he should so
manage that the builder should lose his wages,
let it cost him what it would. And the same
evening, when the builder drove out after stone
with his horse Svadilfare, a mare suddenly ran
out of the woods to the horse and began to neigh
at him. The steed, knowing what sort of horse
this was, grew excited, burst the reins asunder and
ran after the mare, but she ran from him into the
woods. The builder hurried after them with all
his might, and wanted to catch the steed, but
these horses kept running all night, and thus the
time was lost, and at dawn the work had not
made the usual progress. When the builder saw
that his work was not going to be completed, he
resumed his giant form. When the asas thus
became sure that it was really a mountain-giant
that had come among them, they did not heed
their oaths, but called on Thor. He came
straightway, swung his hammer, Mjolner, and
paid the workman his wages,— not with the sun
and moon, but rather by preventing him from
dwelling in Jotunheim; and this was easily done
with the first blow of the hammer, which broke
his skull into small pieces and sent him down
to Niflhel. But Loke had run such a race with
Svadilfare that he some time after bore a foal.
It was gray, and had eight feet, and this is the

best horse among gods and men. Thus it is said in the Vala's Prophecy:

> Then went the gods,
> The most holy gods,
> Onto their judgment-seats,
> And counseled together
> Who all the air
> With guile had blended
> Or to the giant race
> Oder's may had given.
> Broken were oaths,
> And words and promises,—
> All mighty speech
> That had passed between them.
> Thor alone did this,
> Swollen with anger.
> Seldom sits he still
> When such things he hears.*

44. Then asked Ganglere: What is there to be said of Skidbladner, which you say is the best of ships? Is there no ship equally good, or equally great? Made answer Har: Skidbladner is the best of ships, and is made with the finest work-manship; but Naglfare, which is in Muspel, is the largest. Some dwarfs, the sons of Ivalde, made Skidbladner and gave it to Frey. It is so large that all the asas, with their weapons and war-gear, can find room on board it, and as soon as the sails are hoisted it has fair wind, no matter whither it is going. When it is not wanted for a voyage, it is made of so many pieces and with so much skill, that Frey can fold it together like a napkin and carry it in his pocket.

* Elder Edda: The Vala's Prophecy, 29, 30.

CHAPTER XIV.

Then said Ganglere: A good ship is Skidbladner, but much black art must have been re-
sorted to ere it was so fashioned. Has Thor never
come where he has found anything so strong and
mighty that it has been superior to him either
in strength or in the black art? Har answered:
Few men, I know, are able to tell thereof, but
still he has often been in difficult straits. But
though there have been things so mighty and
strong that Thor has not been able to gain the
victory, they are such as ought not to be spoken
of; for there are many proofs which all must
accept that Thor is the mightiest. Then said
Ganglere: It seems to me that I have now asked
about something that no one can answer. Said
Jafnhar: We have heard tell of adventures that
seem to us incredible, but here sits one near who
is able to tell true tidings thereof, and you may
believe that he will not lie for the first time now,
who never told a lie before. Then said Ganglere:
I will stand here and listen, to see if any answer
is to be had to this question. But if you cannot

answer my question I declare you to be defeated.
Then answered Thride: It is evident that he now
is bound to know, though it does not seem proper
for us to speak thereof. The beginning of this
adventure is that Oku-Thor went on a journey
with his goats and chariot, and with him went
the asa who is called Loke. In the evening they
came to a bonde* and got there lodgings for the
night. In the evening Thor took his goats and
killed them both, whereupon he had them flayed
and borne into a kettle. When the flesh was
boiled, Thor and his companion sat down to supper. Thor invited the bonde, his wife and their
children, a son by name Thjalfe, and a daughter
by name Roskva, to eat with them. Then Thor
laid the goat-skins away from the fire-place, and
requested the bonde and his household to cast
the bones onto the skins. Thjalfe, the bonde's
son, had the thigh of one of the goats, which he
broke asunder with his knife, in order to get at
the marrow. Thor remained there over night.
In the morning, just before daybreak, he arose,
dressed himself, took the hammer Mjolner, lifted
it and hallowed the goat-skins. Then the goats
arose, but one of them limped on one of its hind
legs. When Thor saw this he said that either
the bonde or one of his folk had not dealt skill-
fully with the goat's bones, for he noticed that

* Bonde = peasant.

the thigh was broken. It is not necessary to dwell on this part of the story. All can understand how frightened the bonde became when he saw that Thor let his brows sink down over his eyes. When he saw his eyes he thought he must fall down at the sight of them alone. Thor took hold of the handle of his hammer so hard that his knuckles grew white. As might be expected, the bonde and all his household cried aloud and sued for peace, offering him as an atonement all that they possessed. When he saw their fear, his wrath left him. He was appeased, and took as a ransom the bonde's children, Thjalfe and Roskva. They became his servants, and have always accompanied him since that time.

46. He left his goats there and went on his way east into Jotunheim, clear to the sea, and then he went on across the deep ocean, and went ashore on the other side, together with Loke and Thjalfe and Roskva. When they had proceeded a short distance, there stood before them a great wood, through which they kept going the whole day until dark. Thjalfe, who was of all men the fleetest of foot, bore Thor's bag, but the wood was no good place for provisions. When it had become dark, they sought a place for their night lodging, and found a very large hall. At the end of it was a door as wide as the

hall. Here they remained through the night. About midnight there was a great earthquake; the ground trembled beneath them, and the house shook. Then Thor stood up and called his companions. They looked about them and found an adjoining room to the right, in the midst of the hall, and there they went in. Thor seated himself in the door; the others went farther in and were very much frightened. Thor held his hammer by the handle, ready to defend himself. Then they heard a great groaning and roaring. When it began to dawn, Thor went out and saw a man lying not far from him in the wood. He was very large, lay sleeping, and snored loudly. Then Thor thought he had found out what noise it was that they had heard in the night. He girded himself with his Megingjarder, whereby his asa-might increased. Meanwhile the man woke, and immediately arose. It is said that Thor this once forbore to strike him with the hammer, and asked him for his name. He called himself Skrymer; but, said he, I do not need to ask you what your name is,—I know that you are Asa-Thor. But what have you done with my glove? He stretched out his hand and picked up his glove. Then Thor saw that the glove was the hall in which he had spent the night, and that the adjoining room was the thumb of the glove. Skrymer asked whether they would accept of his company. Thor said yes. Skrymer took and loosed his provision-sack and began to eat his breakfast; but Thor and his fellows did the same in another place. Skrymer proposed that they should lay their store of provisions together, to which Thor consented. Then Skrymer bound all their provisions into one bag, laid it on his back, and led the way all the day, taking gigantic strides. Late in the evening he sought out a place for their night quarters under a large oak. Then Skrymer said to Thor that he wanted to lie down to sleep; they might take the provision-sack and make ready their supper. Then Skrymer fell asleep and snored tremendously. When Thor took the provision-sack and was to open it, then happened what seems incredible, but still it must be told,— that he could not get one knot loosened, nor could he stir a single end of the strings so that it was looser than before. When he saw that all his efforts were in vain he became wroth, seized his hammer Mjolner with both his hands, stepped with one foot forward to where Skrymer was lying and dashed the hammer at his head. Skry- mer awoke and asked whether some leaf had fallen upon his head; whether they had taken their supper, and were ready to go to sleep. Thor answered that they were just going to sleep. Then they went under another oak. But the truth must be told, that there was no fearless sleeping. About midnight Thor heard that Skrymer was snoring and sleeping so fast that it thundered in the wood. He arose and went over to him, clutched the hammer tight and hard, and gave him a blow in the middle of the crown, so that he knew that the head of the hammer sank deep into his head. But just then Skrymer awoke and asked: What is that? Did an acorn fall onto my head? How is it with you, Thor? Thor hastened back, answered that he had just waked up, and said that it was midnight and still time to sleep. Then Thor made up his mind that if he could get a chance to give him the third blow, he should never see him again, and he now lay watching for Skrymer to sleep fast. Shortly before daybreak he heard that Skrymer had fallen asleep. So he arose and ran over to him. He clutched the hammer with all his might and dashed it at his temples, which he saw uppermost. The hammer sank up to the handle. Skrymer sat up, stroked his temples, and said: Are there any birds sitting in the tree above me? Methought, as I awoke, that some moss from the branches fell on my head. What! are you awake, Thor? It is now time to get up and dress; but you have not far left to the burg that is called Utgard. I have heard that you have been whispering among yourselves that I am not small of stature, but you will see greater men when you come to Utgard. Now I will give you wholesome advice. Do not brag too much of yourselves, for Utgard-Loke's thanes will not brook the boasting of such insignificant little fellows as you are; otherwise turn back, and that is, in fact, the best thing for you to do. But if you are bound to continue your journey, then keep straight on eastward; my way lies to the north, to those mountains that you there see. Skrymer then took the provision-sack and threw it on his back, and, leaving them, turned into the wood, and it has not been learned whether the asas wished to meet him again in health.

47. Thor and his companions went their way and continued their journey until noon. Then they saw a burg standing on a plain, and it was so high that they had to bend their necks clear back before they could look over it. They drew nearer and came to the burg-gate, which was closed. Thor finding himself unable to open it, and being anxious to get within the burg, they crept between the bars and so came in. They discovered a large hall and went to it. Finding the door open they entered, and saw there many men, the most of whom were immensely large, sitting on two benches. Thereupon they approached the king, Utgard-Loke, and greeted him. He scarcely deigned to look at them, smiled scornfully and

showed his teeth, saying: It is late to ask for tidings of a long journey, but if I am not mis-taken this stripling is Oku-Thor, is it not? It may be, however, that you are really bigger than you look. For what feats are you and your companions prepared? No one can stay with us here, unless he is skilled in some craft or accomplishment beyond the most of men. Then answered he who came in last, namely Loke: I know the feat of which I am prepared to give proof, that there is no one present who can eat his food faster than I. Then said Utgard-Loke: That is a feat, indeed, if you can keep your word, and you shall try it immediately. He then summoned from the bench a man by name Loge, and requested him to come out on the floor and try his strength against Loke. They took a trough full of meat and set it on the floor, whereupon Loke seated himself at one end and Loge at the other. Both ate as fast as they could, and met at the middle of the trough. Loke had eaten all the flesh off from the bones, but Loge had consumed both the flesh and the bones, and the trough too. All agreed that Loke had lost the wager. Then Utgard-Loke asked what game that young man knew? Thjalfe answered that he would try to run a race with anyone that Utgard-Loke might designate. Utgard-Loke said this was a good feat, and added that it was to be

hoped that he excelled in swiftness if he expected
to win in this game, but he would soon have the
matter decided.   He arose and went out.   There
was an excellent race-course along the flat plain.
Utgard-Loke then summoned a young man, whose
name was Huge, and bade him run a race with
Thjalfe.   Then they took the first heat, and Huge
was so much ahead that when he turned at
the goal he met Thjalfe.   Said Utgard-Loke:
You must lay yourself more forward, Thjalfe, if
you want to win the race; but this I confess,
that there has never before come anyone hither
who was swifter of foot than you.   Then they
took a second heat, and when Huge came to the
goal and turned, there was a long bolt-shot to
Thjalfe.   Then said Utgard-Loke: Thjalfe seems
to me to run well; still I scarcely think he will
win the race, but this will be proven when they
run the third heat.   Then they took one more
heat.   Huge ran to the goal and turned back,
but Thjalfe had not yet gotten to the middle
of the course.   Then all said that this game had
been tried sufficiently.   Utgard-Loke now asked
Thor what feats there were that he would be
willing to exhibit before them, corresponding to
the tales that men tell of his great works.   Thor
replied that he preferred to compete with some-
one in drinking.   Utgard-Loke said there would
be no objection to this.   He went into the hall,

called his cup-bearer, and requested him to take
the sconce-horn that his thanes were wont to
drink from. The cup-bearer immediately brought
forward the horn and handed it to Thor. Said
Utgard-Loke: From this horn it is thought to be
well drunk if it is emptied in one draught, some
men empty it in two draughts, but there is no
drinker so wretched that he cannot exhaust it in
three. Thor looked at the horn and did not
think it was very large, though it seemed pretty
long, but he was very thirsty. He put it to his
lips and swallowed with all his might, thinking
that he should not have to bend over the horn
a second time. But when his breath gave out,
and he looked into the horn to see how it had
gone with his drinking, it seemed to him difficult
to determine whether there was less in it than
before. Then said Utgard-Loke: That is well
drunk, still it is not very much. I could never
have believed it, if anyone had told me, that Asa-
Thor could not drink more, but I know you will
be able to empty it in a second draught. Thor
did not answer, but set the horn to his lips, thinking that he would now take a larger draught.
He drank as long as he could and drank deep, as
he was wont, but still he could not make the tip
of the horn come up as much as he would like.
And when he set the horn away and looked into
it, it seemed to him that he had drunk less than

the first time; but the horn could now be borne
without spilling. Then said Utgard-Loke: How
now, Thor! Are you not leaving more for the
third draught than befits your skill? It seems to
me that if you are to empty the horn with the
third draught, then this will be the greatest. You
will not be deemed so great a man here among
us as the asas call you, if you do not distinguish
yourself more in other feats than you seem to me
to have done in this. Then Thor became wroth,
set the horn to his mouth and drank with all
his might and kept on as long as he could, and
when he looked into it its contents had indeed
visibly diminished, but he gave back the horn
and would not drink any more. Said Utgard-
Loke: It is clear that your might is not so great
as we thought. Would you like to try other
games? It is evident that you gained nothing
by the first. Answered Thor: I should like
to try other games, but I should be surprised if
such a drink at home among the asas would be
called small. What game will you now offer me?
Answered Utgard-Loke: Young lads here think
it nothing but play to lift my cat up from the
ground, and I should never have dared to offer
such a thing to Asa-Thor had I not already seen
that you are much less of a man than I thought.
Then there sprang forth on the floor a gray cat,
and it was rather large. Thor went over to it,

put his hand under the middle of its body and tried to lift it up, but the cat bent its back in the same degree as Thor raised his hands; and when he had stretched them up as far as he was able the cat lifted one foot, and Thor did not carry the game any further. Then said Utgard-Loke: This game ended as I expected. The cat is rather large, and Thor is small, and little compared with the great men that are here with us. Said Thor: Little as you call me, let anyone who likes come hither and wrestle with me, for now I am wroth. Answered Utgard-Loke, looking about him on the benches: I do not see anyone here who would not think it a trifle to wrestle with you. And again he said: Let me see first! Call hither that old woman, Elle, my foster-mother, and let Thor wrestle with her if he wants to. She has thrown to the ground men who have seemed to me no less strong than Thor. Then there came into the hall an old woman. Utgard-Loke bade her take a wrestle with Asa-Thor. The tale is not long. The result of the grapple was, that the more Thor tightened his grasp, the firmer she stood. Then the woman began to bestir herself, and Thor lost his footing. They had some very hard tussles, and before long Thor was brought down on one knee. Then Utgard-Loke stepped forward, bade them cease the wrest-ling, and added that Thor did not need to challenge anybody else to wrestle with him in his hall, besides it was now getting late. He showed Thor and his companions to seats, and they spent the night there enjoying the best of hospitality.

48. At daybreak the next day Thor and his companions arose, dressed themselves and were ready to depart. Then came Utgard-Loke and had the table spread for them, and there was no lack of feasting both in food and in drink. When they had breakfasted, they immediately departed from the burg. Utgard-Loke went with them out of the burg, but at parting he spoke to Thor and asked him how he thought his journey had turned out, or whether he had ever met a mightier man than himself. Thor answered that he could not deny that he had been greatly disgraced in this meeting; and this I know, he added, that you will call me a man of little account, whereat I am much mortified. Then said Utgard-Loke: Now I will tell you the truth, since you have come out of the burg, that if I live, and may have my way, you shall never enter it again; and this I know, forsooth, that you should never have come into it had I before known that you were so strong, and that you had come so near bringing us into great misfortune. Know, then, that I have deceived you with illusions. When I first found you in the woods I came to meet you, and when you were

to loose the provision-sack I had bound it with iron threads, but you did not find where it was to be untied. In the next place, you struck me three times with the hammer. The first blow was the least, and still it was so severe that it would have been my death if it had hit me. You saw near my burg a mountain cloven at the top into three square dales, of which one was the deepest,— these were the dints made by your hammer. The mountain I brought before the blows without your seeing it. In like manner I deceived you in your contests with my courtiers. In regard to the first, in which Loke took part, the facts were as follows: He was very hungry and ate fast; but he whose name was Loge was wildfire, and he burned the trough no less rapidly than the meat. When Thjalfe ran a race with him whose name was Huge, that was my thought, and it was impossible for him to keep pace with its swiftness. When you drank from the horn, and thought that it diminished so little, then, by my troth, it was a great wonder, which I never could have deemed possible. One end of the horn stood in the sea, but that you did not see. When you come to the sea-shore you will discover how much the sea has sunk by your drinking; that is now called the ebb. Furthermore he said: Nor did it seem less wonderful to me that you lifted up the cat; and, to tell you the truth, all who saw it were frightened when they saw that you raised one of its feet from the ground, for it was not such a cat as you thought. It was in reality the Midgard-serpent, which surrounds all lands. It was scarcely long enough to touch the earth with its tail and head, and you raised it so high that your hand nearly reached to heaven. It was also a most astonishing feat when you wrestled with Elle, for none has ever been, and none shall ever be, that Elle (eld, old age) will not get the better of him, though he gets to be old enough to abide her coming. And now the truth is that we must part; and it will be better for us both that you do not visit me again. I will again defend my burg with similar or other delusions, so that you will get no power over me. When Thor heard this tale he seized his hammer and lifted it into the air, but when he was about to strike he saw Utgard-Loke nowhere; and when he turned back to the burg and was going to dash that to pieces, he saw a beautiful and large plain, but no burg. So he turned and went his way back to Thrudvang. But it is truthfully asserted that he then resolved in his own mind to seek that meeting with the Midgard-serpent, which afterward took place. And now I think that no one can tell you truer tidings of this journey of Thor.

49. Then said Ganglere: A most powerful

man is Utgard-Loke, though he deals much with delusions and sorcery. His power is also proven by the fact that he had thanes who were so mighty. But has not Thor avenged himself for this? Made answer Har: It is not unknown, though no wise men tell thereof, how Thor made amends for the journey that has now been spoken of. He did not remain long at home, before he busked himself so suddenly for a new journey, that he took neither chariot, nor goats nor any companions with him. He went out of Midgard in the guise of a young man, and came in the evening to a giant by name Hymer.* Thor tarried there as a guest through the night. In the morning Hymer arose, dressed himself, and busked himself to row out upon the sea to fish. Thor also sprang up, got ready in a hurry and asked Hymer whether he might row out with him. Hymer answered that he would get but little help from Thor, as he was so small and young; and he added, you will get cold if I row as far out and remain as long as I am wont. Thor said that he might row as far from shore as he pleased, for all that, and it was yet to be seen who would be the first to ask to row back to land. And Thor grew so wroth at the giant that he came near letting the hammer ring on

* Called Ymer in the Younger Edda, but the Elder Edda calls him Hymer.

his head straightway, but he restrained himself, for he intended to try his strength elsewhere. He asked Hymer what they were to have for bait, but Hymer replied that he would have to find his own bait. Then Thor turned away to where he saw a herd of oxen, that belonged to Hymer. He took the largest ox, which was called Himinbrjot, twisted his head off and brought it down to the sea-strand. Hymer had then shoved the boat off. Thor went on board and seated himself in the stern; he took two oars and rowed so that Hymer had to confess that the boat sped fast from his rowing. Hymer plied the oars in the bow, and thus the rowing soon ended. Then said Hymer that they had come to the place where he was wont to sit and catch flat-fish, but Thor said he would like to row much farther out, and so they made another swift pull. Then said Hymer that they had come so far out that it was dangerous to stay there, for the Midgard-serpent. Thor said he wished to row a while longer, and so he did; but Hymer was by no means in a happy mood. Thor took in the oars, got ready a very strong line, and the hook was neither less nor weaker. When he had put on the ox-head for bait, he cast it overboard and it sank to the bottom. It must be admitted that Thor now beguiled the Midgard-serpent not a whit less than Utgard-

Loke mocked him when he was to lift the serpent with his hand. The Midgard-serpent took the ox-head into his mouth, whereby the hook entered his palate, but when the serpent perceived this he tugged so hard that both Thor's hands were dashed against the gunwale. Now Thor became angry, assumed his asa-might and spurned so hard that both his feet went through the boat and he stood on the bottom of the sea. He pulled the serpent up to the gunwale; and in truth no one has ever seen a more terrible sight than when Thor whet his eyes on the serpent, and the latter stared at him and spouted venom. It is said that the giant Hymer changed hue and grew pale from fear when he saw the serpent and beheld the water flowing into the boat; but just at the moment when Thor grasped the hammer and lifted it in the air, the giant fumbled for his fishing-knife and cut off Thor's line at the gunwale, whereby the serpent sank back into the sea. Thor threw the hammer after it, and it is even said that he struck off his head at the bottom, but I think the truth is that the Midgard-serpent still lives and lies in the ocean. Thor clenched his fist and gave the giant a box on the ear so that he fell backward into the sea, and he saw his heels last, but Thor waded ashore.

CHAPTER XV.

50. Then asked Ganglere: Have there happened any other remarkable things among the asas? A great deed it was, forsooth, that Thor wrought on this journey. Har answered: Yes, indeed, there are tidings to be told that seemed of far greater importance to the asas. The beginning of this tale is, that Balder dreamed dreams great and dangerous to his life. When he told these dreams to the asas they took counsel together, and it was decided that they should seek peace for Balder against all kinds of harm. So Frigg exacted an oath from fire, water, iron and all kinds of metal, stones, earth, trees, sicknesses, beasts, birds and creeping things, that they should not hurt Balder. When this was done and made known, it became the pastime of Balder and the asas that he should stand up at their meetings while some of them should shoot at him, others should hew at him, while others should throw stones at him; but no matter what they did, no harm came to him, and this seemed to all a great honor. When Loke, Laufey's son, saw this, it

displeased him very much that Balder was not scathed. So he went to Frigg, in Fensal, having taken on himself the likeness of a woman. Frigg asked this woman whether she knew what the asas were doing at their meeting. She answered that all were shooting at Balder, but that he was not scathed thereby. Then said Frigg: Neither weapon nor tree can hurt Balder, I have taken an oath from them all. Then asked the woman: Have all things taken an oath to spare Balder? Frigg answered: West of Valhal there grows a little shrub that is called the mistletoe, that seemed to me too young to exact an oath from. Then the woman suddenly disappeared. Loke went and pulled up the mistletoe and proceeded to the meeting. Hoder stood far to one side in the ring of men, because he was blind. Loke addressed himself to him, and asked: Why do you not shoot at Balder? He answered: Because I do not see where he is, and furthermore I have no weapons. Then said Loke: Do like the others and show honor to Balder; I will show you where he stands; shoot at him with this wand. Hoder took the mistletoe and shot at Balder under the guidance of Loke. The dart pierced him and he fell dead to the ground. This is the greatest misfortune that has ever happened to gods and men. When Balder had fallen, the asas were struck speechless with horror, and their hands

failed them to lay hold of the corpse. One looked
at the other, and all were of one mind toward
him who had done the deed, but being assembled
in a holy peace-stead, no one could take vengeance.
When the asas at length tried to speak, the wailing so choked their voices that one could not
describe to the other his sorrow. Odin took this
misfortune most to heart, since he best compre-
hended how great a loss and injury the fall of
Balder was to the asas. When the gods came to
their senses, Frigg spoke and asked who there
might be among the asas who desired to win all
her love and good will by riding the way to Hel
and trying to find Balder, and offering Hel a ransom if she would allow Balder to return home
again to Asgard. But he is called Hermod, the
Nimble, Odin's swain, who undertook this journey. Odin's steed, Sleipner, was led forth. Hermod mounted him and galloped away.

51. The asas took the corpse of Balder and
brought it to the sea-shore. Hringhorn was the
name of Balder's ship, and it was the largest of
all ships. The gods wanted to launch it and
make Balder's bale-fire thereon, but they could
not move it. Then they sent to Jotunheim after
the giantess whose name is Hyrrokken. She
came riding on a wolf, and had twisted serpents
for reins. When she alighted, Odin appointed
four berserks to take care of her steed, but they

were unable to hold him except by throwing him down on the ground. Hyrrokken went to the prow and launched the ship with one single push, but the motion was so violent that fire sprang from the underlaid rollers and all the earth shook. Then Thor became wroth, grasped his hammer, and would forthwith have crushed her skull, had not all the gods asked peace for her. Balder's corpse was borne out on the ship; and when his wife, Nanna, daughter of Nep, saw this, her heart was broken with grief and she died. She was borne to the funeral-pile and cast on the fire. Thor stood by and hallowed the pile with Mjolner. Before his feet ran a dwarf, whose name is Lit. Him Thor kicked with his foot and dashed him into the fire, and he, too, was burned. But this funeral-pile was attended by many kinds of folk. First of all came Odin, accompanied by Frigg and the valkyries and his ravens. Frey came riding in his chariot drawn by the boar called Gullinburste or Slidrugtanne. Heimdal rode his steed Gulltop, and Freyja drove her cats. There was a large number of frost-giants and mountain-giants. Odin laid on the funeral-pile his gold ring, Draupner, which had the property of producing, every ninth night, eight gold rings of equal weight. Balder's horse, fully caparisoned, was led to his master's pile.

52. But of Hermod it is to be told that he rode nine nights through deep and dark valleys, and did not see light until he came to the Gjallar-river and rode on the Gjallar-bridge, which is thatched with shining gold. Modgud is the name of the may who guards the bridge. She asked him for his name, and of what kin he was, saying that the day before there rode five fylkes (kingdoms, bands) of dead men over the bridge; but she added, it does not shake less under you alone, and you do not have the hue of dead men. Why do you ride the way to Hel? He answered: I am to ride to Hel to find Balder. Have you seen him pass this way? She answered that Balder had ridden over the Gjallar-bridge; adding: But downward and northward lies the way to Hel. Then Hermod rode on till he came to Hel's gate. He alighted from his horse, drew the girths tighter, remounted him, clapped the spurs into him, and the horse leaped over the gate with so much force that he never touched it. Thereupon Hermod proceeded to the hall and alighted from his steed. He went in, and saw there sitting on the foremost seat his brother Balder. He tarried there over night. In the morning he asked Hel whether Balder might ride home with him, and told how great weeping there was among the asas. But Hel replied that it should now be tried whether Balder was so

much beloved as was said. If all things, said
she, both quick and dead, will weep for him, then
he shall go back to the asas, but if anything refuses to shed tears, then he shall remain with
Hel. Hermod arose, and Balder accompanied
him out of the hall. He took the ring Draupner
and sent it as a keepsake to Odin. Nanna sent
Frigg a kerchief and other gifts, and to Fulla she
sent a ring. Thereupon Hermod rode back and
came to Asgard, where he reported the tidings
he had seen and heard.

53. Then the asas sent messengers over all the
world, praying that Balder might be wept out of
Hel's power. All things did so,—men and beasts,
the earth, stones, trees and all metals, just as you
must have seen that these things weep when they
come out of frost and into heat. When the messengers returned home and had done their errand
well, they found a certain cave wherein sat a
giantess (gygr=ogress) whose name was Thok.
They requested her to weep Balder from Hel;
but she answered:

> Thok will weep
> With dry tears
> For Balder's burial;
> Neither in life nor in death
> Gave he me gladness.
> Let Hel keep what she has!

It is generally believed that this Thok was
Loke, Laufey's son, who has wrought most evil
among the asas.

54. Then said Ganglere: A very great wrong
did Loke perpetrate; first of all in causing Balder's death, and next in standing in the way of
his being loosed from Hel. Did he get no punishment for this misdeed? Har answered: Yes,
he was repaid for this in a way that he will long
remember. The gods became exceedingly wroth,
as might be expected. So he ran away and hid
himself in a rock. Here he built a house with
four doors, so that he might keep an outlook on
all sides. Oftentimes in the daytime he took
on him the likeness of a salmon and concealed himself in Frananger Force. Then he
thought to himself what stratagems the asas
might have recourse to in order to catch him.
Now, as he was sitting in his house, he took flax
and yarn and worked them into meshes, in the
manner that nets have since been made; but a
fire was burning before him. Then he saw that
the asas were not far distant. Odin had seen
from Hlidskjalf where Loke kept himself. Loke
immediately sprang up, cast the net on the fire
and leaped into the river. When the asas came
to the house, he entered first who was wisest of
them all, and whose name was Kvaser; and when
he saw in the fire the ashes of the net that had

been burned, he understood that this must be a
contrivance for catching fish, and this he told to
the asas. Thereupon they took flax and made
themselves a net after the pattern of that which
they saw in the ashes and which Loke had made.
When the net was made, the asas went to the
river and cast it into the force. Thor held one
end of the net, and all the other asas laid hold on
the other, thus jointly drawing it along the stream.
Loke went before it and laid himself down between two stones, so that they drew the net over
him, although they perceived that some living
thing touched the meshes. They went up to the
force again and cast out the net a second time.
This time they hung a great weight to it, making
it so heavy that nothing could possibly pass
under it. Loke swam before the net, but when
he saw that he was near the sea he sprang over
the top of the net and hastened back to the force.
When the asas saw whither he went they proceeded up to the force, dividing themselves into
two bands, but Thor waded in the middle of the
stream, and so they dragged the net along to the
sea. Loke saw that he now had only two chances
of escape,— either to risk his life and swim out
to sea, or to leap again over the net. He chose
the latter, and made a tremendous leap over the
top line of the net. Thor grasped after him and
caught him, but he slipped in his hand so that

Thor did not get a firm hold before he got to the tail, and this is the reason why the salmon has so slim a tail. Now Loke was taken without truce and was brought to a cave. The gods took three rocks and set them up on edge, and bored a hole through each rock. Then they took Loke's sons, Vale and Nare or Narfe. Vale they changed into the likeness of a wolf, whereupon he tore his brother Narfe to pieces, with whose intestines the asas bound Loke over the three rocks. One stood under his shoulders, another under his loins, and the third under his hams, and the fetters became iron. Skade took a serpent and fastened up over him, so that the venom should drop from the serpent into his face. But Sigyn, his wife, stands by him, and holds a dish under the venom-drops. Whenever the dish becomes full, she goes and pours away the venom, and meanwhile the venom drops onto Loke's face. Then he twists his body so violently that the whole earth shakes, and this you call earthquakes. There he will lie bound until Ragnarok.

CHAPTER XVI.

RAGNAROK.

55. Then said Ganglere: What tidings are to be told of Ragnarok? Of this I have never heard before. Har answered: Great things are to be said thereof. First, there is a winter called the Fimbul-winter, when snow drives from all quarters, the frosts are so severe, the winds so keen and piercing, that there is no joy in the sun. There are three such winters in succession, without any intervening summer. But before these there are three other winters, during which great wars rage over all the world. Brothers slay each other for the sake of gain, and no one spares his father or mother in that manslaughter and adultery. Thus says the Vala's Prophecy:

> Brothers will fight together
> And become each other's bane;
> Sisters' children
> Their sib shall spoil.*
> Hard is the world,
> Sensual sins grow huge.
> There are ax-ages, sword-ages —
> Shields are cleft in twain,—
> There are wind-ages, wolf-ages,
> Ere the world falls dead.†

* Commit adultery.
† Elder Edda: The Vala's Prophecy, 48, 49

Then happens what will seem a great miracle, that the wolf* devours the sun, and this will seem a great loss. The other wolf will devour the moon, and this too will cause great mischief. The stars shall be hurled from heaven. Then it shall come to pass that the earth and the mountains will shake so violently that trees will be torn up by the roots, the mountains will topple down, and all bonds and fetters will be broken and snapped. The Fenris-wolf gets loose. The sea rushes over the earth, for the Midgard-serpent writhes in giant rage and seeks to gain the land. The ship that is called Naglfar also becomes loose. It is made of the nails of dead men; wherefore it is worth warning that, when a man dies with unpared nails, he supplies a large amount of materials for the building of this ship, which both gods and men wish may be finished as late as possible. But in this flood Naglfar gets afloat. The giant Hrym is its steers-man. The Fenris-wolf advances with wide open mouth; the upper jaw reaches to heaven and the lower jaw is on the earth. He would open it still wider had he room. Fire flashes from his eyes and nostrils. The Midgard-serpent vomits forth venom, defiling all the air and the sea; he is very terrible, and places himself by the side of the wolf. In the midst of this clash and din

* Fenris-wolf.

the heavens are rent in twain, and the sons of Muspel come riding through the opening. Surt rides first, and before him and after him flames burning fire. He has a very good sword, which shines brighter than the sun. As they ride over Bifrost it breaks to pieces, as has before been stated. The sons of Muspel direct their course to the plain which is called Vigrid. Thither repair also the Fenris-wolf and the Midgard-serpent. To this place have also come Loke and Hrym, and with him all the frost-giants. In Loke's company are all the friends of Hel. The sons of Muspel have there effulgent bands alone by themselves. The plain Vigrid is one hundred miles (rasts) on each side

56. While these things are happening, Heimdal stands up, blows with all his might in the Gjallar-horn and awakens all the gods, who thereupon hold counsel. Odin rides to Mimer's well to ask advice of Mimer for himself and his folk. Then quivers the ash Ygdrasil, and all things in heaven and earth fear and tremble. The asas and the einherjes arm themselves and speed forth to the battle-field. Odin rides first; with his golden helmet, resplendent byrnie, and his spear Gungner, he advances against the Fenris-wolf. Thor stands by his side, but can give him no assistance, for he has his hands full in his struggle with the Midgard-serpent. Frey encounters

Surt, and heavy blows are exchanged ere Frey
falls. The cause of his death is that he has not
that good sword which he gave to Skirner. Even
the dog Garm, that was bound before the Gnipa-
cave, gets loose. He is the greatest plague. He
contends with Tyr, and they kill each other.
Thor gets great renown by slaying the Midgard-
serpent, but retreats only nine paces when he
falls to the earth dead, poisoned by the venom
that the serpent blows on him. The wolf swallows
Odin, and thus causes his death; but Vidar immediately turns and rushes at the wolf, placing
one foot on his nether jaw. On this foot he has
the shoe for which materials have been gathering
through all ages, namely, the strips of leather
which men cut off for the toes and heels of
shoes; wherefore he who wishes to render assistance to the asas must cast these strips away.
With one hand Vidar seizes the upper jaw of the
wolf, and thus rends asunder his mouth. Thus
the wolf perishes. Loke fights with Heimdal,
and they kill each other. Thereupon Surt flings
fire over the earth and burns up all the world.
Thus it is said in the Vala's Prophecy:

> Loud blows Heimdal
> His uplifted horn.
> Odin speaks
> With Mimer's head.
> The straight-standing ash
> Ygdrasil quivers,

The old tree groans,
And the giant gets loose.

How fare the asas?
How fare the elves?
All Jotunheim roars.
The asas hold counsel;
Before their stone-doors
Groan the dwarfs,
The guides of the wedge-rock.
Know you now more or not?

From the east drives Hrym,
Bears his shield before him.
Jormungand welters
In giant rage
And smites the waves.
The eagle screams,
And with pale beak tears corpses.
Naglfar gets loose.

A ship comes from the east,
The hosts of Muspel
Come o'er the main,
And Loke is steersman.
All the fell powers
Are with the wolf;
Along with them
Is Byleist's brother.*

From the south comes Surt
.With blazing fire-brand,—
The sun of the war-god
Shines from his sword.
Mountains dash together,
Giant maids are frightened,
Heroes go the way to Hel,
And heaven is rent in twain.

*Loke.

Then comes to Hlin
Another woe,
When Odin goes
With the wolf to fight,
And Bele's bright slayer*
To contend with Surt.
There will fall
Frigg's beloved.

Odin's son goes
To fight with the wolf,
And Vidar goes on his way
To the wild beast.†
With his hand he thrusts
His sword to the heart
Of the giant's child,
And avenges his father.

Then goes the famous
Son‡ of Hlodyn
To fight with the serpent.
Though about to die,
He fears not the contest;
All men
Abandon their homesteads
When the warder of Midgard
In wrath slays the serpent.

The sun grows dark,
The earth sinks into the sea,
The bright stars
From heaven vanish;
Fire rages,
Heat blazes,
And high flames play
'Gainst heaven itself. §

* Frey.　　　　† The Fenris-wolf.　　　‡ Thor.
§ Elder Edda: The Vala's Prophecy, 50–52, 54–57. 59. 60, 62, 63.

And again it is said as follows:

> Vigrid is the name of the plain
> Where in fight shall meet
> Surt and the gentle god.
> A hundred miles
> It is every way.
> This field is marked out for them.*

* Elder Edda: Vafthrudner's Lay, 18.

CHAPTER XVII

57. Then asked Ganglere: What happens when heaven and earth and all the world are consumed in flames, and when all the gods and all the einherjes and all men are dead? You have already said that all men shall live in some world through all ages. Har answered: There are many good and many bad abodes. Best it is to be in Gimle, in heaven. Plenty is there of good drink for those who deem this a joy in the hall called Brimer. That is also in heaven. There is also an excellent hall which stands on the Nida mountains. It is built of red gold, and is called Sindre. In this hall good and well-minded men shall dwell. Nastrand is a large and terrible hall, and its doors open to the north. It is built of serpents wattled together, and all the heads of the serpents turn into the hall and vomit forth venom that flows in streams along the hall, and in these streams wade perjurers and murderers. So it is here said:

> A hall I know standing
> Far from the sun
> On the strand of dead bodies.

Drops of venom
Fall through the loop-holes.
Of serpents' backs
The hall is made.

There shall wade
Through heavy streams
Perjurers
And murderers.

But in Hvergelmer it is worst.

There tortures Nidhug
The bodies of the dead.*

58. Then said Ganglere: Do any gods live then? Is there any earth or heaven? (Har answered:) The earth rises again from the sea, and is green and fair. The fields unsown produce their harvests. Vidar and Vale live. Neither the sea nor Surt's fire has harmed them, and they dwell on the plains of Ida, where Asgard was before. Thither come also the sons of Thor, Mode and Magne, and they have Mjolner. Then come Balder and Hoder from Hel. They all sit together and talk about the things that happened aforetime,— about the Midgard-serpent and the Fenris-wolf. They find in the grass those golden tables which the asas once had. Thus it is said:

Vidar and Vale
Dwell in the house of the gods,
When quenched is the fire of Surt.

* Elder Edda: The Vala's Prophecy, 40, 41.

Mode and Magne
Vingner's Mjolner shall have
When the fight is ended.*

In a place called Hodmimer's-holt † are concealed two persons during Surt's fire, called Lif and Lifthraser. They feed on the morning dew. From these so numerous a race is descended that they fill the whole world with people, as is here said:

Lif and Lifthraser
Will lie hid
In Hodmimer's-holt.
The morning dew
They have for food.
From them are the races descended. ‡

But what will seem wonderful to you is that the sun has brought forth a daughter not less fair than herself, and she rides in the heavenly course of her mother, as is here said:

A daughter
Is born of the sun
Ere Fenrer takes her.
In her mother's course
When the gods are dead
This maid shall ride. §

And if you now can ask more questions, said Har to Ganglere, I know not whence that power came to you. I have never heard any one tell

* Elder Edda: Vafthrudner's Lay, 51.
† Holt = grove.
‡ Elder Edda: Vafthrudner's Lay, 45.
§ Elder Edda: Vafthrudner's Lay, 47.

further the fate of the world. Make now the best use you can of what has been told you.

59. Then Ganglere heard a terrible noise on all sides, and when he looked about him he stood out-doors on a level plain. He saw neither hall nor burg. He went his way and came back to his kingdom, and told the tidings which he had seen and heard, and ever since those tidings have been handed down from man to man.

AFTERWORD

The asas now sat down to talk, and held their counsel, and remembered all the tales that were told to Gylfe. They gave the very same names that had been named before to the men and places that were there. This they did for the reason that, when a long time has elapsed, men should not doubt that those asas of whom these tales were now told and those to whom the same names were given were all identical. There was one who is called Thor, and he is Asa-Thor, the old. He is Oku-Thor, and to him are ascribed the great deeds done by Hektor in Troy. But men think that the Turks have told of Ulysses, and have called him Loke, for the Turks were his greatest enemies.

BRAGE'S TALK.

CHAPTER I.

ÆGER'S JOURNEY TO ASGARD.

1. A man by name Æger, or Hler, who dwelt on the island called Hler's Isle, was well skilled in the black art. He made a journey to Asgard. But the asas knew of his coming and gave him a friendly reception; but they also made use of many sorts of delusions. In the evening, when the feast began, Odin had swords brought into the hall, and they were so bright that it glistened from them so that there was no need of any other light while they sat drinking. Then went the asas to their feast, and the twelve asas who were appointed judges seated themselves in their high-seats. These are their names: Thor, Njord, Frey, Tyr, Heimdal, Brage, Vidar, Vale, Uller, Honer, Forsete, Loke. The asynjes (goddesses) also were with them: Frigg, Freyja, Gefjun, Idun, Gerd, Sigyn, Fulla, Nanna. Æger thought all that he saw looked very grand. The panels of the walls

were all covered with beautiful shields. The mead was very strong, and they drank deep. Next to Æger sat Brage, and they talked much together over their drink. Brage spoke to Æger of many things that had happened to the asas.

CHAPTER II.

2. Brage began his tale by telling how three asas, Odin, Loke and Honer, went on a journey over mountains and heaths, where they could get nothing to eat. But when they came down into a valley they saw a herd of cattle. From this herd they took an ox and went to work to boil it. When they deemed that it must be boiled enough they uncovered the broth, but it was not yet done. After a little while they lifted the cover off again, but it was not yet boiled. They talked among themselves about how this could happen. Then they heard a voice in the oak above them, and he who sat there said that he was the cause that the broth did not get boiled. They looked up and saw an eagle, and it was not a small one. Then said the eagle: If you will give me my fill of the ox, then the broth will be boiled. They agreed to this. So he flew down from the tree, seated himself beside the boiling broth, and immediately snatched up first the two thighs of the ox and then both the shoulders. This made Loke wroth: he grasped a large pole, raised it with all

his might and dashed it at the body of the eagle. The eagle shook himself after the blow and flew up. One end of the pole fastened itself to the body of the eagle, and the other end stuck to Loke's hands. The eagle flew just high enough so that Loke's feet were dragged over stones and rocks and trees, and it seemed to him that his arms would be torn from his shoulder-blades. He calls and prays the eagle most earnestly for peace, but the latter declares that Loke shall never get free unless he will pledge himself to bring Idun and her apples out of Asgard. When Loke had promised this, he was set free and went to his companions again; and no more is related of this journey, except that they returned home. But at the time agreed upon, Loke coaxed Idun out of Asgard into a forest, saying that he had found apples that she would think very nice, and he requested her to take with her her own apples in order to compare them. Then came the giant Thjasse in the guise of an eagle, seized Idun and flew away with her to his home in Thrymheim. The asas were ill at ease on account of the disappearance of Idun,—they became gray-haired and old. They met in council and asked each other who last had seen Idun. The last that had been seen of her was that she had gone out of Asgard in company with Loke. Then Loke was seized and brought into the council,

and he was threatened with death or torture.
But he became frightened, and promised to bring
Idun back from Jotunheim if Freyja would lend
him the falcon-guise that she had. He got the
falcon-guise, flew north into Jotunheim, and came
one day to the giant Thjasse. The giant had
rowed out to sea, and Idun was at home alone.
Loke turned her into the likeness of a nut, held
her in his claws and flew with all his might.
But when Thjasse returned home and missed
Idun, he took on his eagle-guise, flew after Loke,
gaining on the latter with his eagle wings. When
the asas saw the falcon coming flying with the
nut, and how the eagle flew, they went to the
walls of Asgard and brought with them bundles
of plane-shavings. When the falcon flew within
the burg, he let himself drop down beside the
burg-wall. Then the asas kindled a fire in the
shavings; and the eagle, being unable to stop
himself when he missed the falcon, caught fire
in his feathers, so that he could not fly any
farther. The asas were on hand and slew the
giant Thjasse within the gates of Asgard, and
that slaughter is most famous.

CHAPTER III.

HOW NJORD GOT SKADE TO WIFE.

Skade, the daughter of the giant Thjasse, donned her helmet, and byrnie, and all her war-gear, and betook herself to Asgard to avenge her father's death. The asas offered her ransom and atonement; and it was agreed to, in the first place, that she should choose herself a husband among the asas, but she was to make her choice by the feet, which was all she was to see of their persons. She saw one man's feet that were wonderfully beautiful, and exclaimed: This one I choose! On Balder there are few blemishes. But it was Njord, from Noatun. In the second place, it was stipulated that the asas were to do what she did not deem them capable of, and that was to make her laugh. Then Loke tied one end of a string fast to the beard of a goat and the other around his own body, and one pulled this way and the other that, and both of them shrieked out loud. Then Loke let himself fall on Skade's knees, and this made her laugh. It is said that Odin did even more than was asked, in that he took Thjasse's eyes and cast them up into heaven, and made two stars of them. Then said Æger: This Thjasse seems to me to have been considerable of a man; of what kin was he? Brage answered: His father's name was Olvalde, and if I told you of him, you would deem it very remarkable. He was very rich in gold, and when he died and his sons were to divide their heritage, they had this way of measuring the gold, that each should take his mouthful of gold, and they should all take the same number of mouthfuls. One of them was Thjasse, another Ide, and the third Gang. But we now have it as a saw among us, that we call gold the mouth-number of these giants. In runes and songs we wrap the gold up by calling it the measure, or word, or tale, of these giants. Then said Æger: It seems to me that it will be well hidden in the runes.

CHAPTER IV.

3. And again said Æger: Whence originated the art that is called skaldship? Made answer Brage: The beginning of this was, that the gods had a war with the people that are called vans. They agreed to hold a meeting for the purpose of making peace, and settled their dispute in this wise, that they both went to a jar and spit into it. But at parting the gods, being unwilling to let this mark of peace perish, shaped it into a man whose name was Kvaser, and who was so wise that no one could ask him any question that he could not answer. He traveled much about in the world to teach men wisdom. Once he came to the home of the dwarfs Fjalar and Galar. They called him aside, saying they wished to speak with him alone, slew him and let his blood run into two jars called Son and Bodn, and into a kettle called Odrarer. They mixed honey with the blood, and thus was produced such mead that whoever drinks from it becomes a skald and sage. The dwarfs told the asas that Kvaser had choked in his wisdom, because no one was so wise that he could ask him enough about learning.

4. Then the dwarfs invited to themselves the giant whose name is Gilling, and his wife; and when he came they asked him to row out to sea with them. When they had gotten a short distance from shore, the dwarfs rowed onto a blind rock and capsized the boat. Gilling, who was unable to swim, was drowned, but the dwarfs righted the boat again and rowed ashore. When they told of this mishap to his wife she took it much to heart, and began to cry aloud. Then Fjalar asked her whether it would not lighten her sorrow if she could look out upon the sea where her husband had perished, and she said it would. He then said to his brother Galar that he should go up over the doorway, and as she passed out he should let a mill-stone drop onto her head, for he said he was tired of her bawling. Galar did so. When the giant Suttung, the son of Gilling, found this out he came and seized the dwarfs, took them out to sea and left them on a rocky island, which was flooded at high tide. They prayed Suttung to spare their lives, and offered him in atonement for their father's blood the precious mead, which he accepted. Suttung brought the mead home with him, and hid it in a place called Hnitbjorg. He set his daughter Gunlad to guard it. For these reasons we call songship Kvaser's blood; the drink of the dwarfs; the dwarfs' fill; some kind of liquor of Odrarer,

or Bodn or Son; the ship of the dwarfs (because
this mead ransomed their lives from the rocky
isle); the mead of Suttung, or the liquor of
Hnitbjorg.

5. Then remarked Æger: It seems dark to me
to call songship by these names; but how came
the asas by Suttung's mead? Answered Brage:
The saga about this is, that Odin set out from
home and came to a place where nine thralls
were mowing hay. He asked them whether they
would like to have him whet their scythes. To
this they said yes. Then he took a whet-stone
from his belt and whetted the scythes. They
thought their scythes were much improved, and
asked whether the whet-stone was for sale. He
answered that he who would buy it must pay
a fair price for it. All said they were willing
to give the sum demanded, and each wanted
Odin to sell it to him. But he threw the whet-
stone up in the air, and when all wished to catch
it they scrambled about it in such a manner
that each brought his scythe onto the other's
neck. Odin sought lodgings for the night at
the house of the giant Bauge, who was a brother
of Suttung. Bauge complained of what had
happened to his household, saying that his nine
thralls had slain each other, and that he did not
know where he should get other workmen. Odin
called himself Bolverk. He offered to undertake

the work of the nine men for Bauge, but asked
in payment therefor a drink of Suttung's mead.
Bauge answered that he had no control over the
mead, saying that Suttung was bound to keep
that for himself alone. But he agreed to go
with Bolverk and try whether they could get
the mead. During the summer Bolverk did the
work of the nine men for Bauge, but when winter
came he asked for his pay. Then they both went
to Suttung. Bauge explained to Suttung his bargain with Bolverk, but Suttung stoutly refused
to give even a drop of the mead. Bolverk then
proposed to Bauge that they should try whether
they could not get at the mead by the aid of
some trick, and Bauge agreed to this. Then
Bolverk drew forth the auger which is called
Rate, and requested Bauge to bore a hole through
the rock, if the auger was sharp enough. He did
so. Then said Bauge that there was a hole
through the rock; but Bolverk blowed into the
hole that the auger had made, and the chips
flew back into his face. Thus he saw that Bauge
intended to deceive him, and commanded him
to bore through. Bauge bored again, and when
Bolverk blew a second time the chips flew inward.
Now Bolverk changed himself into the likeness
of a serpent and crept into the auger-hole. Bauge
thrust after him with the auger, but missed him.
Bolverk went to where Gunlad was, and shared

her couch for three nights. She then promised to give him three draughts from the mead. With the first draught he emptied Odrarer, in the second Bodn, and in the third Son, and thus he had all the mead. Then he took on the guise of an eagle, and flew off as fast as he could. When Suttung saw the flight of the eagle, he also took on the shape of an eagle and flew after him. When the asas saw Odin coming, they set their jars out in the yard. When Odin reached Asgard, he spewed the mead up into the jars. He was, however, so near being caught by Suttung, that he sent some of the mead after him backward, and as no care was taken of this,. anybody that wished might have it. This we call the share of poetasters. But Suttung's mead Odin gave to the asas and to those men who are able to make verses. Hence we call songship Odin's prey, Odin's find, Odin's drink, Odin's gift, and the drink of the asas.

6. Then said Æger: In how many ways do you vary the poetical expressions, or how many kinds of poetry are there? Answered Brage: There are two kinds, and all poetry falls into one or the other of these classes. Æger asks: Which two? Brage answers: Diction and meter. What diction is used in poetry? There are three sorts of poetic diction. Which? One is to name everything by its own name; another is to name it with a pro-

noun, but the third sort of diction is called *ken-ning* (a poetical periphrasis or descriptive name); and this sort is so managed that when we name Odin, or Thor or Tyr, or any other of the asas or elves, we add to their name a reference to some other asa, or we make mention of some of his works. Then the appellation belongs to him who corresponds to the whole phrase, and not to him who was actually named. Thus we speak of Odin as Sigtyr, Hangatyr or Farmatyr, and such names we call simple appellatives. In the same manner he is called Reidartyr.

AFTERWORD

Now it is to be said to young skalds who are
desirous of acquiring the diction of poetry, or of
increasing their store of words with old names,
or, on the other hand, are eager to understand
what is obscurely sung, that they must master
this book for their instruction and pastime. These
sagas are not to be so forgotten or disproved as
to take away from poetry old periphrases which
great skalds have been pleased with. But christian men should not believe in heathen gods, nor
in the truth of these sagas, otherwise than is explained in the beginning of this book, where the
events are explained which led men away from
the true faith, and where it, in the next place, is
told of the Turks how the men from Asia, who
are called asas, falsified the tales of the things that
happened in Troy, in order that the people should
believe them to be gods.

King Priam in Troy was a great chief over all
the Turkish host, and his sons were the most distinguished men in his whole army. That excellent hall, which the asas called Brime's Hall, or

beer-hall, was King Priam's palace. As for the long tale that they tell of Ragnarok, that is the wars of the Trojans. When it is said that Oku-Thor angled with an ox-head and drew on board the Midgard-serpent, but that the serpent kept his life and sank back into the sea, then this is another version of the story that Hektor slew Volukrontes, a famous hero, in the presence of Achilleus, and so drew the latter onto him with the head of the slain, which they likened unto the head of an ox, which Oku-Thor had torn off. When Achilleus was drawn into this danger, on account of his daring, it was the salvation of his life that he fled from the fatal blows of Hektor, although he was wounded. It is also said that Hektor waged the war so mightily, and that his rage was so great when he caught sight of Achilleus, that nothing was so strong that it could stand before him. When he missed Achilleus, who had fled, he soothed his wrath by slaying the champion called Roddros. But the asas say that when Oku-Thor missed the serpent, he slew the giant Hymer. In Ragnarok the Midgard-serpent came suddenly upon Thor and blew venom onto him, and thus struck him dead. But the asas could not make up their minds to say that this had been the fate of Oku-Thor, that anyone stood over him dead, though this had so happened. They rushed headlong over old sagas more than was true when they said that the Midgard-serpent there got his death; and they added this to the story, that Achilleus reaped the fame of Hektor's death, though he lay dead on the same battle-field on that account. This was the work of Elenus and Alexander, and Elenus the asas call Ale. They say that he avenged his brother, and that he lived when all the gods were dead, and after the fire was quenched that burned up Asgard and all the possessions of the gods. Pyrrhos they compared with the Fenris-wolf. He slew Odin, and Pyrrhos might be called a wolf according to their belief, for he did not spare the peace-steads, when he slew the king in the temple before the altar of Thor. The burning of Troy they call the flame of Surt. Mode and Magne, the sons of Oku-Thor, came to crave the land of Ale or Vidar. He is Æneas. He came away from Troy, and wrought thereupon great works. It is said that the sons of Hektor came to Frigialand and established themselves in that kingdom, but banished Elenus.

THE POETICAL DICTION.

(SKALDSKAPARMAL.)*

THOR AND HRUNGNER.

Brage told Æger that Thor had gone eastward to crush trolls. Odin rode on his horse Sleipner to Jotunheim, and came to the giant whose name is Hrungner. Then asked Hrungner what man that was who with a golden helmet rode both through the air and over the sea, and added that he had a remarkably good horse. Odin said that he would wager his head that so good a horse could not be found in Jotunheim. Hrungner admitted that it was indeed an excellent horse, but he had one, called Goldfax, that could take much longer paces; and in his wrath he immediately sprang upon his horse and galloped after Odin, intending to pay him for his insolence. Odin rode so fast that he was a good distance ahead, but Hrungner had worked himself into such a giant rage that, before he was aware of it, he had come within the gates of Asgard.

*This part of the Younger Edda corresponds to the Latin Ars Poetica, and contains the rules and laws of ancient poetry.

When he came to the hall door, the asas invited
him to drink with them. He entered the hall
and requested a drink. They then took the
bowls that Thor was accustomed to drink from,
and Hrungner emptied them all. When he became drunk, he gave the freest vent to his loud
boastings. He said he was going to take Valhal
and move it to Jotunheim, demolish Asgard and
kill all the gods except Freyja and Sif, whom he
was going to take home with him. When Freyja
went forward to refill the bowls for him, he
boasted that he was going to drink up all the
ale of the asas. But when the asas grew weary
of his arrogance, they named Thor's name. At
once Thor was in the hall, swung his hammer
in the air, and, being exceedingly wroth, asked
who was to blame that dog-wise giants were permitted to drink there, who had given Hrungner
permission to be in Valhal, and why Freyja
should pour ale for him as she did in the feasts
of the asas. Then answered Hrungner, looking
with anything but friendly eyes at Thor, and
said that Odin had invited him to drink, and
that he was there under his protection. Thor
replied that he should come to rue that invitation
before he came out. Hrungner again answered
that it would be but little credit to Asa-Thor to
kill him, unarmed as he was. It would be a
greater proof of his valor if he dared fight a duel

with him at the boundaries of his territory, at Grjottungard. It was very foolish of me, he said, that I left my shield and my flint-stone at home; had I my weapons here, you and I would try a holmgang (duel on a rocky island); but as this is not the case, I declare you a coward if you kill me unarmed. Thor was by no means the man to refuse to fight a duel when he was challenged, an honor which never had been shown him before. Then Hrungner went his way, and hastened with all his might back to Jotunheim. His journey became famous among the giants, and the proposed meeting with Thor was much talked of. They regarded it very important who should gain the victory, and they feared the worst from Thor if Hrungner should be defeated, for he was the strongest among them. There-upon the giants made at Grjottungard a man of clay, who was nine rasts tall and three rasts broad under the arms, but being unable to find a heart large enough to be suitable for him, they took the heart from a mare, but even this flut-tered and trembled when Thor came. Hrungner had, as is well-known, a heart of stone, sharp and three-sided; just as the rune has since been risted that is called Hrungner's heart. Even his head was of stone. His shield was of stone, and was broad and thick, and he was holding this shield before him as he stood at Grjottungard waiting for Thor. His weapon was a flint-stone, which he swung over his shoulders, and altogether he presented a most formidable aspect. On one side of him stood the giant of clay, who was named Mokkerkalfe. He was so exceedingly terrified, that it is said that he wet himself when he saw Thor. Thor proceeded to the duel, and Thjalfe was with him. Thjalfe ran forward to where Hrungner was standing, and said to him: You stand illy guarded, giant; you hold the shield before you, but Thor has seen you; he goes down into the earth and will attack you from below. Then Hrungner thrust the shield under his feet and stood on it, but the flint-stone he seized with both his hands. The next that he saw were flashes of lightning, and he heard loud crashings; and then he saw Thor in his asa-might advancing with impetuous speed, swinging his hammer and hurling it from afar at Hrungner. Hrungner seized the flint-stone with both his hands and threw it against the hammer. They met in the air, and the flint-stone broke. One part fell to the earth, and from it have come the flint-mountains; the other part hit Thor's head with such force that he fell forward to the ground. But the hammer Mjolner hit Hrungner right in the head, and crushed his skull in small pieces. He himself fell forward over Thor, so that his foot lay upon Thor's neck. Meanwhile Thjalfe attacked Mokkerkalfe, who fell with but little honor. Then Thjalfe went to Thor and was to take Hrungner's foot off from him, but he had not the strength to do it. When the asas learned that Thor had fallen, they all came to take the giant's foot off, but none of them was able to move it. Then came Magne, the son of Thor and Jarnsaxa. He was only three nights of age. He threw Hrungner's foot off Thor, and said It was a great mishap, father, that I came so late. I think I could have slain this giant with my fist, had I met him. Then Thor arose, greeted his son lovingly, saying that he would become great and powerful; and, added he, I will give you the horse Goldfax, that belonged to Hrungner. Odin said that Thor did wrong in giving so fine a horse to the son of a giantess, instead of to his father. Thor went home to Thrudvang, but the flint-stone still stuck fast in his head. Then came the vala whose name is Groa, the wife of Orvandel the Bold. She sang her magic songs over Thor until the flint-stone became loose. But when Thor perceived this, and was just expecting that the flint-stone would disappear, he desired to reward Groa for her healing, and make her heart glad. So he related to her how he had waded from the north over the Elivogs rivers, and had borne in a basket on his back Orvandel from Jotunheim; and in evidence of this he told her how that one toe of his had protruded from the basket and had frozen, wherefore Thor had broken it off and had cast it up into the sky, and made of it the star which is called Orvandel's toe. Finally he added that it would not be long before Orvandel would come home. But Groa became so glad that she forgot her magic songs, and so the flint-stone became no looser than it was, and it sticks fast in Thor's head yet. For this reason it is forbidden to throw a flint-stone across the floor, for then the stone in Thor's head is moved. Out of this saga Thjodolf of Hvin has made a song:

We have ample evidence
Of the giant-terrifier's* journey
To Grjottungard, to the giant Hrungner,
In the midst of encircling flames.
The courage waxed high in Meile's brother; †
The moon-way trembled
When Jord's son ‡ went
To the steel-gloved contest.

The heavens stood all in flames
For Uller's step-father, §
And the earth rocked.
Svolne's ‖ widow ¶ burst asunder
When the span of goats
Drew the sublime chariot
And its divine master
To the meeting with Hrungner.

* Thor's.   † Thor.   ‡ Jord's (= earth's) son = Thor.
§ Thor.   ‖ Odin's.   ¶ The earth.

Balder's brother* did not tremble
Before the greedy fiend of men;
Mountains quaked and rocks broke;
The heavens were wrapped in flames.
Much did the giant
Get frightened, I learn,
When his bane man he saw
Ready to slay him.

Swiftly the gray shield flew
'Neath the heels of the giant.
So the gods willed it,
So willed it the valkyries.
Hrungner the giant,
Eager for slaughter,
Needed not long to wait for blows
From the valiant friend of the hammer.

The slayer† of Bele's evil race
Made fall the bear of the loud-roaring mountain;‡
On his shield
Bite the dust
Must the giant
Before the sharp-edged hammer,
When the giant-crusher
Stood against the mighty Hrungner,

And the flint-stone
(So hard to break)
Of the friend of the troll-women
Into the skull did whiz
Of Jord's son,§
And this flinty piece
Fast did stick
In Eindride's‖ blood;

Until Orvandel's wife,
Magic songs singing,

---

* Thor. † Thor. ‡ The giant Hrungner. § Thor. ‖ Thor's.

> From the head of Thor
> Removed the giant's
> Excellent flint-stone.
> All do I know
> About that shield-journey.
> A shield adorned
> With hues most splendid
> I received from Thorleif.

THOR'S JOURNEY TO GEIRROD'S.

Then said Æger: Much of a man, it seems to
me, was that Hrungner. Has Thor accomplished
any other great deeds in his intercourse with
trolls (giants)? Then answered Brage: It is
worth giving a full account of how Thor made a
journey to Geirrodsgard. He had with him
neither the hammer Mjolner, nor his belt of
strength, Megingjard, nor his steel gloves; and
that was Loke's fault,—he was with him. For
it had happened to Loke, when he once flew
out to amuse himself in Frigg's falcon-guise, that
he, out of curiosity, flew into Geirrodsgard, where
he saw a large hall. He sat down and looked
in through the window, but Geirrod discovered
him, and ordered the bird to be caught and
brought to him. The servant had hard work
to climb up the wall of the hall, so high was
it. It amused Loke that it gave the servant so
much trouble to get at him, and he thought it
would be time enough to fly away when he

had gotten over the worst. When the latter now caught at him, Loke spread his wings and spurned with his feet, but these were fast, and so Loke was caught and brought to the giant. When the latter saw his eyes he suspected that it was a man. He put questions to him and bade him answer, but Loke refused to speak. Then Geirrod locked him down in a chest, and starved him for three months; and when Geirrod finally took him up again, and asked him to speak, Loke confessed who he was, and to save his life he swore an oath to Geirrod that he would get Thor to come to Geirrodsgard without his hammer or his belt of strength.

On his way Thor visited the giantess whose name is Grid. She was the mother of Vidar the Silent. She told Thor the truth concerning Geirrod, that he was a dog-wise and dangerous giant; and she lent him her own belt of strength and steel gloves, and her staff, which is called Gridarvol. Then went Thor to the river which is called Vimer, and which is the largest of all rivers. He buckled on the belt of strength and stemmed the wild torrent with Gridarvol, but Loke held himself fast in Megingjard. When Thor had come into the middle of the stream, the river waxed so greatly that the waves dashed over his shoulders. Then quoth Thor:

> Wax not Vimer,
> Since I intend to wade
> To the gards of giants.
> Know, if you wax,
> Then waxes my asa-might
> As high as the heavens.

Then Thor looked up and saw in a cleft Gjalp, the daughter of Geirrod, standing on both sides of the stream, and causing its growth. Then took he up out of the river a huge stone and threw at her, saying: At its source the stream must be stemmed.* He was not wont to miss his mark. At the same time he reached the river bank and got hold of a shrub, and so he got out of the river. Hence comes the adage that *a shrub saved Thor*.† When Thor came to Geirrod, he and his companion were shown to the guest-room, where lodgings were given them, but there was but one seat, and on that Thor sat down. Then he became aware that the seat was raised under him toward the roof. He put the Gridarvol against the rafters, and pressed himself down against the seat. Then was heard a great crash, which was followed by a loud screaming. Under the seat were Geirrod's daughters, Gjalp and Greip, and he had broken the backs of both of them. Then quoth Thor:

> Once I employed
> My asa-might
> In the gards of the giants.

---

* Icelandic proverb.   † Icelandic proverb.

> When Gjalp and Greip,
> Geirrod's daughters,
> Wanted to lift me to heaven.

Then Geirrod had Thor invited into the hall to the games. Large fires burned along the whole length of the hall. When Thor came into the hall, and stood opposite Geirrod, the latter seized with a pair of tongs a red-hot iron wedge and threw it at Thor. But he caught it with his steel gloves, and lifted it up in the air. Geirrod sprang behind an iron post to guard himself. But Thor threw the wedge with so great force that it struck through the post, through Geirrod, through the wall, and then went out and into the ground. From this saga, Eilif, son of Gudrun, made the following song, called Thor's Drapa:

> The Midgard-serpent's father exhorted
> Thor, the victor of giants,
> To set out from home.
> A great liar was Loke.
> Not quite confident,
> The companion of the war-god
> Declared green paths to lie
> To the gard of Geirrod.
>
> Thor did not long let Loke
> Invite him to the arduous journey.
> They were eager to crush
> Thorn's descendants.
> When he, who is wont to swing Megingjard,
> Once set out from Odin's home
> To visit Ymer's children in Gandvik.

The giantess Gjalp,
Perjured Geirrod's daughter,
Sooner got ready magic to use
Than the god of war and Loke.
A song I recite.
Those gods noxious to the giants
Planted their feet
In Endil's land,

And the men wont to battle
Went forth.
The message of death
Came of the moon-devourer's women,
When the cunning and wrathful
Conqueror of Loke
Challenged to a contest
The giantess.

And the troll-woman's disgracer
Waded across the roaring stream,—
Rolling full of drenched snow over its banks.
He who puts giants to flight
Rapidly advanced
O'er the broad watery way,
Where the noisy stream's
Venom belched forth.

Thor and his companions
Put before him the staff;
Thereon he rèsted
Whilst over they waded:
Nor sleep did the stones,—
The sonorous staff striking the rapid wave
Made the river-bed ring,—
The mountain-torrent rang with stones.

The wearer of Megingjard
Saw the flood fall
On his hard-waxed shoulders:
He could do no better.

The destroyer of troll-children
Let his neck-strength
Wax heaven high,
Till the mighty stream should diminish.

But the warriors,
The oath-bound protectors of Asgard,—
The experienced vikings,—
Waded fast and the stream sped on.
Thou god of the bow!
The billows
Blown by the mountain-storm
Powerfully rushed
Over Thor's shoulders.

Thjalfe and his companion,
With their heads above water,
Got over the river,—
To Thor's belt they clung.
Their strength was tested,—
Geirrod's daughters made hard the stream
For the iron rod.
Angry fared Thor with the Gridarvol.

Nor did courage fail
Those foes of the giant
In the seething vortex.
Those sworn companions
Regarded a brave heart
Better than gold.
Neither Thor's nor Thjalfe's heart
From fear did tremble.

And the war companions—
Weapons despising—
'Mong the giants made havoc,
Until, O woman!
The giant destroyers
The conflict of helmets
With the warlike race
Did commence.

The giants of Iva's* capes
Made a rush with Geirrod;
The foes of the cold Svithiod
Took to flight.
Geirrod's giants
Had to succumb
When the lightning wielder's† kinsmen
Closely pursued them.

Wailing was 'mongst the cave-dwellers
When the giants,
With warlike spirit endowed,
Went forward.
There was war.
The slayer of troll-women,
By foes surrounded,
The giant's hard head hit.

With violent pressure
Were pressed the vast eyes
Of Gjalp and Greip
Against the high roof.
The fire-chariot's driver
The old backs broke
Of both these maids
For the cave-woman.

The man of the rocky way
But scanty knowledge got;
Nor able were the giants
To enjoy perfect gladness.
● Thou man of the bow-string!
The dwarf's kinsman
An iron beam, in the forge heated,
Threw against Odin's dear son.

* A river in Jotunheim.
† Thor's kinsmen = the asas.

But the battle-hastener,
Freyja's old friend,
With swift hands caught
In the air the beam
As it flew from the hands
Of the father of Greip,—
His breast with anger swollen
Against Thruda's * father.

Geirrod's hall trembled
When he struck,
With his broad head,
'Gainst the old column of the house-wall.
Uller's splendid flatterer
Swung the iron beam
Straight 'gainst the head
Of the knavish giant.

The crusher of the hall-wont troll-women
A splendid victory won
Over Glam's descendants;
With gory hammer fared Thor.
Gridarvol-staff,
Which made disaster
'Mong Geirrod's companion,
Was not used 'gainst that giant himself.

The much worshiped thunderer,
With all his might, slew
The dwellers in Alfheim
With that little willow-twig,
And no shield
Was able to resist
The strong age-diminisher
Of the mountain-king.

---

* Thruda was a daughter of Thor and Sif.

IDUN.

How shall Idun be named? She is called the wife of Brage, the keeper of the apples; but the apples are called the medicine to bar old age (ellilyf, elixir vitæ). She is also called the booty of the giant Thjasse, according to what has before been said concerning how he took her away from the asas. From this saga Thjodolf, of Hvin, composed the following song in his Haustlong:

> How shall the tongue
> Pay an ample reward
> For the sonorous shield
> Which I received from Thorleif,
> Foremost 'mong soldiers?
> On the splendidly made shield
> I see the unsafe journey
> Of three gods and Thjasse.
>
> Idun's robber flew long ago
> The asas to meet
> In the giant's old eagle-guise.
> The eagle perched
> Where the asas bore
> Their food to be cooked.
> Ye women! The mountain-giant
> Was not wont to be timid.
>
> Suspected of malice
> Was the giant toward the gods.
> Who causes this?
> Said the chief of the gods.
> The wise-worded giant-eagle
> From the old tree began to speak.
> The friend of Honer
> Was not friendly to him.

The mountain-wolf from Honer
Asked for his fill
From the holy table:
It fell to Honer to blow the fire.
The giant, eager to kill,
Glided down
Where the unsuspecting gods,
Odin, Loke and Honer, were sitting.

The fair lord of the earth
Bade Farbaute's son
Quickly to share
The ox with the giant;
But the cunning foe of the asas
Thereupon laid
The four parts of the ox
Upon the broad table.

And the huge father of Morn *
Afterward greedily ate
The ox at the tree-root.
That was long ago,
Until the profound
Loke the hard rod laid
'Twixt the shoulders
Of the giant Thjasse.

Then clung with his hands
The husband of Sigyn
To Skade's foster-son,
In the presence of all the gods.
The pole stuck fast
To Jotunheim's strong fascinator,
But the hands of Honer's dear friend
Stuck to the other end.

Flew then with the wise god
The voracious bird of prey
Far away; so the wolf's father
To pieces must be torn.

         * A troll-woman.

Odin's friend got exhausted.
Heavy grew Lopt.
Odin's companion
Must sue for peace.

Hymer's kinsman demanded
That the leader of hosts
The sorrow-healing maid,
Who the asas' youth-preserving apples keeps,
Should bring to him.
Brisingamen's thief
Afterward brought Idun
To the gard of the giant.

Sorry were not the giants
After this had taken place,
Since from the south
Idun had come to the giants.
All the race
Of Yngve-Frey, at the Thing,
Grew old and gray,—
Ugly-looking were the gods.

Until the gods found the blood-dog,
Idun's decoying thrall,
And bound the maid's deceiver,
You shall, cunning Loke,
Spake Thor, die;
Unless back you lead,
With your tricks, that
Good joy-increasing maid.

Heard have I that thereupon
The friend of Honer flew
In the guise of a falcon
(He often deceived the asas with his cunning);
And the strong fraudulent giant,
The father of Morn,
With the wings of the eagle
Sped after the hawk's child.

The holy gods soon built a fire—
They shaved off kindlings—
And the giant was scorched.
This is said in memory
Of the dwarf's heel-bridge.*
A shield adorned with splendid lines
From Thorleif I received.

ÆGER'S FEAST.

How shall gold be named? It may be called Æger's fire; the needles of Glaser; Sif's hair; Fulla's head-gear; Freyja's tears; the chatter, talk or word of the giants; Draupner's drop; Draupner's rain or shower; Freyja's eyes; the otter-ransom, or stroke-ransom, of the asas; the seed of Fyrisvold; Holge's how-roof; the fire of all waters and of the hand; or the stone, rock or gleam of the hand.

Why is gold called Æger's fire? The saga relating to this is, as has before been told, that Æger made a visit to Asgard, but when he was ready to return home he invited Odin and all the asas to come and pay him a visit after the lapse of three months. On this journey went Odin, Njord, Frey, Tyr, Brage, Vidar, Loke; and also the asynjes, Frigg, Freyja, Gefjun, Skade, Idun, Sif. Thor was not there, for he had gone eastward to fight trolls. When the gods had taken their seats, Æger let his servants bring in

*Shield.

on the hall floor bright gold, which shone and lighted up the whole hall like fire, just as the swords in Valhal are used instead of fire. Then Loke bandied hasty words with all the gods, and slew Æger's thrall who was called Fimafeng. The name of his other thrall is Elder. The name of Æger's wife is Ran, and they have nine daughters, as has before been written. At this feast all things passed around spontaneously, both food and ale and all the utensils needed for the feasting. Then the asas became aware that Ran had a net in which she caught all men who perish at sea. Then the saga goes on telling how it happens that gold is called the fire, or light or brightness of Æger, of Ran, or of Æger's daughters; and from these periphrases it is allowed to call gold the fire of the sea, or of any of the periphrases of the sea, since Æger and Ran are found in periphrases of the sea; and thus gold is now called the fire of waters, of rivers, or of all the periphrases of rivers. But these names have fared like other periphrases. The younger skald has composed poetry after the pattern of the old skalds, imitating their songs; but afterward they have expanded the metaphors whenever they thought they could improve upon what was sung before; and thus the water is the sea, the river is the lakes, the brook is the river. Hence all the figures that are expanded more than what has

before been found are called new tropes, and all
seem good that contain likelihood and are natural.
Thus sang the skald Brage:

> From the king I received
> The fire of the brook.
> This the king gave to me
> And a head with song.

Why is gold called the needles or leaves of
Glaser?   In Asgard, before the doors of Valhal,
stands a grove which is called Glaser, and all its
leaves are of red gold, as is here sung:

> Glaser stands
> With golden leaves
> Before Sigtyr's halls.

This is the fairest forest among gods and men.

LOKE'S WAGER WITH THE DWARFS.

Why is gold called Sif's hair?   Loke Laufey's
son had once craftily cut all the hair off Sif; but
when Thor found it out he seized Loke, and
would have broken every bone in him, had he
not pledged himself with an oath to get the
swarthy elves to make for Sif a hair of gold that
should grow like other hair.   Then went Loke
to the dwarfs that are called Ivald's sons, and
they made the hair and Skidbladner, and the
spear that Odin owned and is called Gungner.
Thereupon Loke wagered his head with the dwarf,

who hight Brok, that his brother Sindre would not be able to make three other treasures equally as good as these were. But when they came to the smithy, Sindre laid a pig-skin in the furnace and requested Brok to blow the bellows, and not to stop blowing before he (Sindre) had taken out of the furnace what he had put into it. As soon, however, as Sindre had gone out of the smithy and Brok was blowing, a fly lighted on his hand and stung him; but he kept on blowing as before until the smith had taken the work out of the furnace. That was now a boar, and its bristles were of gold. Thereupon he laid gold in the furnace, and requested Brok to blow, and not to stop plying the bellows before he came back. He went out; but then came the fly and lighted on his neck and stung him still worse; but he continued to work the bellows until the smith took out of the furnace the gold ring called Draupner. Then Sindre placed iron in the furnace, and requested Brok to work the bellows, adding that otherwise all would be worthless. Now the fly lighted between his eyes and stung his eye-lids, and as the blood ran down into his eyes so that he could not see, he let go of the bellows just for a moment and drove the fly away with his hands. Then the smith came back and said that all that lay in the furnace came near being entirely spoiled. Thereupon he took a hammer out of the furnace.

All these treasures he then placed in the hands
of his brother Brok, and bade him go with Loke
to Asgard to fetch the wager. When Loke and
Brok brought forth the treasures, the gods seated
themselves upon their doom-steads. It was agreed
to abide by the decision which should be pronounced by Odin, Thor and Frey. Loke gave to
Odin the spear Gungner, to Thor the hair, which
Sif was to have, and to Frey, Skidbladner; and
he described the qualities of all these treasures,
stating that the spear never would miss its mark,
that the hair would grow as soon as it was placed
on Sif's head, and that Skidbladner would always
have fair wind as soon as the sails were hoisted,
no matter where its owner desired to go; besides,
the ship could be folded together like a napkin
and be carried in his pocket if he desired. Then
Brok produced his treasures. He gave to Odin
the ring, saying that every ninth night eight other
rings as heavy as it would drop from it; to Frey
he gave the boar, stating that it would run through
the air and over seas, by night or by day, faster
than any horse; and never could it become so dark
in the night, or in the worlds of darkness, but
that it would be light where this boar was present, so bright shone his bristles. Then he gave
to Thor the hammer, and said that he might strike
with it as hard as he pleased; no matter what was
before him, the hammer would take no scathe,

and wherever he might throw it he would never
lose it; it would never fly so far that it did not
return to his hand; and if he desired, it would
become so small that he might conceal it in his
bosom; but it had one fault, which was, that the
handle was rather short. The decision of the
gods was, that the hammer was the best of all
these treasures and the greatest protection against
the frost-giants, and they declared that the dwarf
had fairly won the wager. Then Loke offered to
ransom his head. The dwarf answered saying
there was no hope for him on that score. Take
me, then! said Loke; but when the dwarf was to
seize him Loke was far away, for he had the shoes
with which he could run through the air and
over the sea. Then the dwarf requested Thor to
seize him, and he did so. Now the dwarf wanted
to cut the head off Loke, but Loke said that the
head was his, but not the neck. Then the dwarf
took thread and a knife and wanted to pierce
holes in Loke's lips, so as to sew his mouth together, but the knife would not cut. Then said
he, it would be better if he had his brother's awl,
and as soon as he named it the awl was there
and it pierced Loke's lips. Now Brok sewed
Loke's mouth together, and broke off the thread
at the end of the sewing. The thread with which
the mouth of Loke was sewed together is called
Vartare (a strap).

THE NIFLUNGS AND GJUKUNGS.

The following is the reason why gold is called otter-ransom: It is related that three asas went abroad to learn to know the whole world, Odin, Honer and Loke. They came to a river, and walked along the river-bank to a force, and near the force was an otter. The otter had caught a salmon in the force, and sat eating it with his eyes closed. Loke picked up a stone, threw it at the otter and hit him in the head. Loke bragged of his chase, for he had secured an otter and a salmon with one throw. They took the salmon and the otter with them, and came to a byre, where they entered. But the name of the bonde who lived there was Hreidmar. He was a mighty man, and thoroughly skilled in the black art. The asas asked for night-lodgings, stating that they had plenty of food, and showed the bonde their game. But when Hreidmar saw the otter he called his sons, Fafner and Regin, and said that Otter, their brother, was slain, and also told who had done it. Then the father and the sons attacked the asas, seized them and bound them, and then said, in reference to the otter, that he was Hreidmar's son. The asas offered, as a ransom for their lives, as much money as Hreidmar himself might demand, and this was agreed to, and confirmed with an oath. Then the otter was flayed. Hreidmar took the otter-belg and said to them that they should fill the belg with red gold, and then cover it with the same metal, and when this was done they should be set free. Thereupon Odin sent Loke to the home of the swarthy elves, and he came to the dwarf whose name is Andvare, and who lived as a fish, in the water. Loke caught him in his hands, and demanded of him, as a ransom for his life, all the gold that he had in his rock. And when they entered the rock, the dwarf produced all the gold that he owned, and that was a very large amount. Then the dwarf concealed in his hand a small gold ring. Loke saw this, and requested him to hand forth the ring. The dwarf begged him not to take the ring away from him, for with this ring he could increase his wealth again if he kept it. Loke said the dwarf should not keep as much as a penny, took the ring from him and went out. But the dwarf said that that ring should be the bane of every one who possessed it. Loke replied that he was glad of this, and said that all should be fulfilled according to his prophecy: he would take care to bring the curse to the ears of him who was to receive it. He went to Hreidmar and showed Odin the gold; but when the latter saw the ring, it seemed to him a fair one, and he took it and put it aside, giving Hreidmar the rest of the gold. They filled the otter-belg as full as it would hold, and raised it up when it was full. Then came Odin, and was to cover the belg with gold; and when this was done, he requested Hreidmar to come and see whether the belg was sufficiently covered. But Hreidmar looked at it, examined it closely, and saw a mouth-hair, and demanded that it should be covered, too, otherwise the agreement would be broken. Then Odin brought forth the ring and covered with it the mouth-hair, saying that now they had paid the otter-ransom. But when Odin had taken his spear, and Loke his shoes, so that they had nothing more to fear, Loke said that the curse that Andvare had pronounced should be fulfilled, and that the ring and that gold should be the bane of its possessor; and this curse was afterward fulfilled. This explains why gold is called the otter-ransom, or forced payment of the asas, or strife-metal.

What more is there to be told of this gold? Hreidmar accepted the gold as a ransom for his son, but Fafner and Regin demanded their share of it as a ransom for their brother. Hreidmar was, however, unwilling to give them as much as a penny of it. Then the brothers made an agreement to kill their father for the sake of the gold. When this was done, Regin demanded that Fafner should give him one half of it. Fafner answered that there was but little hope that he would share the gold with his brother, since he had himself slain his father to obtain it; and he commanded Regin to get him gone, for else the same thing would happen to him as had happened to Hreidmar. Fafner had taken the sword hight Hrotte, and the helmet which had belonged to his father, and the latter he had placed on his head. This was called the Æger's helmet, and it was a terror to all living to behold it. Regin had the sword called Refil. With it he fled. But Fafner went to Gnita-heath (the glittering heath), where he made himself a bed, took on him the likeness of a serpent (dragon), and lay brooding over the gold.

Regin then went to Thjode, to king Hjalprek, and became his smith. There he undertook the fostering of Sigurd (Sigfrid), the son of Sigmund, the son of Volsung and the son of Hjordis, the daughter cf Eylime. Sigurd was the mightiest of all the kings of hosts, in respect to both family and power and mind. Regin explained to him where Fafner was lying on the gold, and egged him on to try to get possession thereof. Then Regin made the sword which is hight Gram (wrath), and which was so sharp that when Sigurd held it in the flowing stream it cut asunder a tuft of wool which the current carried down against the sword's edge. In the next place, Sigurd cut with his sword Regin's anvil in twain.

Thereupon Sigurd and Regin repaired to Gnita-heath. Here Sigurd dug a ditch in Fafner's path and sat down in it; so when Fafner crept to the water and came directly over this ditch, Sigurd pierced him with the sword, and this thrust caused his death. Then Regin came and declared that Sigurd had slain his brother, and demanded of him as a ransom that he should cut out Fafner's heart and roast it on the fire; but Regin kneeled down, drank Fafner's blood, and laid himself down to sleep. While Sigurd was roasting the heart, and thought that it must be done, he touched it with his finger to see how tender it was; but the fat oozed out of the heart and onto his finger and burnt it, so that he thrust his finger into his mouth. The heart-blood came in contact with his tongue, which made him comprehend the speech of birds, and he understood what the eagles said that were sitting in the trees. One of the birds said:

> There sits Sigurd,
> Stained with blood.
> On the fire is roasting
> Fafner's heart.
> Wise seemed to me
> The ring-destroyer,
> If he the shining
> Heart would eat.

Another eagle sang:

> There lies Regin,
> Contemplating

> How to deceive the man
> Who trusts him;
> Thinks in his wrath
> Of false accusations.
> The evil smith plots
> Revenge 'gainst the brother.*

Then Sigurd went to Regin and slew him, and thereupon he mounted his horse hight Grane, and rode until he came to Fafner's bed, took out all the gold, packed it in two bags and laid it on Grane's back, then got on himself and rode away. Now is told the saga according to which gold is called Fafner's bed or lair, the metal of Gnita-heath, or Grane's burden.

Then Sigurd rode on until he found a house on the mountain. In it slept a woman clad in helmet and coat-of-mail. He drew his sword and cut the coat-of-mail off from her. Then she awaked and called herself Hild. Her name was Brynhild, and she was a valkyrie. Thence Sigurd rode on and came to the king whose name was Gjuke. His wife was called Grimhild, and their children were Gunnar, Hogne, Gudrun, Gudny; Gothorm was Gjuke's step-son. Here Sigurd remained a long time. Then he got the hand of Gudrun, Gjuke's daughter, and Gunnar and Hogne entered into a sworn brotherhood with Sigurd. Afterward Sigurd and the sons of Gjuke went to Atle, Budle's son, to ask for his sister,

---

* Elder Edda: the Lay of Fafner, 32, 33.

Brynhild, for Gunnar's wife. She sat on Hind-fell, and her hall was surrounded by the bicker-ing flame called the Vafurloge, and she had made a solemn promise not to wed any other man than him who dared to ride through the bickering flame. Then Sigurd and the Gjukungs (they are also called Niflungs) rode upon the mountain, and there Gunnar was to ride through the Vafurloge. He had the horse that was called Gote, but this horse did not dare to run into the flame. So Sigurd and Gunnar changed form and weapons, for Grane would not take a step under any other man than Sigurd. Then Sigurd mounted Grane and rode through the bickering flame. That same evening he held a wedding with Brynhild; but when they went to bed he drew his sword Gram from the sheath and placed it between them. In the morning when he had arisen, and had donned his clothes, he gave to Brynhild, as a bridal gift, the gold ring that Loke had taken from Andvare, and he received another ring as a memento from her. Then Sigurd mounted his horse and rode to his companions. He and Gunnar exchanged forms again and went back to Gjuke with Brynhild. Sigurd had two children with Gudrun. Their names were Sigmund and Swanhild.

Once it happened that Brynhild and Gudrun went to the water to wash their hair. When they came to the river Brynhild waded from the

river bank into the stream, and said that she
could not bear to have that water in her hair that
ran from Gudrun's hair, for she had a more high-
minded husband. Then Gudrun followed her
into the stream, and said that she was entitled
to wash her hair farther up the stream than
Brynhild, for the reason that she had the husband who was bolder than Gunnar, or any other
man in the world; for it was he who slew Fafner
and Regin, and inherited the wealth of both.
Then answered Brynhild: A greater deed it was
that Gunnar rode through the Vafurloge, which
Sigurd did not dare to do. Then laughed Gudrun and said: Do you think it was Gunnar
who rode through the bickering flame? Then I
think you shared the bed with him who gave me
this gold ring. The gold ring which you have
on your finger, and which you received as a
bridal-gift, is called Andvaranaut (Andvare's
Gift), and I do not think Gunnar got it on Gnita-
heath. Then Brynhild became silent and went
home. Thereupon she egged Gunnar and Hogne
to kill Sigurd; but being sworn brothers of
Sigurd, they egged Guthorm, their brother, to
slay Sigurd. Guthorm pierced him with his
sword while he was sleeping; but as soon as
Sigurd was wounded he threw his sword, Gram,
after Guthorm, so that it cut him in twain
through the middle. There Sigurd fell, and his

son, three winters old, by name Sigmund, whom
they also killed. Then Brynhild pierced herself
with the sword and was cremated with Sigurd.
But Gunnar and Hogne inherited Fafner's gold
and the Gift of Andvare, and now ruled the
lands.

King Atle, Budle's son, Brynhild's brother, then
got in marriage Gudrun, who had been Sigurd's
wife, and they had children. King Atle invited
Gunnar and Hogne to visit him, and they accepted his invitation. But before they started on
their journey they concealed Fafner's hoard in
the Rhine, and that gold has never since been
found. King Atle had gathered together an
army and fought a battle with Gunnar and
Hogne, and they were captured. Atle had the
heart cut out of Hogne alive. This was his
death. Gunnar he threw into a den of snakes,
but a harp was secretly brought to him, and he
played the harp with his toes (for his hands were
fettered), so that all the snakes fell asleep excepting the adder, which rushed at him and bit him
in the breast, and then thrust its head into the
wound and clung to his liver until he died. Gunnar and Hogne are called Niflungs (Niblungs)
and Gjukungs. Hence gold is called the Niflung
treasure or inheritance. A little later Gudrun
slew her two sons and made from their skulls
goblets trimmed with gold, and thereupon the

funeral ceremonies took place. At the feast, Gudrun poured for King Atle in these goblets mead that was mixed with the blood of the youths. Their hearts she roasted and gave to the king to eat. When this was done she told him all about it, with many unkind words. There was no lack of strong mead, so that the most of the people sitting there fell asleep. On that night she went to the king when he had fallen asleep, and had with her her son Hogne. They slew him, and thus he ended his life. Then they set fire to the hall, and with it all the people who were in it were burned. Then she went to the sea and sprang into the water to drown herself; but she was carried across the fjord, and came to the land which belonged to King Jonaker. When he saw her he took her home and made her his wife. They had three children, whose names were Sorle, Hamder and Erp. They all had hair as black as ravens, like Gunnar and Hogne and the other Niflungs.

There was fostered Swanhild, the daughter of Sigurd, and she was the fairest of all women. That Jormunrek, the rich, found out. He sent his son, Randver, to ask for her hand for him; and when he came to Jonaker, Swanhild was delivered to him, so that he might bring her to King Jormunrek. Then said Bikke that it would be more fitting that Randver should marry Swanhild, he being young and she too, but Jormunrek being old. This plan pleased the two young people well. Soon afterward Bikke informed the king of it, and so King Jormunrek seized his son and had him brought to the gallows. Then Randver took his hawk, plucked the feathers off him, and requested that it should be sent to his father, whereupon he was hanged. But when King Jormunrek saw the hawk, it came to his mind that as the hawk was flightless and featherless, so his kingdom was without preservation ; for he was old and sonless. Then King Jormunrek riding out of the woods from the chase with his courtiers, while Queen Swanhild sat dressing her hair, had the courtiers ride onto her, and she was trampled to death beneath the feet of the horses. When Gudrun heard of this, she begged her sons to avenge Swanhild. While they were busking themselves for the journey, she brought them byrnies and helmets, so strong that iron could not scathe them. She laid the plan for them, that when they came to King Jormunrek, they should attack him in the night whilst he was sleeping. Sorle and Hamder should cut off his hands and feet, and Erp his head. On the way they asked Erp what assistance they were to get from him, when they came to King Jormunrek. He answered them that he would give them such assistance as the hand gives the foot. They said that the feet got no support from the hands whatsoever. They were angry at their mother, because she had forced them to undertake this journey with harsh words, and hence they were going to do that which would displease her most. So they killed Erp, for she loved him the most. A little later, while Sorle was walking, he slipped with one foot, and in falling supported himself with his hands. Then said he: Now the hands helped the foot; better were it now if Erp were living. When they came to Jormunrek, the king, in the night, while he was sleeping, they cut off both his hands and his feet. Then he awaked, called his men and bade them arise. Said Hamder then: The head would now have been off had Erp lived. The courtiers got up, attacked them, but could not overcome them with weapons. Then Jormunrek cried to them that they should stone them to death. This was done, Sorle and Hamder fell, and thus perished the last descendants of Gjuke.

After King Sigurd lived a daughter hight Aslaug, who was fostered at Heimer's in Hlymdaler. From her mighty races are descended. It is said that Sigmund, the son of Volsung, was so powerful, that he drank venom and received no harm therefrom. But Sinfjotle, his son, and Sigurd, were so hard-skinned that no venom coming onto them could harm them. Therefore the skald Brage has sung as follows:

> When the tortuous serpent,
> Full of the drink of the Volsungs,*
> Hung in coils
> On the bait of the giant-slayer.†

Upon these sagas very many skalds have made lays, and from them they have taken various themes. Brage the Old made the following song about the fall of Sorle and Hamder in the drapa, which he composed about Ragnar Lodbrok:

> Jormunrek once,
> In an evil dream, waked
> In that sword-contest
> Against the blood-stained kings.
> A clashing of arms was heard
> In the house of Randver's father,
> When the raven-blue brothers of Erp
> The insult avenged.
>
> Sword-dew flowed
> Off the bed on the floor.
> Bloody hands and feet of the king
> One saw cut off.
> On his head fell Jormunrek,
> Frothing in blood.
> On the shield
> This is painted.
>
> The king saw
> Men so stand
> That a ring they made
> 'Round his house.

----

* The drink of the Volsungs = venom; the tortuous venom-serpent = the Midgard-serpent.

† Thor.

Sorle and Hamder
Were both at once,
With slippery stones,
Struck to the ground.
King Jormunrek
Ordered Gjuke's descendants
Violently to be stoned
When they came to take the life
Of Swanhild's husband.
All sought to pay
Jonaker's sons
With blows and wounds.

This fall of men
And sagas many
On the fair shield I see.
Ragnar gave me the shield.

MENJA AND FENJA.

Why is gold called Frode's meal? The saga
giving rise to this is the following:

Odin had a son by name Skjold, from whom
the Skjoldungs are descended. He had his throne
and ruled in the lands that are now called Denmark, but were then called Gotland. Skjold had
a son by name Fridleif, who ruled the lands
after him. Fridleif's son was Frode. He took
the kingdom after his father, at the time when
the Emperor Augustus established peace in all
the earth and Christ was born. But Frode being
the mightiest king in the northlands, this peace
was attributed to him by all who spake the
Danish tongue, and the Norsemen called it the

peace of Frode. No man injured the other, even though he might meet, loose or in chains, his father's or brother's bane. There was no thief or robber, so that a gold ring would be a long time on Jalanger's heath. King Frode sent messengers to Svithjod, to the king whose name was Fjolner, and bought there two maid-servants, whose names were Fenja and Menja. They were large and strong. About this time were found in Denmark two mill-stones, so large that no one had the strength to turn them. But the nature belonged to these mill-stones that they ground whatever was demanded of them by the miller. The name of this mill was Grotte. But the man to whom King Frode gave the mill was called Hengekjapt. King Frode had the maid-servants led to the mill, and requested them to grind for him gold and peace, and Frode's happiness. Then he gave them no longer time to rest or sleep than while the cuckoo was silent or while they sang a song. It is said that they sang the song called the Grottesong, and before they ended it they ground out a host against Frode; so that on the same night there came the sea-king, whose name was Mysing, and slew Frode and took a large amount of booty. Therewith the Frode-peace ended. Mysing took with him Grotte, and also Fenja and Menja, and bade them grind salt, and in the middle of the night they asked Mysing whether he did not have salt enough. He bade them grind more. They ground only a short time longer before the ship sank. But in the ocean arose a whirlpool (Maelstrom, mill-stream) in the place where the sea runs into the mill-eye. Thus the sea became salt.

THE GROTTESONG.

Now are come
To the house of the king
The prescient two,
Fenja and Menja.
There must the mighty
Maidens toil
For King Frode,
Fridleif's son.

Brought to the mill
Soon they were;
The gray stones
They had to turn.
Nor rest nor peace
He gave to them:
He would hear the maidens
Turn the mill.

They turned the mill,
The prattling stones
The mill ever rattling.
What a noise it made!
Lay the planks!
Lift the stones! *

---

* These words are spoken by the maidens while they put the mill together.

But he* bade the maids
Yet more to grind.

They sang and swung
The swift mill-stone,
So that Frode's folk
Fell asleep.
Then, when she came
To the mill to grind,
With a hard heart
And with loud voice
Did Menja sing:

We grind for Frode
Wealth and happiness,
And gold abundant
On the mill of luck.
Dance on roses!
Sleep on down!
Wake when you please!
That is well ground.

Here shall no one
Hurt the other,
Nor in ambush lie,
Nor seek to kill;
Nor shall any one
With sharp sword hew,
Though bound he should find
His brother's bane.

They stood in the hall,
Their hands were resting;
Then was it the first
Word that he spoke:
Sleep not longer
Than the cuckoo on the hall,
Or only while
A song I sing:

* Frode.

Frode! you were not
Wary enough,—
You friend of men,—
When maids you bought!
At their strength you looked,
And at their fair faces,
But you asked no questions
About their descent.

Hard was Hrungner
And his father;
Yet was Thjasse
Stronger than they,
And Ide and Orner,
Our friends, and
The mountain-giants' brothers,
Who fostered us two.

Not would Grotte have come
From the mountain gray,
Nor this hard stone
Out from the earth;
The maids of the mountain-giants
Would not thus be grinding
If we two knew
Nothing of the mill.

Through winters nine
Our strength increased,
While below the sod
We played together.
Great deeds were the maids
Able to perform;
Mountains they
From their places moved.

The stone we rolled
From the giants' dwelling,
So that all the earth
Did rock and quake.

So we hurled
The rattling stone,
The heavy block,
That men caught it.

In Svithjod's land
Afterward we
Fire-wise women,
Fared to the battle,
Byrnies we burst,
Shields we cleaved,
Made our way
Through gray-clad hosts.

One chief we slew,
Another we aided,—
To Guthorm the Good
Help we gave.
Ere Knue had fallen
Nor rest we got.
Then bound we were
And taken prisoners.

Such were our deeds
In former days,
That we heroes brave
Were thought to be.
With spears sharp
Heroes we pierced,
So the gore did run
And our swords grew red.

Now we are come
To the house of the king,
No one us pities.
Bond-women are we.
Dirt eats our feet,
Our limbs are cold,
The peace-giver* we turn.
Hard it is at Frode's.

*The mill.

The hands shall stop,
The stone shall stand;
Now have I ground
For my part enough.
Yet to the hands
No rest must be given,
'Till Frode thinks
Enough has been ground.

Now hold shall the hands
The lances hard,
The weapons bloody,—
Wake now, Frode!
Wake now, Frode!
If you would listen
To our songs,—
To sayings old.

Fire I see burn
East of the burg,—
The warnews are awake.
That is called warning.
A host hither
Hastily approaches
To burn the king's
Lofty dwelling

No longer you will sit
On the throne of Hleidra
And rule o'er red
Rings and the mill.
Now must we grind
With all our might,
No warmth will we get
From the blood of the slain.

Now my father's daughter
Bravely turns the mill.
The death of many
Men she sees.

Now broke the large
Braces 'neath the mill,—
The iron-bound braces.
Let us yet grind!

Let us yet grind!
Yrsa's son
Shall on Frode revenge
Halfdan's death.
He shall Yrsa's
Offspring be named,
And yet Yrsa's brother.
Both of us know it.

The mill turned the maidens,—
Their might they tested;
Young they were,
And giantesses wild.
The braces trembled.
Then fell the mill,—
In twain was broken
The heavy stone.

All the old world
Shook and trembled,
But the giant's maid
Speedily said:
We have turned the mill, Frode!
Now we may stop.
By the mill long enough
The maidens have stood.

ROLF KRAKE.

A king in Denmark hight Rolf Krake, and
was the most famous of all kings of olden times;
moreover, he was more mild, brave and conde-
scending than all other men. A proof of his con-
descension, which is very often spoken of in olden
stories, was the following: There was a poor
little fellow by name Vog. He once came into
King Rolf's hall while the king was yet a young
man, and of rather delicate growth. Then Vog
went before him and looked up at him. Then
said the king: What do you mean to say, my
fellow, by looking so at me? Answered Vog:
When I was at home I heard people say that
King Rolf, at Hleidra, was the greatest man in
the northlands, but now sits here in the high-seat
a little crow (krake), and it they call their king.
Then made answer the king: You, my fellow,
have given me a name, and I shall henceforth be
called Rolf Krake, but it is customary that a gift
accompanies the name. Seeing that you have no
gift that you can give me with the name, or that
would be suitable to me, then he who has must
give to the other. Then he took a gold ring off
his hand and gave it to the churl. Then said
Vog: You give as the best king of all, and therefore I now pledge myself to become the bane of

him who becomes your bane. Said the king,
laughing: A small thing makes Vog happy.

Another example is told of Rolf Krake's bravery. In Upsala reigned a king by name Adils,
whose wife was Yrsa, Rolf Krake's mother. He
was engaged in a war with Norway's king, Ale.
They fought a battle on the ice of the lake called
Wenern. King Adils sent a message to Rolf
Krake, his stepson, asking him to come and help
him, and promising to furnish pay for his whole
army during the campaign. Furthermore King
Rolf himself should have any three treasures that
he might choose in Sweden. But Rolf Krake
could not go to his assistance, on account of the
war which he was then waging against the
Saxons. Still he sent twelve berserks to King
Adils. Among them were Bodvar Bjarke, Hjalte
the Valiant, Hvitserk the Keen, Vot, Vidsete, and
the brothers Svipday and Beigud. In that war
fell King Ale and a large part of his army. Then
King Adils took from the dead King Ale the
helmet called Hildesvin, and his horse called
Rafn. Then the berserks each demanded three
pounds of gold in pay for their service, and also
asked for the treasures which they had chosen
for Rolf Krake, and which they now desired to
bring to him. These were the helmet Hildegolt;
the byrnie Finnsleif, which no steel could scathe;
and the gold ring called Sviagris, which had

belonged to Adils' forefathers. But the king
refused to surrender any of these treasures, nor
did he give the berserks any pay. The berserks
then returned home, and were much dissatisfied.
They reported all to King Rolf, who straightway
busked himself to fare against Upsala; and when
he came with his ships into the river Fyre, he
rode against Upsala, and with him his twelve
berserks, all peaceless. Yrsa, his mother, received
him and took him to his lodgings, but not to the
king's hall. Large fires were kindled for them,
and ale was brought them to drink. Then came
King Adils' men in and bore fuel onto the fire-
place, and made a fire so great that it burnt the
clothes of Rolf and his berserks, saying: Is it
true that neither fire nor steel will put Rolf
Krake and his berserks to flight? Then Rolf
Krake and all his men sprang up, and he said:

> Let us increase the blaze
> In Adils' chambers.

He took his shield and cast it into the fire, and
sprang over the fire while the shield was burning, and cried:

> From the fire flees not he
> Who over it leaps.

The same did also his men, one after the other,
and then they took those who had put fuel on
the fire and cast them into it. Now Yrsa came

and handed Rolf Krake a deer's horn full of gold, and with it she gave him the ring Sviagris, and requested them to ride straightway to their army. They sprang upon their horses and rode away over the Fyrisvold. Then they saw that King Adils was riding after them with his whole army, all armed, and was going to slay them. Rolf Krake took gold out of the horn with his right hand, and scattered it over the whole way. But when the Swedes saw it they leaped out of their saddles, and each one took as much as he could. King Adils bade them ride, and he him-self rode on with all his might. The name of his horse was Slungner, the fastest of all horses. When Rolf Krake saw that King Adils was riding near him, he took the ring Sviagris and threw it to him, asking him to take it as a gift. King Adils rode to the ring, picked it up with the end of his spear, and let it slide down to his hand. Then Rolf Krake turned round and saw that the other was stooping. Said he: Like a swine I have now bended the foremost of all Swedes. Thus they parted. Hence gold is called the seed of Krake or of Fyrisvold.

HOGNE AND HILD.

A king by name Hogne had a daughter by name Hild. Her a king, by name Hedin, son of Hjarrande, made a prisoner of war, while King Hogne had fared to the trysting of the kings. But when he learned that there had been harrying in his kingdom, and that his daughter had been taken away, he rode with his army in search of Hedin, and learned that he had sailed northward along the coast. When King Hogne came to Norway, he found out that Hedin had sailed westward into the sea. Then Hogne sailed after him to the Orkneys. And when he came to the island called Ha, then Hedin was there before him with his host. Then Hild went to meet her father, and offered him as a reconciliation from Hedin a necklace; but if he was not willing to accept this, she said that Hedin was prepared for a battle, and Hogne might expect no clemency from him. Hogne answered his daughter harshly. When she returned to Hedin, she told him that Hogne would not be reconciled, and bade him busk himself for the battle. And so both parties did; they landed on the island and marshaled their hosts. Then Hedin called to Hogne, his father-in-law, offering him a reconciliation and much gold as a ransom. Hogne answered: Too late do you offer to make peace with me, for now I have drawn the sword Dains-leif, which was smithied by the dwarfs, and must be the death of a man whenever it is drawn; its blows never miss the mark, and the wounds made by it never heal. Said Hedin: You boast the sword, but not the victory. That I call a good sword that is always faithful to its master Then they began the battle which is called the Hjadninga-vig (the slaying of the Hedin*ians*); they fought the whole day, and in the evening the kings fared back to their ships. But in the night Hild went to the battlefield, and waked up with sorcery all the dead that had fallen. The next day the kings went to the battlefield and fought, and so did also all they who had fallen the day before. Thus the battle continued from day to day; and all they who fell, and all the swords that lay on the field of battle, and all the shields, became stone. But as soon as day dawned all the dead arose again and fought, and all the weapons became new again, and in songs it is said that the Hjadnings will so con-tinue until Ragnarok.

NOTES.

ENEA.

The **Enea** mentioned in the Foreword to Gylfe's
Fooling refers to the settlement of western Europe,
where Æneas is said to have founded a city on the
Tiber. Bergmann, however, in his Fascination de
Gulfi, page 28, refers it to the Thracian town Ainos.

HERIKON.

Herikon is undoubtedly a mutilated form for Erich-
thonios. The genealogy here given corresponds with
the one given in the Iliad, Book 20, 215.

THE HISTORICAL ODIN.

The historical or anthropomorphized Odin, described in the Foreword to the Fooling of Gylfe, becomes interesting when we compare it with Snorre's
account of that hero in Heimskringla, and then compare both accounts with the Roman traditions about
Æneas. Of course the whole story is only a myth;
but we should remember that in the minds and hearts
of our ancestors it served every purpose of genuine
history. Our fathers accepted it in as good faith as
any christian ever believed in the gospel of Christ,
and so it had a similar influence in moulding the
social, religious, political and literary life of our ancestors. We become interested in this legend as

much as if it were genuine history, on account of the influence it wielded upon the minds and hearts of a race destined to act so great a part in the social, religious and political drama of Europe. We look into this and other ancestral myths, and see mirrored in them all that we afterward find to be reliable history of the old Teutons. In the same manner we are interested in the story told about Romulus and Remus, about Mars and the wolf. This Roman myth is equally prophetic in reference to the future career of Rome. The warlike Mars, the rapacity of the wolf, and the fratricide Romulus, form a mirror in which we see reflected the whole historical development of the Romans; so that the story of Romulus is a vest-pocket edition of the history of Rome.

There are many points of resemblance between this old story of Odin and the account that Virgil gives us of Æneas, the founder of the Latin race; and it is believed that, while Virgil imitated Homer, he based his poem upon a legend current among his countrymen. The Greeks in Virgil's poem are Pompey and the Romans in our Teutonic story. The Trojans correspond to Mithridates and his allies. Æneas and Odin are identical. Just as Odin, a heroic defender of Mithridates, after traversing various unknown countries, finally reaches the north of Europe, organizes the various Teutonic kingdoms, settles his sons upon the thrones of Germany, England, Denmark, Sweden and Norway, and instructs his people to gather strength and courage, so as eventually to take revenge on the cursed Romans; so Æneas, one of the most valiant defenders of Troy, after many adventures in various lands, at length settles in Italy,

and becomes the founder of a race that in course of
time is to wreak vengeance upon the Greeks. The
prophecy contained in the Roman legend was fulfilled
by Metellus and Mummius, in the years 147 and 146
before Christ, when the Romans became the con-
querors of Greece. The prophecy contained in our
Teutonic legend foreshadowed with no less unrelent-
ing necessity the downfall of proud Rome, when the
Teutonic commander Odoacer, in the year 476 after
Christ, dethroned, not Romulus, brother of Remus,
but Romulus Augustulus, son of Orestes. Thus history
repeats itself. Roman history begins and ends with
Romulus; and we fancy we can see some connection
between Od-in and Od-oacer. "As the twig is bent
the tree is inclined."

It might be interesting to institute a similar com-
parison between our Teutonic race-founder Odin and
Ulysses, king of Ithaca, but the reader will have to
do this for himself.

In one respect our heroes differ. The fall of Troy
and the wanderings of Ulysses became the theme of
two great epic poems among the Greeks. The wanderings and adventures of Æneas, son of Anchises,
were fashioned into a lordly epic by Virgil for the Romans. But the much-traveled man, the ἀνὴρ πολύθροπος,
the weapons and the hero, Odin, who, driven by the
norns, first came to Teutondom and to the Baltic
shores, has not yet been sung. This wonderful expedition of our race-founder, which, by giving a historic
cause to all the later hostilities and conflicts between
the Teutons and the Romans, might, as suggested by
Gibbon, supply the noble ground-work of an epic
poem as thrilling as the Æneid of Virgil, has not yet

been woven into a song for our race, and we give our readers this full account of Odin from the Heimskringla in connection with the Foreword to Gylfe's Fooling, with the hope that among our readers there may be found some descendant of Odin, whose skaldic wings are but just fledged for the flights he hopes to take, who will take a draught, first from Mimer's gushing fountain, then from Suttung's mead, brought by Odin to Asgard, and consecrate himself and his talents to this legend with all the ardor of his soul. For, as William Morris so beautifully says of the Volsung Saga, this is the great story of the Teutonic race, and should be to us what the tale of Troy was to the Greeks, and what the tale of Æneas was to the Romans, to all our race first and afterward, when the evolution of the world has made the Teutonic race nothing more than a name of what it has been; a story, too, then, should it be to the races that come after us, no less than the Iliad, and the Odyssey and the Æneid have been to us.* We sincerely trust that we shall see Odin wrought into a Teutonic epic, that will present in grand outline the contrast between the Roman and the Teuton. And now we are prepared to give the Heimskringla account of the historical Odin. We have adopted Samuel Laing's translation, with a few verbal alterations where such seemed necessary.

It is said that the earth's circle (Heimskringla), which the human race inhabits, is torn across into many bights, so that great seas run into the land from the out-ocean. Thus it is known that a great

---

* Quoted from memory.

sea goes into Njorvasound,* and up to the land of Jerusalem. From the same sea a long sea-bight stretches toward the northeast, and is called the Black Sea, and divides the three parts of the earth ; of which the eastern part is called Asia, and the western is called by some Europe, by some Enea.† Northward of the Black Sea lies Svithjod the Great,‡ or the Cold. The Great Svithjod is reckoned by some not less than the Saracens' land,§ others compare it to the Great Blueland.‖ The northern part of Svithjod lies uninhabited on account of frost and cold, as likewise the southern parts of Blueland are waste from the burning sun. In Svithjod are many great domains, and many wonderful races of men, and many kinds of languages. There are giants,¶ and there are dwarfs,** and there are also blue men.†† There are wild beasts and dreadfully large dragons. On the north side of the mountains, which lie outside of all inhabited lands, runs a river through Svithjod, which is properly called by the name of Tanais,‡‡ but was formerly called Tanaquisl or Vanaquisl, and which falls into the ocean at

---

* Njorvasound, the Straits of Gibraltar; so called from the first Norseman who sailed through them. His name was Njorve. See Ann. for nordisk Oldkyndighed, Vol. I, p. 58.

† See note, page 221.

‡ Svithjod the Great, or the Cold, is the ancient Sarmatia and Scythia Magna, and formed the great part of the present European Russia. In the mythological sagas it is also called Godheim; that is, the home of Odin and the other gods. Svithjod the Less is Sweden proper, and is called Mannheim; that is, the home of the kings, the descendants of the gods.

§ The Saracens' land (Serkland) means North Africa and Spain, and the Saracen countries in Asia; that is, Persia, Assyria, etc.

‖ Blueland, the country of the blacks in Africa, the country south of Serkland, the modern Ethiopia.

¶ Tartareans.   ** Kalmuks.   †† Mongolians.

‡‡ The Tanais is the present Don river, which empties into the Sea of Asov.

the Black Sea. The country of the people on the Vanaquisl was called Vanaland or Vanaheim, and the river separates the three parts of the world, of which the easternmost is called Asia and the westernmost Europe.

The country east of the Tanaquisl in Asia was called Asaland or Asaheim, and the chief city in that land was called Asgard.* In that city was a chief called Odin, and it was a great place for sacrifice. It was the custom there that twelve temple-priests † should both direct the sacrifices and also judge the people. They were called priests or masters, and all the people served and obeyed them. Odin was a great and very far-traveled warrior, who conquered many kingdoms, and so successful was he that in every battle the victory was on his side. It was the belief of his people that victory belonged to him in every battle. It was his custom when he sent his men into battle, or on any expedition, that he first laid his hand upon their heads, and called down a blessing upon them; and then they believed their undertaking would be successful. His people also were accustomed, whenever they fell into danger by land or sea, to call upon his name; and they thought

---

* Asgard is supposed, by those who look for historical fact in mythological tales, to be the present Assor; others, that it is Chasgar in the Caucasian ridge, called by Strabo Aspargum the Asburg, or castle of the asas. We still have in the Norse tongue the word Aas, meaning a ridge of high land. The word asas is not derived from Asia, as Snorre supposed. It is the O. H. Ger. *ans;* Anglo-Sax. *os* = a hero. The word also means a pillar; and in this latter sense the gods are the pillars of the universe. Connected with the word is undoubtedly Aas, a mountain-ridge, as supporter of the skies; and this reminds us of *Atlas,* as bearer of the world.

† The temple-priests performed the functions of priest and judge, and their office continued hereditary throughout the heathen period of Norse history.

that always they got comfort and aid by it, for where he was they thought help was near. Often he went away so long that he passed many seasons on his journeys.

Odin had two brothers, the one hight Ve, the other Vile,* and they governed the kingdom when he was absent. It happened once when Odin had gone to a great distance, and had been so long away that the people of Asia doubted if he would ever return home, that his two brothers took it upon themselves to divide his estate; but both of them took his wife Frigg to themselves. Odin soon after returned home, and took his wife back.

Odin went out with a great army against the Vanaland people; but they were well prepared, and defended their land, so that victory was changeable, and they ravaged the lands of each other and did great damage. They tired of this at last, and, on both sides appointing a meeting for establishing peace, made a truce and exchanged hostages. The Vanaland people sent their best men,—Njord the Rich and his son Frey; the people of Asaland sent a man hight Hœner,† as he was a stout and very handsome man, and with him they sent a man of great understanding, called Mimer; and on the other side the Vanaland people sent the wisest man in their community, who was called Quaser. Now when Hœner came to Vanaheim he was immediately made a chief, and Mimer came to him with good counsel on all occasions. But when Hœner stood in the Things, or other meetings, if Mimer was not near him, and any difficult matter was

* See Norse Mythology, page 174.
† See Brage's Talk, p. 160; and Norse Mythology, pp. 247 and 342.

laid before him, he always answered in one way:
Now let others give their advice; so that the Vanaland people got a suspicion that the Asaland people
had deceived them in the exchange of men. They
took Mimer, therefore, and beheaded him, and sent
his head to the Asaland people. Odin took the head,
smeared it with herbs, so that it should not rot, and
sang incantations over it. Thereby he gave it the
power that it spoke to him, and discovered to him
many secrets.* Odin placed Njord and Frey as priests
of the sacrifices, and they became deities of the Asaland people. Njord's daughter, Freyja, was priestess
of the sacrifices, and first taught the Asaland people
the magic art, as it was in use and fashion among the
Vanaland people. While Njord was with the Vanaland people he had taken his own sister in marriage,
for that was allowed by their law; and their children
were Frey and Freyja. But among the Asaland
people it was forbidden to come together in so near
relationship.†

There goes a great mountain barrier from northeast
to southwest, which divides the Great Svithjod from
other kingdoms. South of this mountain ridge is not

---

* In the Vala's Prophecy of the Elder Edda it is said that Odin
talks with the head of Mimer before the coming of Ragnarok. See
Norse Mythology, p. 421.

† This shows that the vans must have belonged to the mythological system of some older race that, like the ancient Romans (Liber
and Libera), recognized the propriety of marriage between brothers
and sisters, at least among their gods. Such marriages were not
allowed among our Odinic ancestors. Hence we see that when Njord,
Frey and Freyja were admitted to Asgard, they entered into new marriage relations. Njord married Skade, Frey married Gerd, and Freyja
married Oder. Our ancestors were never savages!

far to Turkland, where Odin had great possessions.*
But Odin, having foreknowledge and magic-sight, knew
that his posterity would come to settle and dwell in
the northern half of the world. In those times the
Roman chiefs went wide around the world, subduing
to themselves all people; and on this account many
chiefs fled from their domains.† Odin set his brothers

* Turkland was usually supposed to mean Moldau and Wallachia.
Some, who regard the great mountain barrier as being the Ural
Mountains, think Turkland is Turkistan in Asia. Asia Minor is
also frequently styled Turkland.

† Ancient Norse writers connect this event with Mithridates and
Pompey the Great. They tell how Odin was a heroic prince who,
with his twelve peers or apostles, dwelt in the Black Sea region.
He became straightened for room, and so led the asas out of Asia
into eastern Europe. Then they go on to tell how the Roman empire
had arrived at its highest point of power, and saw all the then
known world — the orbis terrarum — subject to its laws, when an
unforeseen event raised up enemies against it from the very heart of
the forests of Scythia, and on the banks of the Don river. The
leader was Mithridates the Great, against whom the Romans waged
three wars, and the Romans looked upon him as the most formidable enemy the empire had ever had to contend with. Cicero delivered
his famous oration, Pro lege Manilia, and succeeded in getting Pompey appointed commander of the third war against Mithridates.
The latter, by flying, had drawn Pompey after him into the wilds of
Scythia. Here the king of Pontus sought refuge and new means of
vengeance. He hoped to arm against the ambition of Rome all his
neighboring nations whose liberties she threatened. He was successful at first, but all those Scythian peoples, ill-united as allies,
ill-armed as soldiers, and still worse disciplined, were at length
forced to yield to the genius of the great general Pompey. And here
traditions tell us that Odin and the other asas were among the allies
of Mithridates. Odin had been one of the gallant defenders of Troy,
and at the same time, with Æneas and Anchises, he had taken flight
out of the burning and falling city. Now he was obliged to withdraw
a second time by flight, but this time it was not from the Greeks,
but from the Romans, whom he had offended by assisting Mithridates. He was now compelled to go and seek, in lands unknown
to his enemies, that safety which he could no longer find in the
Scythian forests. He then proceeded to the north of Europe, and
laid the foundations of the Teutonic nations. As fast as he subdued the countries in the west and north of Europe he gave them
to one or another of his sons to govern. Thus it comes to pass that
so many sovereign families throughout Teutondom are said to be
descended from Odin. Hengist and Horsa, the chiefs of those Saxons

Vile and Ve over Asgard, and he himself, with all the gods and a great many other people, wandered out, first westward to Gardarike (Russia), and then south to Saxland (Germany). He had many sons, and

who conquered Britain in the fifth century, counted Odin in the number of their ancestors. The traditions go on to tell how he conquered Denmark, founded Odinse (Odinsve = Odin's Sanctuary; comp. *ve* with the German *Wei* in *Weinacht*), and gave the kingdom to his son Skjold (shield); how he conquered Sweden, founded the Sigtuna temple, and gave the country to his son Yngve; how finally Norway had to submit to him, and be ruled by a third son of Odin, Saming.

It has been seriously contended,— and it would form an important element in an epic based on the historical Odin,— that a desire of being revenged on the Romans was one of the ruling principles of Odin's whole conduct. Driven by those foes of universal liberty from his former home in the east, his resentment was the more violent, since the Teutons thought it a sacred duty to revenge all injuries, especially those offered to kinsmen or country. Odin had no other view in traversing so many distant lands, and in establishing with so much zeal his doctrines of valor, than to arouse all Teutonic nations, and unite them against so formidable and odious a race as the Romans. And we, who live in the light of the nineteenth century, and with the records before us, can read the history of the convulsions of Europe during the decline of the Roman empire; we can understand how that leaven, which Odin left in the bosoms of the believers in the asa-faith, first fermented a long time in secret; but we can also see how in the fullness of time, the signal given, the descendants of Odin fell like a swarm of locusts upon this unhappy empire, and, after giving it many terrible shocks, eventually overturned it, thus completely avenging the insult offered so many centuries before by Pompey to their founder Odin. We can understand how it became possible for "those vast multitudes, which the populous north poured from her frozen loins, to pass the Rhine and the Danube, and come like a deluge on the south, and spread beneath Gibraltar and the Libyan sands;" how it were possible, we say, for them so largely to remodel and invigorate a considerable part of Europe, nay, how they could succeed in overrunning and overturning "the rich but rotten, the mighty but marrowless, the disciplined but diseased, Roman empire; that gigantic and heartless and merciless usurpation of soulless materialism and abject superstition of universal despotism, of systemized and relentless plunder, and of depravity deep as hell." In connection with this subject we would refer our readers to Mallet's Northern Antiquities, pp. 79-83, where substantially the same account is given; to Norse Mythology, pp. 232-236; to George Stephen's Runic Monuments, Vol. 1; and to Charles Kingsley's The Roman and the Teuton.

after having subdued an extensive kingdom in Saxland he set his sons to defend the country. He himself went northward to the sea, and took up his abode
in an island which is called Odinse (see note below),
in Funen. Then he sent Gefjun across the sound
to the north to discover new countries, and she came
to King Gylfe, who gave her a ploughland. Then
she went to Jotunheim and bore four sons to a giant,
and transformed them into a yoke of oxen, and yoked
them to a plough and broke out the land into the
ocean, right opposite to Odinse, which was called
Seeland, where she afterward settled and dwelt.*
Skjold, a son of Odin, married her, and they dwelt at
Leidre.† Where the ploughed land was, is a lake or
sea called Laage.‡ In the Swedish land the fjords of
Laage correspond to the nesses of Seeland. Brage
the old sings thus of it:

> Gefjun glad
> Drew from Gylfe
> The excellent land,
> Denmark's increase,
> So that it reeked
> From the running beasts.
> Four heads and eight eyes
> Bore the oxen,
> As they went before the wide
> Robbed land of the grassy isle.§

Now when Odin heard that things were in a pros-
perous condition in the land to the east beside Gylfe,

---

* Compare this version of the myth with the one given in the first
chapter of The Fooling of Gylfe. Many explain the myth to mean
the breaking through of the Baltic between Sweden and Denmark.

† Leidre or Leire, at the end of Isefjord, in the county of Lithra-
borg, is considered the oldest royal seat in Denmark.

‡ Laage is a general name for lakes and rivers. It here stands
for Lake Malar, in Sweden.　　　§ The grassy isle is Seeland.

he went thither, and Gylfe made a peace with him, for Gylfe thought he had no strength to oppose the people of Asaland. Odin and Gylfe had many tricks and enchantments against each other; but the Asaland people had always the superiority. Odin took up his residence at the Malar lake, at the place now called Sigtun.* There he erected a large temple, where there were sacrifices according to the customs of the Asaland people. He appropriated to himself the whole of that district of country, and called it Sigtun. To the temple gods he gave also domains. Njord dwelt in Noatun, Frey in Upsal, Heimdal in Himinbjorg, Thor in Thrudvang, Balder in Breidablik; † to all of them he gave good domains.

When Odin of Asaland came to the north, and the gods with him, he began to exercise and to teach others the arts which the people long afterward have practiced. Odin was the cleverest of all, and from him all others learned their magic arts; and he knew them first, and knew many more than other people. But now, to tell why he is held in such high respect, we must mention various causes that contributed to it. When sitting among his friends his countenance was so beautiful and friendly, that the spirits of all were exhilarated by it; but when he was in war, he appeared fierce and dreadful. This arose from his being able to

---

*Sigtun. *Sige*, Ger. Sieg, (comp. Sigfrid,) means victory, and is one of Odin's names; *tun* means an inclosure, and is the same word as our modern English *town*. Thus Sigtun would, in modern English, be called Odinstown; like our Johnstown, Williamstown, etc.

†Noatun, Thrudvang, Breidablik and Himinbjorg are purely mythological names, and for their significance the reader is referred to The Fooling of Gylfe. Snorre follows the lay of Grimner in the Elder Edda.

change his color and form in any way he liked. Another cause was, that he conversed so cleverly and smoothly, that all who heard were persuaded. He spoke everything in rhyme, such as is now composed, and which we call skald-craft. He and his temple gods were called song-smiths, for from them came that art of song into the northern countries. Odin could make his enemies in battle blind or deaf, or terror-struck, and their weapons so blunt that they could no more cut than a willow-twig; on the other hand, his men rushed forward without armor, were as mad as dogs or wolves, bit their shields, and were strong as bears or wild bulls, and killed people at a blow, and neither fire nor iron told upon them. These were called berserks.*

Odin could transform his shape; his body would lie as if dead or asleep, but then he would be in the shape of a fish, or worm, or bird, or beast, and be off

* Berserk. The etymology of this word has been much contested. Some, upon the authority of Snorre in the above quoted passage, derive it from berr (*bare*) and serkr (comp. *sark*, Scotch for shirt); but this etymology is inadmissible, because serkr is a substantive, not an adjective. Others derive it from berr (Germ. *Bär* = *ursus*), which is greatly to be preferred, for in olden ages athletes and champions used to wear hides of bears, wolves and reindeer (as skins of lions in the south), hence the names Bjalfe, Bjarnhedinn, Ulfhedinn (hedinn, *pellis*),—"pellibus aut parvis rhenonum tegimentis utuntur." Cæsar, Bell. Gall. VI, 22. Even the old poets understood the name so, as may be seen in the poem of Hornklofi (beginning of the 10th century), a dialogue between a valkyrie and a raven, where the valkyrie says at berserkja reiðu vil ek þik spyrja, to which the raven replies, Ulfhednar heita, *they are called wolf coats*. In battle the berserks were subject to fits of frenzy, called *berserksgangr* (*furor bersercicus*), when they howled like wild beasts, foamed at the mouth, and gnawed the iron rim of their shields. During these fits they were, according to a popular belief, proof against steel and fire, and made great havoc in the ranks of the enemy. But when the fever abated they were weak and tame. Vigfusson Cleasby's Icelandic-English Dictionary, *sub voce*.

in a twinkling to distant lands upon his own or other peoples' business. With words alone he could quench fire, still the ocean in tempest, and turn the wind to any quarter he pleased. Odin had a ship, which he called Skidbladner,* in which he sailed over wide seas, and which he could roll up like a cloth. Odin carried with him Mimer's head, which told him all the news of other countries. Sometimes even he called the dead out of the earth, or set himself beside the burial-mounds; whence he was called the ghost-sovereign, and the lord of the mounds. He had two ravens,† to whom he had taught the speech of man; and they flew far and wide through the land, and brought him the news. In all such things he was preëminently wise. He taught all these arts in runes and songs, which are called incantations, and therefore the Asaland people are called incantation-smiths. Odin also understood the art in which the greatest power is lodged, and which he himself practiced, namely, what is called magic. By means of this he could know beforehand the predestined fate ‡ of men, or their not yet completed lot, and also bring on the death, ill-luck or bad health of people, or take away the strength or wit from one person and give it to another. But after such witchcraft followed such

---

* In the mythology this ship belongs to Frey, having been made for him by the dwarfs.

† Hugin and Munin.

‡ The old Norse word is örlög, which is plural, (from ör = Ger. *ur,* and lög, *laws,*) and means the primal law, fate, weird, doom; the Greek μοῖρα. The idea of predestination was a salient feature in the Odinic religion. The word örlog, O. H. G. *urlac,* M. H. G. *urlone,* Dutch *orlog,* had special reference to a man's fate in war. Hence Orlogschiffe in German means a naval fleet. The Danish orlog means warfare at sea.

weakness and anxiety, that it was not thought respectable for men to practice it; and therefore the priestesses were brought up in this art. Odin knew definitely where all missing cattle were concealed under the earth, and understood the songs by which the earth, the hills, the stones and mounds were opened to him; and he bound those who dwell in them by the power of his word, and went in and took what he pleased. From these arts he became very celebrated. His enemies dreaded him; his friends put their trust in him, and relied on his power and on himself. He taught the most of his arts to his priests of the sacrifices, and they came nearest to himself in all wisdom and witch-knowledge. Many others, however, occupied themselves much with it; and from that time witchcraft spread far and wide, and continued long. People sacrificed to Odin, and the twelve chiefs of Asaland,— called them their gods, and believed in them long after. From Odin's name came the name Audun, which people gave to his sons; and from Thor's name came Thorer, also Thorarinn; and it was also sometimes augmented by other additions, as Steinthor, Hafthor, and many kinds of alterations.

Odin established the same law in his land that had been before in Asaland. Thus he established by law that all dead men should be burned, and their property laid with them upon the pile, and the ashes be cast into the sea or buried in the earth. Thus, said he, everyone will come to Valhal with the riches he had with him upon the pile; and he would also enjoy whatever he himself had buried in the earth. For men of consequence a mound should be raised to their memory, and for all other warriors who had been distinguished for manhood, a standing stone; which custom remained long after Odin's time. Toward winter there should be a blood-sacrifice for a good year, and in the middle of winter for a good crop; and the third sacrifice should be in summer, for victory in battle. Over all Svithjod * the people paid Odin a scatt, or tax,— so much on each head; but he had to defend the country from enemy or disturbance, and pay the expense of the sacrifice-feasts toward winter for a good year.

Njord took a wife hight Skade; but she would not live with him, but married afterward Odin, and had many sons by him, of whom one was called Saming, and of this Eyvind Skaldespiller sings thus:

> To Asason† Queen Skade bore
> Saming, who dyed his shield in gore,—
> The giant queen of rock and snow
> Who loves to dwell on earth below,
> The iron pine-tree's daughter she,
> Sprung from the rocks that rib the sea,
> To Odin bore full many a son,—
> Heroes of many a battle won.

To Saming Jarl Hakon the Great reckoned up his pedigree.‡ This Svithjod (Sweden) they call Mannheim, but the great Svithjod they call Godheim, and of Godheim great wonders and novelties were related.

Odin died in his bed in Sweden; and when he was near his death he made himself be marked with the point of a spear,§ and said he was going to Godheim,

---

* Svithjod, which here means Sweden, is derived from Odin's name, Svidr and thjod = folk, people. Svithjod thus means Odin's people, and the country takes its name from the people.

† Odin.   ‡ Norway was given to Saming by Odin.

§ He gave himself nine wounds in the form of the head of a spear, or Thor's hammer; that is, he marked himself with the sign of the cross, an ancient heathen custom.

and would give a welcome there to all his friends,
and all brave warriors should be dedicated to him;
and the Swedes believed that he was gone to the
ancient Asgard, and would live there eternally. Then
began the belief in Odin, and the calling upon him.
The Swedes believed that he often showed himself
to them before any great battle. To some he gave
victory, others he invited to himself; and they
reckoned both of these to be well off in their fate.
Odin was burnt, and at his pile there was great
splendor. It was their faith that the higher the
smoke arose in the air, the higher would he be raised
whose pile it was; and the richer he would be the
more property that was consumed with him.

Njord of Noatun was then the sole sovereign of
the Swedes; and he continued the sacrifices, and was
called the drot, or sovereign, by the Swedes, and he
received scatt and gifts from them. In his days were
peace and plenty, and such good years in all respects
that the Swedes believed Njord ruled over the growth
of seasons and the prosperity of the people. In his
time all the diars, or gods, died, and blood-sacrifices
were made for them. Njord died on a bed of sickness, and before he died made himself be marked for
Odin with the spear-point. The Swedes burned him,
and all wept over his grave-mound.

Frey took the kingdom after Njord, and was called
drot by the Swedes, and they paid taxes to him. He
was like his father, fortunate in friends and in good
seasons. Frey built a great temple at Upsala, made
it his chief seat, and gave it all his taxes, his land and
goods. Then began the Upsala domains, which have
remained ever since. Then began in his day the

Frode-peace; and then there were good seasons in all the land, which the Swedes ascribed to Frey, so that he was more worshiped than the other gods, as the people became much richer in his days by reason of the peace and good seasons. His wife was called Gerd, daughter of Gymer, and their son was called Fjolner. Frey was called by another name, Yngve; and this name Yngve was considered long after in his race as a name of honor, so that his descendants have since been called Ynglings (*i. e.* Yngvelings). Frey fell into a sickness, and as his illness took the upper hand, his men took the plan of letting few approach him. In the meantime they raised a great mound, in which they placed a door with three holes in it. Now when Frey died they bore him secretly into the mound, but told the Swedes he was alive, and they kept watch over him for three years. They brought all the taxes into the mound, and through the one hole they put in the gold, through the other the silver, and through the third the copper money that was paid. Peace and good seasons continued.

Freyja alone remained of the gods, and she became on this account so celebrated that all women of distinction were called by her name, whence they now have the title Frue (Germ. *Frau*), so that every woman is called frue (that is, mistress) over her property, and the wife is called the house-frue. Freyja continued the blood-sacrifices. Freyja had also many other names. Her husband was called Oder, and her daughters Hnos and Gersame. They were so very beautiful that afterward the most precious jewels were called by their names.

When it became known to the Swedes that Frey was dead, and yet peace and good seasons continued, they believed that it must be so as long as Frey remained in Sweden, and therefore they would not burn his remains, but called him the god of this world, and afterward offered continually blood-sacrifices to him, principally for peace and good seasons.*

FORNJOT AND THE SETTLEMENT OF NORWAY.

In the asa-faith we find various foreign elements introduced. Thus, for example, the vans did not originally belong to the Odinic system. As the Teutons came in contact with other races, the religious ideas of the latter were frequently adopted in some modified form. Especially do Finnish elements enter into the asa-system. The Finnish god of thunder was Ukko. He is supposed to have been confounded with our Thor, whence the latter got the name Öku-Thor (Ukko-Thor). The vans may be connected with the Finnish Wainamoinen, and in the same manner a number of Celtic elements have been mixed with Teutonic mythology. And this is not all. There must have flourished a religious system in the North before the arrival of Odin and

---

* Here ends Snorre's account of the asas in Heimskringla. The reader will, of course, compare the account here given of Odin, Njord, Frey, Freyja, etc., with the purely mythological description of them in the Younger Edda, and with that in Norse Mythology. Upon the whole, Snorre has striven to accommodate his sketch to the Eddas, while he has had to clothe mythical beings with the characteristics of human kings. Like Saxo-Grammaticus, Snorre has striven to show that the deities, which we now recognize as personified forces and phenomena of nature, were extraordinary and enterprising persons, who formerly ruled in the North, and inaugurated the customs, government and religion of Norway, Sweden, Denmark, Germany, England, and the other Teutonic lands.

his apostles. This was probably either Tshudic or Celtic, or a mixture of the two. The asa-doctrine superseded it, but there still remain traces in some of the oldest records of the North. Thus we have in the prehistoric sagas of Iceland an account of the finding of Norway, wherein it is related that Fornjot,* in Jotland, which is also called Finland or Quenland, east of the Gulf of Bothnia, had three sons: Hler. also called Æger, Loge and Kare.† Of Loge it is related that he was of giant descent, and, being very tall of stature, he was called Haloge, that is, High Loge; and after him the northern part of Norway is called Halogaland (now Helgeland). He was married to Glod (a red-hot coal), and had with her two daughters, Eysa and Eimyrja; both words meaning glowing embers. Haloge had two jarls, Vifil (the one taking a vif = wife) and Vesete (the one who sits at the ve = the sanctuary, that is, the dweller by the hearth, the first sanctuary), who courted his daughters; the former addressing himself to Eimyrja, the latter to Eysa, but the king refusing to give his consent, they carried them away secretly. Vesete settled in Borgundarholm (Bornholm), and had a son, Bue (one who settles on a farm); Vifil sailed further east and settled on the island Vifilsey, on the coast of Sweden, and had a son, Viking (the pirate).

The third son, Kare, had a numerous offspring. He had one son by name Jokul (iceberg), another Froste

---

* The word fornjot can be explained in two ways: either as fornjot = the first enjoyer, possessor; or as forn-jot, the ancient giant. He would then correspond to Ymer.

† Notice this trinity: Hler is the sea (comp. the Welsh word *llyr* = sea); Loge is fire (comp. the Welsh *llwg*), he reminds us both by his name and his nature of Loke; Kare is the wind.

(frost), and Froste's son was named Sna (snow). He
had a third son, by name Thorri (bare frost), after
whom the mid-winter month, Thorra-month, was called;
and his daughters hight Fonn (packed snow), Drifa
(snow-drift), and Mjoll (meal, fine snow). All these
correspond well to Kare's name, which, as stated,
means wind. Thorri had two sons, Nor and Gor, and
a daughter, Goe. The story goes on to tell how Goe,
the sister, was lost, and how the brothers went to
search for her, until they finally found him who had
robbed her. He was Hrolf, from the mountain, a son
of the giant Svade, and a grandson of Asa-Thor. They
settled their trouble, and thereupon Hrolf married
Goe, and Nor married Hrolf's sister, settled in the
land and called it after his own name, Norvegr, that
is, Norway. By this story we are reminded of Kad-
mos, who went to seek his lost sister Europa. In the
Younger Edda the winds are called the sons of Fornjot, the sea is called the son of Fornjot, and the
brother of the fire and of the winds, and Fornjot is
named among the old giants. This makes it clear
that Fornjot and his offspring are not historical persons, but cosmological impersonations. And additional proof of this is found by an examination of the
beginning of the Saga of Thorstein, Viking's Son.
(See Viking Tales of the North, pp. 1 and 2).

THE FOOLING OF GYLFE.

This story about the ploughing of Gylfe reminds us of the legend told in the first book of Virgil's Æneid, about the founding of Carthage by Dido, who bought from the Libyan king as much ground as she could cover with a bull's hide. Elsewhere it is related that she cut the bull's hide into narrow strips and encircled therewith all the ground upon which Carthage was afterward built. Thus Dido deceived the Libyan king nearly as effectually as Gefjun deluded King Gylfe. The story is also told by Snorre in Heimskringla, see p. 231.

The passage in verse, which has given translators so much trouble in a transposed form, would read as follows: Gefjun glad drew that excellent land (djúprödul = the deep sun = gold; öðla = udal = property; djüprödul öðla = the golden property), Denmark's increase (Seeland), so that it reeked (steamed) from the running oxen. The oxen bore four heads and eight eyes, as they went before the wide piece of robbed land of the isle so rich in grass.

Gefjun is usually interpreted as a goddess of agriculture, and her name is by some derived from $\gamma\bar{\eta}$ and *fjon*, that is, *terræ separatio;* others compare it with the Anglo-Saxon *geofon* = the sea. The etymology remains very uncertain.

CHAPTER II.

It is to the delusion or eye-deceit mentioned in this chapter that Snorre Sturlasson refers in his Heimskringla, in Chapter VI of Ynglingla Saga.

Thjodolf of Hvin was a celebrated skald at the court of Harald Fairhair.

Thinking thatchers, etc. Literally transposed, this passage would read: Reflecting men let shields (literally Svafner's, that is Odin's roof-trees,) glisten on the back. They were smitten with stones. To let shields glisten on the back, is said of men who throw their shields on their backs to protect themselves against those who pursue the flying host.

Har means the High One, Jafnhar the Equally High One, and Thride the Third One. By these three may be meant the three chief gods of the North: Odin, Thor and Frey; or they may be simply an expression of the Eddic trinity. This trinity is represented in a number of ways: by Odin, Vile and Ve in the creation of the world, and by Odin, Hœner and Loder in the creation of Ask and Embla, the first human pair. The number three figures extensively in all mythological systems. In the pre-chaotic state we have Muspelheim, Niflheim and Ginungagap. Fornjot had three sons: Hler, Loge and Kare. There are three norns: Urd, Verdande and Skuld. There are three fountains: Hvergelmer, Urd's and Mimer's; etc. (See Norse Mythology, pp. 183, 195, 196.)

Har being Odin, Har's Hall will be Valhal. You will not come out from this hall unless you are wiser. In the lay of Vafthrudner, of the Elder Edda, we

have a similar challenge, where Vafthrudner says to
Odin:

> Out will you not come
> From our halls
> Unless I find you to be wiser (than I am).

CHAPTER III.

This chapter gives twelve names of Odin. In the
Eddas and in the skaldic lays he has in all nearly two
hundred names. His most common name is Odin
(in Anglo-Saxon and in Old High German *Wodan*),
and this is thought by many to be of the same origin
as our word *god*. The other Old Norse word for
god, *tivi*, is identical in root with Lat. *divus;* Sansk.
divas; Gr. Διός (Ζεύς); and this is again connected
with *Tyr*, the Tivisco in the Germania of Tacitus.
(See Max Müller's Lectures on the Science of Language, 2d series, p. 425). Paulus Diakonus states that
Wodan, or Gwodan, was worshiped by all branches
of the Teutons. Odin has also been sought and found
in the Scythian *Zalmoxis*, in the Indian *Buddha*, in
the Celtic Budd, and in the Mexican Votan. Zalmoxis, derived from the Gr. Ζαλμός, helmet, reminds
us of Odin as the helmet-bearer (Grimm, Gesch. der
Deutschen Sprache). According to Humboldt, a race
in Guatemala, Mexico, claim to be descended from
Votan (Vues des Cordillères, 1817, I, 208). This sug-
gests the question whether Odin's name may not have
been brought to America by the Norse discoverers
in the 10th and 11th centuries, and adopted by some
of the native races. In the Lay of Grimner (Elder
Edda) the following names of Odin are enumerated:

Grim is my name
And Ganglere,
Herjan and Helmet-bearer,
Thekk and Thride,
Thud and Ud,
Helblinde and Har,

Sad and Svipal,
And Sanngetal,
Herteit and Hnikar,
Bileyg and Baleyg,
Bolverk, Fjolner,
Grim and Grimner,
Glapsvid and Fjolsvid,

Sidhot, Sidskeg,
Sigfather, Hnikud,
Alfather, Valfather,
Atrid and Farmatyr.
With one name
Was I never named
When I fared 'mong the peoples.

Grimner they called me
Here at Geirrod's,
But Jalk at Asmund's,
And Kjalar the time
When sleds (kjalka) I drew,
And Thror at the Thing,
Vidur on the battle-field,
Oske and Ome,
Jafnhar and Biflinde,
Gondler and Harbard 'mong the gods.

Svidur and Svidre
Hight I at Sokmimer's,
And fooled the ancient giant
When I alone Midvitne's,
The mighty son's,
Bane had become.

> Odin I now am called,
> Ygg was my name before,
> Before that I hight Thund,
> Vak and Skilfing,
> Vafud and Hroptatyr,
> Got and Jalk 'mong the gods,
> Ofner and Svafner.
> All these names, I trow,
> Have to me alone been given.

What the etymology of all these names is, it is not easy to tell. The most of them are clearly Norse words, and express the various activities of their owner. It is worthy of notice that it is added when and where Odin bore this or that name (his name was Grim at Geirrod's, Jalk at Asmund's, etc.), and that the words sometimes indicate a progressive development, as Thund, then Ygg, and then Odin. First he was a mere sound in the air (Thund), then he took to thinking (Ygg), and at last he became the inspiring soul of the universe. Although we are unable to define all these names, they certainly each have a distinct meaning, and our ancestors certainly understood them perfectly. Har = the High One; Jafnhar = the Equally High One; Thride = the Third (Ζεὺς ἄλλος and Τρίτος); Alfather probably contracted from *Alda*father = the Father of the Ages and the Creations; Veratyr = the Lord of Beings; Rögner = the Ruler (from regin); Got (Gautr, from *gjóta*, to cast) = the Creator, Lat. Instillator; Mjotud = the Creator, the word being allied to Anglo-Saxon *meotod*, *metod*, Germ. *Messer*, and means originally cutter; but to cut and to make are synonymous. Such names as these have reference to Odin's divinity as creator, arranger and ruler of gods and men. Svid and Fjolsvid = the swift, the wise ; Ganglere, Gangrad and Vegtam = the wanderer, the waywont ; Vidrer = the weather-ruler, together with serpent-names like Ofner, Svafner, etc., refer to Odin's knowledge, his journeys, the various shapes he assumes. Permeating all nature, he appears in all its forms. Names like Sidhot = the slouchy hat; Sidskeg = the long-beard; Baleyg = the burning-eye ; Grimner = the masked ; Jalk (Jack) = the youth, etc., express the various forms in which he was thought to appear,— to his slouchy hat, his long beard, or his age, etc. Such names as Sanngetal = the true investigator ; Farmatyr = the cargo-god, etc., refer to his various occupations as inventor, discoverer of runes, protector of trade and commerce, etc. (Finally, all such names as Herfather = father of hosts; Herjan = the devastator ; Sigfather = the father of victory ; Sigtyr = god of victory ; Skilfing = producing trembling ; Hnikar = the breaker, etc., represent Odin as the god of war and victory. Oske = wish, is thus called because he gratifies our desires. Gimle, as will be seen later, is the abode of the blessed after Ragnarok. Vingolf (Vin and golf) means *friends' floor*, and is the hall of the goddesses. Hel is the goddess of death, and from her name our word *hell* is derived.

Our ancestors divided the universe into nine worlds: the uppermost was Muspelheim (the world of light); the lowest was Niflheim (the world of darkness). Compare the Greek word νεφέλη = *mist*. (See Norse Mythology, p. 187.)

GINUNGAGAP. Ginn means wide, large, far-reaching, perhaps also void (compare the Anglo-Saxon *gin* = gaping, open, spacious; ginian = to gap; and ginnung = a yawning). Ginungagap thus means the yawning gap or abyss, and represents empty space. The poets use ginnung in the sense of a fish and of a hawk, and in geographical saga-fragments it is used as the name of the Polar Sea.

HVERGELMER. This word is usually explained as a transposition for Hvergemler, which would then be derived from Hver and gamall (old) = the old kettle; but Petersen shows that gelmir must be taken from galm, which is still found in the Jutland dialect, and means a gale (compare Golmstead = a windy place, and *golme* = to roar, blow). Gelmer is then the one producing galm, and Hvergelmer thus means the roaring kettle. The twelve rivers proceeding from Hvergelmer are called the Elivogs (Élivágar) in the next chapter. Éli-vágar means, according to Vigfusson, ice-waves. The most of the names occur in the long list of river names given in the Lay of Grimner, of the Elder Edda. Svol = the cool; Gunnthro = the battle-trough. Slid is also mentioned in the Vala's Prophecy, where it is represented as being full of mud and swords. Sylg (from *svelgja* = to swallow) = the devourer; Ylg (from *yla* = to roar) = the roaring one; Leipt = the glowing, is also mentioned in the Lay of Helge Hunding's Bane, where it is stated that they swore by it (compare Styx); Gjoll (from *gjalla* = to glisten and clang) = the shining, clanging one. The meaning of the other words is not clear, but they doubtless all, like those explained, express cold, violent motion, etc. The most noteworthy of these rivers are Leipt and Gjoll. In the Lay of Grimner they are said to flow nearest to the abode of man, and fall thence into Hel's realm. Over Gjoll was the bridge which Hermod, after the death of Balder, crossed on his way to Hel. It is said to be thatched with shining gold, and a maid by name Modgud watches it. In the song of Sturle Thordson, on the death of Skule Jarl, it is said that "the king's kinsman went over the Gjoll-bridge." The farther part of the horizon, which often appears like a broad bright stream, may have suggested this river.

Surt means the swarthy or black one. Many have regarded him as the unknown (dark) god, but this is probably an error. But there was some one in Muspelheim who sent the heat, and gave life to the frozen drops of rime. The latter, and not Surt, who is a giant, is the eternal god, the mighty one, whom the skald in the Lay of Hyndla dare not name. It is interesting to notice that our ancestors divided the evolution of the world into three distinct periods: (1) a pre-chaotic condition (Niflheim, Muspelheim and Ginungagap); (2) a chaotic condition (Ymer and the cow Audhumbla); (3) and finally the three gods, Odin (spirit), Vile (will) and Ve (sanctity), transformed chaos into cosmos. And away back in this pre-chaotic state of the world we find this mighty being who sends the heat. It is not definitely stated, but it can be inferred from other passages, that just as the good principle existed from everlasting in Muspelheim, so the evil principle existed co-eternally with it in Hvergelmer in Niflheim. Hvergelmer is the source out of which all matter first proceeded, and the dragon or devil Nidhug, who dwells in Hvergelmer, is, in our opinion, the evil principle who is from eternity. The good principle shall continue forever, but the evil shall cease to exist after Ragnarok.

Ymer is the noisy one, and his name is derived from *ymja* = to howl (compare also the Finnish deity Jumo, after whom the town Umea takes its name, like Odinse).

Aurgelmer, Thrudgelmer and Bergelmer express the gradual development from aur (clay) to thrud (that which is compressed), and finally to berg (rock).

Vidolf, Vilmeide and Svarthofde are mentioned nowhere else in the mythology.

Bure and Bor mean the bearing and the born; that is, father and son.

Bolthorn means the miserable one, from bol = evil; and Bestla may mean that which is best. The idea then is that Bor united himself with that which was best of the miserable material at hand.

That the flood caused by the slaying of Ymer reminds us of Noah and his ark, and of the Greek flood, needs only to be suggested.

CHAPTER IV.

Ask means an ash-tree, and Embla an elm-tree.

While the etymology of the names in the myths are very obscure, the myths themselves are clear enough. Similar myths abound in Greek mythology. The story about Bil and Hjuke is our old English rhyme about Jack and Gill, who went up the hill to fetch a pail of water.

CHAPTER V.

In reference to the golden age, see Norse Mythology, pp. 182 and 197.

In the appendix to the German so-called Hero-Book we are told that the dwarfs were first created

to cultivate the desert lands and the mountains;
thereupon the giants, to subdue the wild beasts; and
finally the heroes, to assist the dwarfs against the
treacherous giants. While the giants are always
hostile to the gods, the dwarfs are usually friendly
to them.

DWARFS. Both giants and dwarfs shun the light.
If surprised by the breaking forth of day, they become changed to stone. In one of the poems of the
Elder Edda (the Alvismál), Thor amuses the dwarf
Alvis with various questions till daylight, and then
cooly says to him: With great artifices, I tell you,
you have been deceived; you are surprised here,
dwarf, by daylight! The sun now shines in the hall.
In the Helgakvida Atle says to the giantess Hrimgerd: It is now day, Hrimgerd! But Atle has de-
tained you, to your life's perdition. It will appear
a laughable harbor-mark, where you stand as a stone-
image.

In the German tales the dwarfs are described as
deformed and diminutive, coarsely clad and of dusky
hue: "a little black man," "a little gray man." They
are sometimes of the height of a child of four years,
sometimes as two spans high, a thumb high (hence,
Tom Thumb). The old Danish ballad of Eline of
Villenwood mentions a troll not bigger than an ant.
Dvergmál (the speech of the dwarfs) is the Old Norse
expression for the echo in the mountains.

In the later popular belief, the dwarfs are generally
called the subterraneans, the brown men in the moor,
etc. They make themselves invisible by a hat or
hood. The women spin and weave, the men are smiths.
In Norway rock-crystal is called dwarf-stone. Certain

stones are in Denmark called dwarf-hammers. They borrow things and seek advice from people, and beg aid for their wives when in labor, all which services they reward. But they also lame cattle, are thievish, and will carry off damsels. There have been instances of dwarf females having married and had children with men. (Thorpe's Northern Mythology.)

WAR. It was the first warfare in the world, says the Elder Edda, when they pierced Gullveig (gold-thirst) through with a spear, and burned her in Odin's hall. Thrice they burned her, thrice she was born anew: again and again, but still she lives. When she comes to a house they call her Heide (the bright, the welcome), and regard her as a propitious vala or prophetess. She can tame wolves, understands witchcraft, and delights wicked women. Hereupon the gods consulted together whether they should punish this misdeed, or accept a blood-fine, when Odin cast forth a spear among mankind, and now began war and slaughter in the world. The defenses of the burgh of the asas was broken down. The vans anticipated war, and hastened over the field. The valkyries came from afar, ready to ride to the gods' people: Skuld with the shield, Skogul, Gunn, Hild, Gondul and Geirr Skogul. (Quoted by Thorpe.)

CHAPTER VI.

In reference to Ygdrasil, we refer our readers to Norse Mythology, pp. 205–211, and to Thomas Carlyle's Heroes and Hero-worship.

A connection between the norns Urd, Verdande and Skuld and the weird sisters in Shakspeare's *Macbeth* has long since been recognized; but new light has recently been thrown upon the subject by the philosopher Karl Blind, who has contributed valuable articles on the subject in the German periodical "Die Gegenwart" and in the "London Academy." We take the liberty of reproducing here an abstract of his article in the "Academy":

*　　*　　*　　*　　*　　*

The fact itself of these Witches being simply transfigurations, or later disguises, of the Teutonic Norns is fully established — as may be seen from Grimm or Simrock. In delineating these hags, Shakspeare has practically drawn upon old Germanic sources, perhaps upon current folk-lore of his time.

It has always struck me as noteworthy that in the greater part of the scene between the Weird Sisters, Macbeth and Banquo, and wherever the Witches come in, Shakspeare uses the staff-rime in a remarkable manner. Not only does this add powerfully to the archaic impressiveness and awe, but it also seems to bring the form and figure of the Sisters of Fate more closely within the circle of the Teutonic idea. I have pointed out this striking use of the alliterative system in *Macbeth* in an article on "An old German Poem and a Vedic Hymn," which appeared in *Fraser* in June, 1877, and in which the derivation of the Weird Sisters from the Germanic Norns is mentioned.

The very first scene in the first act of *Macbeth* opens strongly with the staff-rime:

1st Witch. When shall we three meet again —
In thunder, lightning or in rain?
2d Witch. When the hurly-burly's done,
When the battle's lost and won.
3d Witch. That will be ere set of sun.
1st Witch. Where the place?
2d Witch. 　　　Upon the heath.
3d Witch. There to meet with Macbeth.
1st Witch. I come, Graymalkin!
All. Paddock calls. Anon.
Fair is foul, and foul is fair.
Hover through the fog and filthy air.

Not less marked is the adoption of the fullest staff-rime — together (as above) with the end-rime — in the third scene, when the Weird Sisters speak. Again, there is the staff-rime when Banquo addresses them. Again, the strongest alliteration, combined with the end-rime, runs all through the Witches' spell-song in Act iv, scene 1. This feature in Shakspeare appears to me to merit closer investigation; all the more so because a less regular alliteration, but still a marked one, is found in not a few passages of a number of his plays. Only one further instance of the systematic employment of alliteration may here be noted in passing. It is in Ariel's songs in the *Tempest*, Act i, scene 2. Schlegel and Tieck evidently did not observe this alliterative peculiarity. Their otherwise excellent translation does not render it, except so far as the obvious similarity of certain English and German words involuntarily made them do so. But in the notes to their version of *Macbeth* the character of the Weird Sisters is also misunderstood, though Warburton is referred to, who had already suggested their derivations from the Valkyrs or Norns.

It is an error to say that the Witches in *Macbeth* "are never called witches" (compare Act i, scene 3: "'Give me!' quoth I. 'A-roint thee, *witch!*' the rump-fed ronyon cries"). However, their designation as Weird Sisters fully settles the case of their Germanic origin.

This name "Weird" is derived from the Anglo-Saxon Norn Wyrd (Sax. *Wurth;* O. H. Ger. *Wurd;* Norse, *Urd*), who represents the Past, as her very name shows. Wurd is *die Gewordene* — the "Has Been," or rather the "Has Become," if one could say so in English.

*　　*　　*　　*　　*　　*

In Shakspeare the Witches are three in number — even as in Norse, German, as well as in Keltic and other mythologies. Urd, properly speaking, is the Past. Skuld is the Future, or "That Which shall Be." Verdandi, usually translated as the Present, has an even deeper meaning. Her name is not to be derived from *vera* (to be), but from *verda* (Ger. *werden*). This verb, which has a mixed meaning of "to be," "to become," or to "grow," has been lost in English. Verdandi is, therefore, not merely a representative of present Being, but of the process of Growing, or of Evolution — which gives her figure a profounder aspect. Indeed, there is generally more significance in mythological tales than those imagine who look upon them chiefly as a barren play of fancy.

Incidentally it may be remarked that, though Shakspeare's Weird Sisters are three in number — corresponding to Urd, Verdandi and Skuld — German and Northern mythology and folk-lore occasionally speak of twelve or seven of them. In the German tale of *Dorn-*

röschen, or the Sleeping Beauty, there are twelve good fays; and a thirteenth, who works the evil spell. Once, in German folk-lore, we meet with but two Sisters of Fate — one of them called *Kann*, the other *Muss*. Perhaps these are representatives of man's measure of free will (that which he " can "), and of that which is his inevitable fate — or, that which he " must " do.

Though the word " Norn " has been lost in England and Germany, it is possibly preserved in a German folk-lore ditty, which speaks of three Sisters of Fate as " Nuns." Altogether, German folk-lore is still full of rimes about three Weird Sisters. They are sometimes called Wild Women, or Wise Women, or the Measurers (*Metten*) — namely, of Fate; or, euphemistically, like the Eumenides, the Advisers of Welfare (*Heil-Räthinnen*), reminding us of the counsels given to Macbeth in the apparition scene; or the Quick Judges (*Gach-Schepfen*). Even as in the Edda, these German fays weave and twist threads or ropes, and attach them to distant parts, thus fixing the weft of Fate. One of these fays is sometimes called Held, and described as black, or as half dark half white — like Hel, the Mistress of the Nether World. That German fay is also called Rachel, clearly a contraction of Rach-Hel, i. e. the Avengeress Hel.

Now, in *Macbeth* also the Weird Sisters are described as " black." The coming up of Hekate·with them in the cave-scene might not unfitly be looked upon as a parallel with the German Held, or Rach-Hel, and the Norse Hel; these Teutonic deities being originally Goddesses of Nocturnal Darkness, and of the Nether World, even as Hekate.

In German folk-lore, three Sisters of Fate bear the names of Wilbet, Worbet and Ainbet. Etymologically these names seem to refer to the well-disposed nature of a fay representing the Past; to the warring or worrying troubles of the Present; and to the terrors (*Ain = Agin*) of the Future. All over southern Germany, from Austria to Alsace and Rhenish Hesse, the three fays are known under various names besides Wilbet, Worbet, and Ainbet — for instance, as Mechtild, Ottilia, and Gertraud; as Irmina, Adela, and Chlothildis, and so forth. The fay in the middle of this trio is always a good fay, a white fay — but blind. Her treasure (the very names of Ottilia and Adela point to a treasure) is continually being taken from her by the third fay, a dark and evil one, as well as by the first. This myth has been interpreted as meaning that the Present, being blinded as to its own existence, is continually being encroached upon, robbed as it were, by the dark Future and the Past.

Of this particular trait there is no vestige in Shakspeare's Weird Sisters. They, like the Norns, "go hand in hand." But there is another point which claims attention: Shakspeare's Witches are bearded. ("You should be women, and yet your beards forbid me to interpret that you are so." Act i, scene 3.)

It need scarcely be brought to recollection that a commingling of the female and male character occurs in the divine and semi-divine figures of various mythological systems—including the Bearded Venus. Of decisive importance is, however, the fact of a bearded Weird Sister having apparently been believed in by our heathen German forefathers.

Near Wessobrunn, in Upper Bavaria, where the semi-heathen fragment of a cosmogonic lay, known as "Wessobrunn Prayer," was discovered, there has also been found, of late, a rudely-sculptured three-headed image. It is looked upon as an ancient effigy of the German Norns. The Cloister of the three Holy Bournes, or Fountains, which stands close by the place of discovery, is supposed to have been set up on ground that had once served for pagan worship. Probably the later monkish establishment of the Three Holy Bournes had taken the place of a similarly named heathen sanctuary where the three Sisters of Fate were once adored. Indeed, the name of all the corresponding fays in yet current German folk-lore is connected with holy wells. This quite fits in with the three Eddic Bournes near the great Tree of Existence, at one of which—apparently at the oldest, which is the very Source of Being —the Norns live, "the maidens that over the Sea of Age travel in deep foreknowledge," and of whom it is said that:

> They laid the lots; they ruled the life
> To the sons of men, their fate foretelling.

Now, curiously enough, the central head of the slab found near Wessobrunn, in the neighborhood of the Cloister of the Three Holy Bournes, is *bearded*. This has puzzled our archæologists. Some of them fancied that what appears to be a beard might after all be the hair of one of the fays or Norns, tied round the chin. By the light of the description of the Weird Sisters in Shakspeare's *Macbeth* we, however, see at once the true connection.

In every respect, therefore, his "Witches" are an echo from the ancient Germanic creed—an echo, moreover, coming to us in the oldest Teutonic verse-form; that is, in the staff-rime.

KARL BLIND.

Elves. The elves of later times seem a sort of middle thing between the light and dark elves. They are fair and lively, but also bad and mischievous. In some parts of Norway the peasants describe them as diminutive naked boys with hats on. Traces of their dance are sometimes to be seen on the wet grass, especially on the banks of rivers. Their exhalation is injurious, and is called *alfgust* or *elfblæst*, causing a swelling, which is easily contracted by too nearly approaching places where they have spat, etc. They have a predilection for certain spots, but particularly for large trees, which on that account the owners do not venture to meddle with, but look on them as something sacred, on which the weal or woe of the place depends. Certain diseases among their cattle are attributed to the elves, and are, therefore, called elf-fire or elf-shot. The dark elves are often confounded with the dwarfs, with whom they, indeed, seem identical, although they are distinguished in Odin's Raven's Song. The Norwegians also make a distinction between dwarfs and elves, believing the former to live solitary and in quiet, while the latter love music and dancing. (Faye, p. 48; quoted by Thorpe.)

The fairies of Scotland are precisely identical with the above. They are described as a diminutive race of beings of a mixed or rather dubious nature, capricious in their dispositions and mischievous in their resentment. They inhabit the interior of green hills, chiefly those of a conical form, in Gaelic termed *Sighan*, on which they lead their dances by moonlight; impressing upon the surface the marks of circles, which sometimes appear yellow and blasted, sometimes of a deep green hue, and within which it is dangerous to sleep, or to be found after sunset. Cattle which are suddenly seized with the cramp, or some similar disorder, are said to be *elf-shot*. (Scott's Minstrelsy of the Scottish Border; quoted by Thorpe.)

Of the Swedish elves, Arndt gives the following sketch: Of giants, of dwarfs, of the alp, of dragons, that keep watch over treasures, they have the usual stories; nor are the kindly elves forgotten. How often has my postillion, when he observed a circular mark in the dewy grass, exclaimed: See! there the elves have been dancing. These elf-dances play a great part in the spinning-room. To those who at midnight happen to enter one of these circles, the elves become visible, and may then play all kinds of pranks with them; though in general they are little, merry, harmless beings, both male and female. They often sit in small stones, that are hollowed out in circular form, and which are called elf-querns or mill-stones. Their voice is said to be soft like the air. If a loud cry is heard in the forest, it is that of the Skogsrå (spirit of the wood), which should be answered only by a *He!* when it can do no harm. (Reise durch Sweden; quoted by Thorpe.)

The elf-shot was known in England in very remote times, as appears from the Anglo-Saxon incantation, printed by Grimm in his Deutsche Mythologie, and in the appendix to Kemble's Saxons in England: Gif hit wære esa gescot oððe hit wære ylfa gescot; that is, if it were an asa-shot or an elf-shot. On this subject Grimm says: It is a very old belief that dangerous arrows were shot by the elves from the air. The thunder-bolt is also called elf-shot, and in Scot-

land a hard, sharp, wedge-shaped stone is known by
the name of elf-arrow, elf-flint, elf-bolt, which, it is
supposed, has been sent by the spirits. (Quoted by
Thorpe.)

CHAPTER VII.

Our ancestors divided the universe into nine worlds,
and these again into three groups:

1. Over the earth. Muspelheim, Ljosalfaheim and
Asaheim.

2. On the earth. Jotunheim, Midgard and Van-
heim.

3. Below the earth. Svartalfaheim, Niflheim and
Niflhel.

The gods had twelve abodes:

1. THRUDHEIM. The abode of Thor. His realm is
Thrudvang, and his palace is Bilskirner.

2. YDALER. Uller's abode.

3. VALASKJALF. Odin's hall.

4. SOKVABEK. The abode of Saga.

5. GLADSHEIM, where there are twelve seats for
the gods, besides the throne occupied by Alfather.

6. THRYMHEIM. Skade's abode.

7. BREIDABLIK. Balder's abode.

8. HIMMINBJORG. Heimdal's abode.

9. FOLKVANG. Freyja's abode.

10. GLITNER. Forsete's abode.

11. NOATUN. Njord's abode

12. LANDVIDE. Vidar's abode.

According to the Lay of Grimner, the gods had
twelve horses, but the owner of each horse is not
given:

(1) Sleipner (Odin's), (2) Goldtop (Heimdal's),

(3) Glad, (4) Gyller, (5) Gler, (6) Skeidbrimer, (7) Silvertop, (8) Siner, (9) Gisl, (10) Falhofner, (11) Lightfoot, (12) Blodughofdi (Frey's).

The owners of nine of them are not given, and, moreover, it is stated that Thor had no horse, but always either went on foot or drove his goats.

The favorite numbers are three, nine and twelve. Monotheism was recognized in the unknown god, who is from everlasting to everlasting. A number of trinities were established, and the nine worlds were classified into three groups. The week had nine days, and originally there were probably but nine gods, that is, before the vans were united with the asas. The number nine occurs where Heimdal is said to have nine mothers, Menglad is said to have nine maid-servants, Æger had nine daughters, etc. When the vans were united with the asas, the number rose to twelve:

(1) Odin, (2) Thor, (3) Tyr, (4) Balder, (5) Hoder, (6) Heimdal, (7) Hermod, (8) Njord, (9) Frey, (10) Uller, (11) Vidar, (12) Forsete.

If we add to this list Brage, Vale and Loke, we get fifteen; but the Eddas everywhere declare that there are twelve gods, who were entitled to divine worship.

The number of the goddesses is usually given as twenty-six.

CHAPTER VIII.

Loke and his offspring are so fully treated in our Norse Mythology, that we content ourselves by referring our readers to that work.

CHAPTER IX.

Freyja's ornament Brising. In the saga of Olaf Tryggvason, there is a rather awkward story of the manner in which Freyja became possessed of her ornament. Freyja, it is told, was a mistress of Odin. Not far from the palace dwelt four dwarfs, whose names were Alfrig, Dvalin, Berling and Grer; they were skillful smiths. Looking one day into their stony dwelling, Freyja saw them at work on a beautiful golden necklace, or collar, which she offered to buy, but which they refused to part with, except on conditions quite incompatible with the fidelity she owed to Odin, but to which she, nevertheless, was tempted to accede. Thus the ornament became hers. By some means this transaction came to the knowledge of Loke, who told it to Odin. Odin commanded him to get possession of the ornament. This was no easy task, for no one could enter Freyja's bower without her consent. He went away whimpering, but most were glad on seeing him in such tribulation. When he came to the locked bower, he could nowhere find an entrance, and, it being cold weather, he began to shiver. He then transformed himself into a fly and tried every opening, but in vain; there was nowhere air enough to make him to get through [Loke (fire) requires air]. At length he found a hole in the roof, but not bigger than the prick of a needle. Through this he slipt. On his entrance he looked around to see if anyone were awake, but all were buried in sleep. He peeped in at Freyja's bed, and saw that she had the ornament round her neck, but that the lock was on the side she lay on. He then transformed himself to a flea, placed himself on Freyja's cheek, and stung her so that she awoke, but only turned herself round and slept again. He then laid aside his assumed form, cautiously took the ornament, unlocked the bower, and took his prize to Odin. In the morning, on waking, Freyja seeing the door open, without having been forced, and that her ornament was gone, instantly understood the whole affair. Having dressed herself, she repaired to Odin's hall, and upbraided him with having stolen her ornament, and insisted on its restoration, which she finally obtained. (Quoted by Thorpe.)

Mention is also made of the Brósinga-men in the Beowulf (verse 2394). Here it is represented as belonging to Hermanric, but the legend concerning it has never been found.

CHAPTER X.

This myth about Frey and Gerd is the subject of one of the most fascinating poems in the Elder Edda, the Journey of Skirner. It is, as Auber Forestier, in Echoes from Mistland, says, the germ of the Niblung story. Frey is Sigurd or Sigfrid, and Gerd is Brynhild. The myth is also found in another poem of the Elder Edda, the Lay of Fjolsvin, in which the god himself — there called Svipday (the hastener of the day) — undertakes the journey to arouse from the winter sleep the cold giant nature of the maiden Menglad (the sun-radiant daughter), who is identical with Freyja (the goddess of spring, promise, or of love between man and woman, and who can easily be compared with Gerd). Before the bonds which enchain the maiden can in either case be broken, Bele (the giant of spring storms, corresponding to the dragon Fafner in the Niblung story,) must be conquered, and Wafurloge (the wall of bickering flames that surrounded the castle) must be penetrated. The fanes symbolize the funeral pyre, for whoever enters the nether world must scorn the fear of death. (Auber Forestier's Echoes from Mistland; Introduction, xliii, xliv.) We also find this story repeated again and again, in numberless variations, in Teutonic folk-lore; for instance, in The Maiden on the Glass Mountain, where the glass mountain takes the place of the bickering flame.

CHAPTER XI.

The tree Lerad (furnishing protection) must be regarded as a branch of Ygdrasil.

CHAPTER XII.

In Heimskringla Skidbladner is called Odin's ship. This is correct. All that belonged to the gods was his also.

CHAPTER XIII.

For a thorough analysis of Thor as a spring god, as the god who dwells in the clouds, as the god of thunder and lightning, as the god of agriculture, in short, as the god of culture, we can do no better than to refer our readers to Der Mythus von Thor, nach Nordischen Quellen, von Ludwig Uhland, Stuttgart, 1836; and to Handbuch der Deutschen Mythologie, mit Einschluss der Nordischen, von Karl Simrock, Vierte Auflage, Bonn, 1874.

CHAPTER XIV.

The death of Balder is justly regarded as the most beautiful myth in Teutonic mythology.   It is connected with the Lay of Vegtam in the Elder Edda. Like so many other myths (Frey and Gerd, The Robbing of Idun, etc.) the myth symbolizes originally the end of summer and return of spring.   Thus Balder dies every year and goes to Hel.   But in the following spring he returns to the asas, and gladdens all things living and dead with his pure shining light. Gradually, however, the myth was changed from a symbol of the departing and returning summer, and applied to the departing and returning of the world year, and thus the death of Balder prepares the way for Ragnarok and Regeneration.   Balder goes to Hel and does not return to this world.   Thokk refuses to weep for him.   His return is promised after Ragnarok.   The next spring does not bring him back, but the rejuvenated earth.   Thus the death of Balder becomes the central thought in the drama of the fate of the gods and of the world.   It is inseparably connected with the punishment of Loke and the twilight of the gods.   The winter following the death of Balder is not an ordinary winter, but the Fimbul-winter, which is followed by no summer, but by the destruction of the world.   The central idea in the Odinic religion, the destruction and regeneration of the world, has taken this beautiful sun-myth of Balder into its service.   Balder is then no more merely the pure holy light of heaven; he symbolizes at the same time the purity and innocence of the gods; he is changed from a physical to an ethical myth.   He impersonated al

that was good and holy in the life of the gods; and so
it came to pass that when the golden age had ceased,
when thirst for gold (Gulveig), when sin and crime
had come into the world, he was too good to live
in it. As in Genesis fratricide (Cain and Abel) followed upon the eating of the forbidden fruit, and the
loss of paradise; so, when the golden age (paradise)
had ended among the asas, Loke (the serpent) brought
fratricide (Hoder and Balder) among the gods; themselves and our ancestors regarded fratricide as the
lowest depth of moral depravity. After the death of
Balder

> Brothers slay brothers,
> Sisters' children
> Shed each other's blood,
> Hard grows the world,
> Sensual sin waxes huge.

> There are sword-ages, ax-ages —
> Shields are cleft in twain,—
> Storm-ages, murder-ages,
> Till the world falls dead,
> And men no longer spare
> Or pity one another.

Upon the whole we may say that a sun-myth first
represents the death of the day at sunset, when the sky
is radiant as if dyed in blood. In the flushing morn
light wins its victory again. Then this same myth becomes transferred to the death and birth of summer.
Once more it is lifted into a higher sphere, while still
holding on to its physical interpretation, and is applied
to the world year. Finally, it is clothed with ethical at-
tributes, becomes thoroughly anthropomorphized, and
typifies the good and the evil, the virtues and vices
(light and darkness), in the character and life of gods

and of men. Thus we get four stages in the development of the myth.

CHAPTER XV.

RAGNAROK. The word is found written in two ways, Ragnarök and ragnarökr. Ragna is genitive plural, from the word regin (god), and means of the gods. Rök means reason, ground, origin, a wonder, sign, marvel. It is allied to the O. H. G. *rahha* = sentence, judgment. Ragnarök would then mean *the history of the gods*, and applied to the dissolution of the world, might be translated *the last judgment, doomsday, weird of gods and the world*. Rökr means *twilight*, and Ragnarokr, as the Younger Edda has it, thus means *the twilight of the gods*, and the latter is adopted by nearly all modern writers, although Gudbr. Vigfusson declares that Ragnarok (doomsday) is no doubt the correct form. And this is also to be said in favor of doomsday, that Ragnarok does not involve only the *twilight*, but the whole *night* of the gods and the world.

THE NIFLUNGS AND GJUKUNGS.

This chapter of *Skaldkaparmal* contains much valuable material for a correct understanding of the Nibelungen-Lied, especially as to the origin of the Niblung hoard, and the true character of Brynhild. The material given here, and in the Icelandic Volsunga Saga, has been used by Wm. Morris in his Sigurd the Volsung and the Fall of the Niblungs. In the Nibelungen-Lied, as transposed by Auber Forestier, in Echoes from Mist-Land, we have a perfect gem of literature from the middle high German period, but its author had lost sight of the divine and mythical origin of the material that he wove into his poem. It is only by combining the German Nibelungen-Lied with the mythical materials found in Norseland that our national Teutonic epic can be restored to us. Wagner has done this for us in his famous drama; Jordan has done it in his Sigfrid's saga; Morris has done it in the work mentioned above; but will not Auber Forestier gather up all the scattered fragments relating to Sigurd and Brynhild, and weave them together into a prose narrative, that shall delight the young and the old of this great land?

We are glad to welcome at this time a new book in the field of Niblung literature. We refer to Geibel's Brunhild, translated, with introduction and notes, by Prof. G. Theo. Dippold, and recently published in Boston.

MENJA AND FENJA.

This is usually called the peace of Frode, which corresponds to the golden age in the life of the asas. Avarice is the root of crime, and all other evils. Avarice is at the bottom of all the endless woes of the Niblung story. The myth explaining why the sea is salt is told in a variety of forms in different countries. In Germany there are several folk-lore stories and traditions in regard to it. In Norway, where folk-lore tales are so abundant, we find the myth about Menja and Fenja recurring in the following form:

WHY THE SEA IS SALT.

Long, long ago there were two brothers, the one was rich and the other was poor. On Christmas eve the poor one had not a morsel of bread or meat in his house, and so he went to his brother and asked him for mercy's sake to give him something for Christmas. It was not the first time the brother had had to give him, and he was not very much pleased to see him this time either.

"If you will do what I ask of you, I will give you a whole ham of pork," said he.

The poor man promised immediately, and was very thankful besides.

"There you have it, now go to hell," said the rich one, and threw the ham at him.

"What I have promised, I suppose, I must keep," said the other. He took the ham and started. He walked and walked the whole day, and at twilight he came to a place where everything looked so bright and splendid.

"This must be the place," thought the man with the ham.

Out in the wood-shed stood an old man with a long white beard, cutting wood for Christmas.

"Good evening," said the man with the ham.

"Good evening, sir. Where are you going so late?" said the man.

"I am on my way to hell, if I am on the right road," said the poor man.

"Yes, you have taken the right road; it is here," said the old man. "Now when you get in, they will all want to buy your ham, for pork is rare food in hell; but you must not sell it, unless you get the hand-mill that stands back of the door for it. When you come out again I will show you how to regulate it. You will find it useful in more than one respect."

The man with the ham thanked the old man for this valuable information, and rapped at the devil's door.

When he came in it happened as the old man had said. All the devils, both the large ones and the small ones, crowded around him like ants around a worm, and the one bid higher than the other for the ham.

"It is true my wife and I were to have it for our Christmas dinner, but, seeing that you are so eager for it, I suppose I will have to let you have it," said the man. "But if I am to sell it, I want that hand-mill that stands behind the door there for it."

The devil did not like to spare it, and kept dickering and bantering with the man, but he insisted, and so the devil had to give him the hand-mill. When the man came out in the yard he asked the old wood-chopper how he should regulate the mill; and when he had learned how to do it, he said "thank you," and made for home as fast as he could. But still he did not reach home before twelve o'clock in the night Christmas eve.

"Why, where in the world have you been?" said the woman. "Here I have been sitting hour after hour waiting and waiting, and I haven't as much as two sticks to put on the fire so as to cook the Christmas porridge."

"Oh, I could not come any sooner. I had several errands to do, and I had a long way to go too. But now I will show you," said the man. He set the mill on the table, and had it first grind light, then a table-cloth, then food and ale and all sorts of good things for Christmas, and as he commanded the mill ground. The woman expressed her great astonishment again and again, and wanted to know where her husband had gotten the mill, but this he would not tell.

"It makes no difference where I have gotten it; you see the mill is a good one, and that the water does not freeze," said the man.

Then he ground food and drink, and all good things, for the whole Christmas week, and on the third day he invited his friends: he was going to have a party. When the rich brother saw all the nice and good things at the party, he became very wroth, for he could not bear to see his brother have anything.

"Christmas eve he was so needy that he came to me and asked me for mercy's sake to give him a little food, and now he gives a feast as though he were both count and king," said he to the others.

"But where in hell have you gotten all your riches from?" said he to his brother.

"Behind the door," answered he who owned the mill. He did not care to give any definite account, but later in the evening, when he began to get a little tipsy, he could not help himself and brought out the mill.

"There you see the one that has given me all the riches." said he, and then he let the mill grind both one thing and another. When the brother saw this he was bound to have the mill, and after a long bantering about it, he finally was to have it; but he was to pay three hundred dollars for it, and his brother was to keep it until harvest.

"When I keep it until then, I shall have ground food enough to last many years," thought he.

Of course the mill got no chance to grow rusty during the next six months, and when harvest-time came, the rich brother got it; but the other man had taken good care not to show him how to regulate it. It was in the evening that the rich man brought the mill home, and in the morning he bade his wife go and spread the hay after the mowers,— he would get dinner ready, he said. Toward dinner he put the mill on the table.

"Grind fish and gruel: Grind both well and fast!" said the man, and the mill began to grind fish and gruel. It first filled all the dishes and tubs full, and after that it covered the whole floor with fish and gruel. The man kept puttering and tinkering, and tried to get the mill to stop; but no matter how he turned it and fingered at it, the mill kept on, and before long the gruel got so deep in the room that the man was on the point of drowning. Then he opened the door to the sitting-room, but before long that room was filled too, and the man had all he could do to get hold of the door-latch down in this flood of gruel. When he got the door open he did not remain long in the room. He ran out as fast as he could, and there was a perfect flood of fish gruel behind, deluging the yard and his fields.

The wife, who was in the meadow making hay, began to think that it took a long time to get dinner ready.

"Even if husband does not call us, we will have to go anyway. I suppose he does not know much about making gruel; I will have to go and help him," said the woman to the mowers.

They went homeward, but on coming up the hill they met the flood of fish and gruel and bread, the one mixed up with the other, and the man came running ahead of the flood.

"Would that each one of you had an hundred stomachs, but have a care that you do not drown in the gruel flood," cried the husband. He ran by them as though the devil had been after him, and hastened down to his brother. He begged him in the name of everything sacred to come and take the mill away immediately.

"If it grinds another hour the whole settlement will perish in fish and gruel," said he.

But the brother would not take it unless he got three hundred dollars, and this money had to be paid to him.

Now the poor brother had both money and the mill, and so it did not take long before he got himself a farm, and a much nicer one than his brother's. With his mill he ground out so much gold that he covered his house all over with sheets of gold. The house stood down by the sea-shore, and it glistened far out upon the sea. All who sailed past had to go ashore and visit the rich man in the golden house, and all wanted to see the wonderful mill, for its fame spread far and wide, and there was none who had not heard speak of it.

After a long time there came a sea-captain who

wished to see the mill. He asked whether it could grind salt.

"Yes, it can grind salt," said he who owned the mill; and when the captain heard this, he was bound to have it, let it cost what it will. For if he had that, thought he, he would not have to sail far off over dangerous waters after cargoes of salt. At first the man did not wish to sell it, but the captain teased and begged and finally the man sold it, and got many thousand dollars for it. When the captain had gotten the mill on his back, he did not stay there long, for he was afraid the man might reconsider the bargain and back out again. He had no time to ask how to regulate it; he went to his ship as fast as he could, and when he had gotten some distance out upon the sea, he got his mill out.

"Grind salt both fast and well," said the captain. The mill began to grind salt, and that with all its might. When the captain had gotten the ship full he wanted to stop the mill; but no matter how he worked, and no matter how he handled it, the mill kept grinding as fast as ever, and the heap of salt kept growing larger and larger, and at last the ship sank. The mill stands on the bottom of the sea grinding this very day, and so it comes that the sea is salt.

VOCABULARY.

ADILS. A king who reigned in Upsala.

AE. A dwarf.

ÆGER. The god presiding over the stormy sea.

ALF. A dwarf.

ALFATHER. A name of Odin.

ALFHEIM. The home of the elves.

ALFRIG. A dwarf.

ALSVID. One of the horses of the sun.

ALTHJOF. A dwarf.

ALVIS. A dwarf.

AMSVARTNER. The name of the lake in which the island was situated where the wolf Fenrer was chained.

ANDHRIMNER. The cook in Valhal.

ANDLANG. The second heaven.

ANDVARE. A dwarf.

ANDVARE-NAUT. The ring in the Niblung story.

ANGERBODA. A giantess; mother of the Fenris-wolf.

ANNAR. Husband of Night and father of Jord.

ARVAK. The name of one of the horses of the sun.

ASAHEIM. The home of the asas.

ASALAND. The land of the asas.

ASAS. The Teutonic gods.

ASA-THOR. A common name for Thor.

ASGARD. The residence of the gods.

ASK. The name of the first man created by Odin, Honer and Loder.

ASLAUG. Daughter of Sigurd and Brynhild.

ASMUND. A man visited by Odin.

ASYNJES. The Teutonic goddesses

ATLE. Gudrun's husband after the death of Sigurd.

ATRID. A name of Odin.

AUD. The son of Night and Naglfare.

AUDHUMBLA. The cow that nourished the giant Ymer.

AUDUN. A name derived from Odin.

AURGELMER. A giant; grandfather of Bergelmer; the same as Ymer.

AURVANG. A dwarf.

AUSTRE. A dwarf.

BAFUR. A dwarf.

BALDER. Son of Odin and Frigg, slain by Hoder.

BALEYG. A name of Odin.

BAR-ISLE. A cool grove in which Gerd agreed with Skirner to meet Frey.

BAUGE. A brother of Suttung. Odin worked for him one summer, in order to get his help in obtaining Suttung's mead of poetry.

BEIGUD. One of Rolf Krake's berserks.

BELE. A giant, brother of Gerd, slain by Frey.

BERGELMER. A giant; son of Thrudgelmer and grandson of Aurgelmer.

BERLING. A dwarf.

BESTLA. Wife of Bure and mother of Odin.

BIFLIDE. A name of Odin.

BIFLINDE. A name of Odin.

BIFROST. The rainbow.

BIFUR. A dwarf.

BIKKE. A minister of Jormunrek; causes Randver to be hanged, and Svanhild trodden to death by horses.

BIL. One of the children that accompany Moon.

BILEYG. A name of Odin.

BILSKIRNER. Thor's abode.

BLAIN. A dwarf.

BLODUGHOFDE. Frey's horse.

BODN. One of the three jars in which the poetic mead is kept.

BODVAR BJARKE. One of Rolf Krake's berserks.

BOL. One of the rivers flowing out of Hvergelmer.

BOLTHORN. A giant; father of Bestla, mother of Odin.

BOLVERK. A name of Odin.

BOMBUR. A dwarf.

BOR. Son of Bure; father of Odin.

BRAGE. A son of Odin; the best of skalds.

BREIDABLIK. The abode of Balder.

BRIMER. One of the heavenly halls after Ragnarok.

BRISING. Freyja's necklace.

BROK. A dwarf.

BRYNHILD. One of the chief heroines in the Niblung story.

BUDLE. Father of Atle and Brynhild.

BUE. A son of Vesete, who settled in Borgundarholm.

Bure. Grandfather of Odin.

Byleist. A brother of Loke.

Byrger. A well from which Bil and Hjuke were going when they were taken by Moon.

Dain. A dwarf.

Dain. One of the stags that bite the leaves of Ygdrasil.

Dainsleif. Hogne's sword.

Day. Son of Delling.

Daybreak. The father of Day.

Delling. Daybreak.

Dolgthvare. A dwarf.

Dore. A dwarf.

Draupner. Odin's ring.

Drome. One of the fetters with which the Fenris-wolf was chained.

Duf. A dwarf.

Duney. One of the stags that bite the leaves of Ygdrasil.

Durathro. One of the stags that bite the leaves of Ygdrasil.

Durin. A dwarf.

Dvalin. One of the stags that bite the leaves of Ygdrasil.

Dvalin. A dwarf.

Eikinskjalde. A dwarf.

Eikthyrner. A hart that stands over Odin's hall.

Eilif. Son of Gudrun; a skald.

Eimyrja. One of the daughters of Haloge and Glod.

Eindride. A name of Thor.

Eir. An attendant of Menglod, and the best of all in the healing art.

Ekin. One of the rivers flowing from Hvergelmer.

Elder. A servant of Æger.

Eldhrimner. The kettle in which the boar Sahrimner is cooked in Valhal.

Elivogs. The ice-cold streams that flow out of Niflheim.

Eljudner. Hel's hall.

Elle. An old woman (old age) with whom Thor wrestled in Jotunheim.

Embla. The first woman created by Odin, Honer and Loder.

Endil. The name of a giant.

Erp. A son of Jonaker, murdered by Sorle and Hamder.

Eylime. The father of Hjordis, mother of Volsung.

Eysa. One of the daughters of Haloge and Glod.

Fafner. Son of Hreidmar, killed by Sigurd.

FAL. A dwarf.

FALHOFNER. One of the horses of the gods.

FARBAUTE. The father of Loke.

FARMAGOD. One of the names of Odin.

FARMATYR. One of the names of Odin.

FENJA. A female slave who ground at Frode's mill.

FENRIS-WOLF. The monster wolf, son of Loke.

FENSALER. The abode of Frigg.

FID. A dwarf.

FILE. A dwarf.

FIMAFENG. Æger's servant.

FIMBUL. One of the streams flowing from Hvergelmer.

FIMBULTHUL. One of the streams flowing from Hvergelmer.

FIMBUL-TYR. The unknown god.

FIMBUL-WINTER. The great and awful winter of three years' duration preceding Ragnarok.

FINNSLEIF. A byrnie belonging to King Adils, of Upsala.

FJALAR. A dwarf.

FJOLNER. A name of Odin.

FJOLSVID. A name of Odin.

FJORGVIN. The mother of Frigg and of Thor.

FJORM. One of the streams flowing from Hvergelmer.

FOLKVANG. Freyja's abode.

FORM. One of the streams flowing from Hvergelmer.

FORNJOT. The ancient giant; the father of Æger.

FORSETE. The peace-maker; son of Balder and Nanna.

FRANANGER FORCE. The waterfall into which Loke cast himself in the likeness of a salmon.

FREKE. One of Odin's wolves.

FREY. Son of Njord and husband of Skade.

FREYJA. The daughter of Njord and sister of Frey.

FRIDLEIF. A son of Skjold.

FRIGG. Wife of Odin and mother of the gods.

FRODE. Grandson of Skjold.

FROSTE. A dwarf.

FULLA. Frigg's attendant.

FUNDIN. A dwarf.

FYRE. A river in Sweden.

GAGNRAD. A name of Odin.

GALAR. A dwarf.

GANDOLF. A dwarf.

GANG. A giant.

GANGLARE. A name of Odin.

GANGLATE. Hel's man-servant.

GANGLERE. A name of Odin.

GANGLOT. Hel's maid-servant.

GANGRAD. A name of Odin.

GARDROFA. A horse.

GARM. A dog that barks at Ragnarok.

GAUT. A name of Odin.

GEFJUN. A goddess; she is present at Æger's feast.

GEFN. One of the names of Freyja.

GEIRAHOD. A valkyrie.

GEIRROD. A giant visited by Thor.

GEIR SKOGUL. A valkyrie.

GEIRVIMUL. One of the streams flowing from Hvergelmer.

GELGJA. The fetter with which the Fenris-wolf was chained.

GERD A beautiful giantess, daughter of Gymer.

GERE One of Odin's wolves.

GERSAME. One of the daughters of Freyja.

GILLING. Father of Suttung, who possessed the poetic mead.

GIMLE. The abode of the righteous after Ragnarok.

GINNAR. A dwarf.

GINUNGAGAP. The premundane abyss.

GIPUL. One of the streams flowing from Hvergelmer.

GISL. One of the horses of the gods.

GJAILAR-BRIDGE. The bridge across the river Gjol, near Helheim.

GJAILAR-HORN. Heimdal's horn.

GJAILAR-RIVER. The river near Helheim.

GJALP. One of the daughters of Geirrod.

GJUKE. A king in Germany, visited by Sigurd.

GLADSHEIM. Odin's dwelling.

GLAM. The name of a giant.

GLAPSVID. A name of Odin.

GLASER. A grove in Asgard.

GLEIPNER. The last fetter with which the wolf Fenrer was bound.

GLENER. The husband of Sol (sun).

GLER. One of the horses of the gods.

GLITNER. Forsete's hall.

GLOIN. A dwarf.

GNA. Frigg's messenger.

GNIPA-CAVE. The cave before which the dog Garm barks.

GNITA-HEATH. Fafner's abode, where he kept the treasure of the
  Niblungs.
GOIN. A serpent under Ygdrasil.
GOL. A valkyrie.
GOLDFAX. The giant Hrungner's horse.
GOMUL. One of the streams flowing from Hvergelmer.
GONDLER. One of the names of Odin.
GONDUL. A valkyrie.
GOPUL. One of the streams flowing from Hvergelmer.
GOT. A name of Odin.
GOTE. Gunnar's horse.
GOTHORM. A son of Gjuke; murders Sigurd, and is slain by him.
GRABAK. One of the serpents under Ygdrasil.
GRAD. One of the streams flowing from Hvergelmer.
GRAFVITNER. A serpent under Ygdrasil.
GRAFVOLLUD. A serpent under Ygdrasil.
GRAM. Sigurd's sword.
GRANE. Sigurd's horse.
GREIP. One of the daughters of Geirrod.
GRID. A giantess visited by Thor.
GRIDARVOL. Grid's staff.
GRIM. A name of Odin.
GRIMHILD. Gjuke's queen.
GRIMNER. One of the names of Odin.
GRJOTTUNGARD. The place where Thor fought with Hrungner.
GROA. A giantess, mother of Orvandel.
GROTTE. The name of King Frode's mill.
GUD. A valkyrie.
GUDNY. One of the children of Gjuke.
GUDRUN. The famous daughter of Gjuke.
GULLINBURSTE. The name of Frey's boar.
GULLINTANNE. A name of Heimdal.
GULLTOP. Heimdal's horse.
GULLVEIG. A personification of gold; she is pierced and burnt.
GUNGNER. Odin's spear.
GUNLAD. The daughter of the giant Suttung.
GUNN. A valkyrie.
GUNNAR. The famous son of Gjuke.
GUNTHRAIN. One of the rivers flowing from Hvergelmer.
GWODAN. An old name for Odin.

GYLFE. A king of Svithjod, who visited Asgard under the name of Ganglere.

GYLLER. One of the horses of the gods.

GYMER. Another name of the ocean divinity Æger.

HABROK. A celebrated hero.

HALLINSKIDE. Another name of Heimdal.

HALOGE. A giant, son of Fornjot; also called Loge.

HAMDER. Son of Jonaker and Gudrun, incited by his mother to avenge his sister's death.

HAMSKERPER. A horse; the sire of Hofvarpner, which was Gna's horse.

HANGAGOD. A name of Odin.

HANGATYR. A name of Odin.

HAPTAGOD. A name of Odin.

HAR. The High One; applied to Odin.

HARBARD. A name assumed by Odin.

HATE. The wolf bounding before the sun, and will at last catch the moon.

HEIDE. Another name for Gullveig.

HEIDRUN. A goat that stands over Valhal.

HEIMDAL. The god of the rainbow.

HEIMER. Brynhild's foster-father.

HEL. The goddess of death; daughter of Loke.

HELBLINDE. A name of Odin.

HELMET-BEARER. A name of Odin.

HENGEKJAPT. The man to whom King Frode gave his mill.

HEPTE. A dwarf.

HERAN. A name of Odin.

HERFATHER. A name of Odin.

HERJAN. A name of Odin.

HERMOD. The god who rode on Sleipner to Hel, to get Balder back.

HERTEIT. A name of Odin.

HILD. A valkyrie.

HILDESVIN. A helmet, which King Adils took from King Ale.

HIMINBJORG. Heimdal's dwelling.

HINDFELL. The place where Brynhild sat in her hall, surrounded by the Vafurloge.

HJALMBORE. A name of Odin.

HJALPREK. A king in Denmark; collects a fleet for Sigurd.

HJATLE THE VALIANT. One of Rolf Krake's berserks.

HJORDIS. Married to Sigmund, and mother of Sigurd.

HJUKE. One of the children that accompany Moon.

HLEDJOLF. A dwarf.

HLER. Another name of Æger.

HLIDSKJALF. The seat of Odin, whence he looked out over all the world.

HLIN. One of the attendants of Frigg; Frigg herself is sometimes called by this name.

HLODYN. Thor's mother.

HLOK. A valkyrie.

HLORIDE. A name of Thor.

HNIKAR. A name of Odin.

HNIKUD. A name of Odin.

HNITBJORG. The place where Suttung hid the poetic mead.

HNOS. Freyja's daughter.

HODER. The slayer of Balder; he is blind.

HODMIMER'S-HOLT. The grove where the two human beings, Lif and Lifthraser, were preserved during Ragnarok.

HOFVARPNER. Gna's horse.

HOGNE. A son of Gjuke.

HONER. One of the three creating gods; with Odin and Loder he creates Ask and Embla.

HOR. A dwarf.

HORN. A name of Freyja.

HRASVELG. A giant in an eagle's plumage, who produces the wind.

HREIDMAR. The father of Regin and Fafner.

HRID. One of the streams flowing from Hvergelmer.

HRIMFAXE. The horse of Night.

HRINGHORN. The ship upon which Balder's body was burned.

HRIST. A valkyrie.

HRODVITNER. A wolf; father of the wolf Hate.

HRON. One of the streams flowing from Hvergelmer.

HROPTATYR. A name of Odin.

HROTTE. Fafner's sword.

HRUNGNER. A giant; Thor slew him.

HRYM. A giant, who steers the ship Naglfar at Ragnarok.

HVERGELMER. The fountain in the middle of Niflheim.

HUGE. A person (Thought) who ran a race with Thjalfe, in Jotunheim.

HUGIN. One of Odin's ravens.

HUGSTORE. A dwarf.

HYMER. A giant with whom Thor went fishing when he caught the Midgard-serpent.

HYNDLA. A vala visited by Freyja.

HYRROKEN. A giantess who launched the ship on which Balder was burned.

IDA. A plain where the gods first assemble, and where they assemble again after Ragnarok.

IDAVOLD. The same.

IDE. A giant, son of Olvalde.

IDUN. Wife of Brage; she kept the rejuvenating apples.

IRONWOOD. The abode of giantesses called Jarnveds.

IVA. A river in Jotunheim.

IVALD. The father of the dwarfs that made Sif's hair, the ship Skidbladner, and Odin's spear Gungner.

JAFNHAR. A name of Odin.

JALG. A name of Odin.

JALK. A name of Odin.

JARNSAXA. One of Heimdal's nine giant mothers.

JARNVED. The same as Ironwood.

JARNVIDJIS. The giantesses dwelling in Ironwood.

JORD. Wife of Odin, mother of Thor.

JORMUNDGAND. The Midgard-serpent.

JORMUNREK. King of Goths, marries Svanhild.

JORUVOLD. The country where Aurvang is situated. Thence come several dwarfs.

JOTUNHEIM. The home of the giants.

KERLAUGS. The rivers that Thor every day must cross.

KILE. A dwarf.

KJALER. A name of Odin.

KORMT. A river which Thor every day must cross.

KVASER. The hostage given by the vans to the asas; his blood, when slain, was the poetical meed kept by Suttung.

LADING. One of the fetters with which the Fenris-wolf was bound.

LANDVIDE. Vidar's abode.

LAUFEY. Loke's mother.

LEIPT. One of the rivers flowing out of Hvergelmer.

LERAD. A tree near Valhal.

LETFET. One of the horses of the gods.

LIF. } The two persons preserved in Hodmimer's-holt
LIFTHRASER. } during Ragnarok.

LIT. A dwarf.

LJOSALFAHEIM. The home of the light elves.

LODER. One of the three gods who created Ask and Embla.

LOFN. One of the asynjes.

LOGE. A giant who tried his strength at eating with Loke in Jotunheim.

LOKE. The giant-god of the Norse mythology.

LOPT. Another name for Loke.

LOVAR. A dwarf.

LYNGVE. The island where the Fenris-wolf was chained.

MAGNE. A son of Thor.

MANNHEIM. The home of man; our earth.

MARDOL. One of the names of Freyja.

MEGINGJARDER. Thor's belt.

MEILE. A son of Odin.

MENGLAD. Svipdag's betrothed.

MENJA. A female slave who ground at Frode's mill.

MIDGARD. The name of the earth in the mythology.

MIDVITNE. A giant.

MIMER. The name of the wise giant; keeper of the holy well

MIST. A valkyrie.

MJODVITNER. A dwarf.

MJOLNER. Thor's hammer.

MJOTUD. A name of Odin.

MODE. One of Thor's sons.

MODGUD. The may who guards the Gjallar-bridge.

MODSOGNER. A dwarf.

MOIN. A serpent under Ygdrasil.

MOKKERKALFE. A clay giant in the myth of Thor and Hrungner.

MOON, BROTHER OF SUN. Both children of Mundilfare.

MOONGARM. A wolf of Loke's offspring; he devours the moon.

MORN. A troll-woman.

MUNDILFARE. Father of the sun and moon.

MUNIN. One of Odin's ravens.

MUSPEL. The name of an abode of fire.

MUSPELHEIM. The world of blazing light before the creation.

NA. A dwarf.

NAGLFAR. A mythical ship made of nail-parings; it appears in
Ragnarok.

NAIN. A dwarf.

NAL. Mother of Loke.

NANNA. Daughter of Nep; mother of Forsete, and wife of Balder.

NARE. Son of Loke; also called Narfe.

NARFE. *See* Nare.

NASTRAND. A place of punishment for the wicked after Ragnarok.

NEP. Father of Nanna.

NIBLUNGS. Identical with Gjukungs.

NIDA MOUNTAINS. A place where there is, after Ragnarok, a golden hall for the race of Sindre (the dwarfs).

NIDE. A dwarf.

NIDHUG. A serpent in the nether world.

NIFLHEIM. The world of mist before the creation.

NIFLUNGS. Identical with Niblungs.

NIGHT. Daughter of Norfe.

NIKAR. A name of Odin.

NIKUZ. A name of Odin.

NIPING. A dwarf.

NJORD. A van; husband of Skade, and father of Frey and Freyja.

NOATUN. Njord's dwelling.

NON. One of the streams flowing from Hvergelmer.

NOR. The man after whom Norway was supposed to have been named.

NORDRE. A dwarf.

NORFE. A giant, father of Night.

NORNS. The weird sisters.

NOT. One of the streams flowing from Hvergelmer.

NY. A dwarf.

NYE. A dwarf.

NYRAD. A dwarf.

ODER. Freyja's husband.

ODIN. Son of Bor and Bestla; the chief of Teutonic gods.

ODRARER. One of the vessels in which the poetic mead was kept.

OFNER. A serpent under Ygdrasil.

OIN. A dwarf.

OKU-THOR. A name of Thor.

OLVALDE. A giant; father of Thjasse, Ide and Gang.

OME. A name of Odin.

ONAR. A dwarf.

ORBODA. Wife of the giant Gymer.

ORE. A dwarf.

ORMT. One of the rivers that Thor has to cross.

ORNER. The name of a giant.

ORVANDEL. The husband of Groa, the vala who sang magic songs over Thor after he had fought with Hrungner.

OSKE. A name of Odin.

OTTER. A son of Hreidmar; in the form of an otter he was killed by Loke.

QUASER. *See* Kvaser.

RADGRID. A valkyrie.

RADSVID. A dwarf.

RAFNAGUD. A name of Odin.

RAGNAROK.. The last day; the dissolution of the gods and the world; the twilight of the gods.

RAN. The goddess of the sea; wife of Æger.

RANDGRID. A valkyrie.

RANDVER. A son of Jormunrek.

RATATOSK. A squirrel in Ygdrasil.

RATE. An auger used by Odin in obtaining the poetic mead.

REGIN. Son of Hreidmar.

REGINLEIF. A valkyrie.

REIDARTYR. A name of Odin.

REK. A dwarf.

RIND. Mother of Vale.

ROGNER. A name of Odin.

ROSKVA. Thor's maiden follower.

SAHRIMNER. The boar on which the gods and heroes in Valhal live.

SAD. A name of Odin.

SAGA. The goddess of history.

SAGER. The bucket carried by Bil and Hjuke.

SANGETAL. A name of Odin.

SEKIN. One of the streams flowing from Hvergelmer.

SESSRYMNER. Freyja's palace.

SIAR. A dwarf.

SID. A stream flowing from Hvergelmer.

SIDHOT. A name of Odin.

SIDSKEG. A name of Odin.

SIF. Thor's wife.

SIGFATHER. A name of Odin.

SIGFRID. The hero in the Niblung story; the same as Sigurd.

SIGMUND. Son of Volsung. Also son of Sigurd and Gudrun.

SINDRE. A dwarf.

SIGTYR. A name of Odin.

SIGYN. Loke's wife.

SIGURD. The hero in the Niblung story; identical with Sigfrid.

SILVERTOP. One of the horses of the gods.

SIMUL. The pole on which Bil and Hjuke carried the bucket.

SINFJOTLE. Son of Sigmund.

SINER. One of the horses of the gods.

SJOFN. One of the asynjes.

SKADE. A giantess; daughter of Thjasse and wife of Njord.

SKEGGOLD. A valkyrie.

SKEIDBRIMER. One of the horses of the gods.

SKIDBLADNER. Frey's ship.

SKIFID. A dwarf.

SKIFIR. A dwarf.

SKILFING. A name of Odin.

SKINFAXE. The horse of Day.

SKIRNER. Frey's messenger.

SKOGUL. A valkyrie.

SKOL. The wolf that pursues the sun.

SKRYMER. The name assumed by Utgard-Loke; a giant.

SKULD. The norn of the future.

SLEIPNER. Odin's eight-footed steed.

SLID. One of the streams flowing from Hvergelmer.

SLIDRUGTANNE. Frey's boar.

SNOTRA. One of the asynjes.

SOKMIMER. A giant slain by Odin.

SOKVABEK. A mansion, where Odin and Saga quaff from golden beakers.

SOL. Daughter of Mundilfare.

SON. One of the vessels containing the poetic mead.

SORLE. Son of Jonaker and Gudrun; avenges the death of Svanhild.

SUDRE. A dwarf.

SUN. Identical with Sol.

SURT. Guards Muspelheim. A fire-giant in Ragnarok.

SUTTUNG. The giant possessing the poetic mead.

SVADE. A giant.

SVADILFARE. A horse, the sire of Sleipner.

SVAFNER. A serpent under Ygdrasil.

SVANHILD. Daughter of Sigurd and Gudrun.

SVARIN. A dwarf.

SVARTALFAHEIM. The home of the swarthy elves.

SVARTHOFDE. The ancestor of all enchanters.

SVASUD. The name of a giant; father of summer.

SVIAGRIS. A ring demanded by the berserks for Rolf Krake.
SVID. A name of Odin.
SVIDAR. A name of Odin.
SVIDR. A name of Odin.
SVIDRE. A name of Odin.
SVIDRIR. A name of Odin.
SVIDUR. A name of Odin.
SVIPDAG. The betrothed of Menglad.
SVIPOL. A name of Odin.
SVOL. One of the streams flowing from Hvergelmer.
SVOLNE. A name of Odin.
SYLG. A stream flowing from Hvergelmer.
SYN. A minor goddess.
SYR. A name of Freyja.
TANGNJOST. } Thor's goats.
TANGRISNER. }
THEK. A dwarf; also a name of Odin.
THJALFE. The name of Thor's man-servant.
THJASSE. A giant; the father of Njord's wife, Skade.
THJODNUMA. One of the streams flowing from Hvergelmer.
THOK. Loke in the disguise of a woman.
THOL. One of the streams flowing from Hvergelmer.
THOR. Son of Odin and Fjorgyn. The god of thunder.
THORIN. A dwarf.
THORN. A giant.
THRIDE. A name of Odin.
THRO. A dwarf; also a name of Odin.
THROIN. A dwarf.
THROR. A name of Odin.
THRUD. A valkyrie.
THUD. A name of Odin.
THUL. A stream flowing from Hvergelmer.
THUND. A name of Odin.
THVITE. A stone used in chaining the Fenris-wolf.
THYN. One of the streams flowing from Hvergelmer.
TYR. The one-armed god of war.
UD. A name of Odin.
UKKO. The god of thunder in Tshudic mythology.
UKKO-THOR. A name for Thor.
ULLER. Son of Sif and step-son of Thor.
URD. The norn of the past.

UTGARD. The abode of the giant Utgard-Loke.

UTGARD-LOKE. A giant visited by Thor; identical with Skrymer.

VAFTHRUDNER. A giant visited by Odin.

VAFUD. A name of Odin.

VAFURLOGE. The bickering flame surrounding Brynhild on Hind-fell.

VAK. A name of Odin.

VALASKJALF. One of Odin's dwellings.

VALE. Brother of Balder; kills Hoder.

VALFATHER. A name of Odin.

VALHAL. The hall to which Odin invites those slain in battle.

VANADIS. A name of Freyja.

VANAHEIM. The home of the vans.

VAR. The goddess of betrothals and marriages.

VARTARE. The thread with which the mouth of Loke was sewed together.

VASAD. The grandfather of Winter.

VE. A brother of Odin. (Odin, Vile and Ve).

VEDFOLNER. A hawk in Ygdrasil.

VEGSVIN. One of the streams flowing from Hvergelmer.

VEGTAM. A name of Odin.

VERATYR. A name of Odin.

VERDANDE. The norn of the present.

VESTRE. A dwarf.

VID. One of the streams flowing from Hvergelmer.

VIDAR. Son of Odin and the giantess Grid.

VIDBLAIN. The third heaven.

VIDFIN. The father of Bil and Hjuke.

VIDOLF. The ancestor of the valas.

VIDRER. A name of Odin.

VIDUR. A name of Odin.

VIG. A dwarf.

VIGRID. The field of battle where the gods and the hosts of Surt meet in Ragnarok.

VILE. Brother of Odin and Ve.

VILMEIDE. The ancestor of all wizards.

VIMER. A river that Thor crosses.

VIN. A river that flows from Hvergelmer.

VINA. A river that flows from Hvergelmer.

VINDALF. A dwarf.

VINDLONG. One of the names of the father of winter.

VINDSVAL. One of the names of the father of winter.

VINGNER. A name of Thor.

VINGOLF. The palace of the asynjes.

VINGTHOR. A name of Thor.

VIRFIR. A dwarf.

VIT. A dwarf.

VOLSUNGS. The descendants of Volsung.

VON. A river formed by the saliva running from the mouth of the chained Fenris-wolf.

VOR. One of the asynjes.

WODAN. A name of Odin.

YDALER. Uller's dwelling.

YG. A name of Odin.

YGDRASIL. The world-embracing ash-tree.

YLG. One of the streams flowing from Hvergelmer.

YMER. The huge giant out of whose body the world was created.

INDEX.

BOOKS PUBLISHED BY
S. C. GRIGGS & COMPANY,
CHICAGO.

**ANDERSON—AMERICA NOT DISCOVERED BY CO-
LUMBUS.** A historical Sketch of the Discovery of America
by the Norsemen in the 10th century. By Prof. R. B. ANDER-
SON. With an Appendix on the Historical, Literary and Scientific value of the Scandinavian Languages. 12mo, cloth, $1.

" A valuable addition to American history."—*Notes and Queries*, London.

**ANDERSON—NORSE MYTHOLOGY; or, the Religion of
our Forefathers.** Containing all the Myths of the Eddas
carefully systematized and interpreted; with an Introduction,
Vocabulary and Index. By R. B. ANDERSON, Prof. of Scandinavian Languages in the University of Wisconsin. Crown 8vo,
cloth, $2.50; cloth, gilt edges, $3; half calf, $4.50.

" Prof. Anderson's work is incomparably superior to the already existing
books of this order."—*Scribner's Monthly.*

" The exposition, analysis and interpretation of the Norse Mythology leave
nothing to be desired. The whole structure and framework of the system are
here; and, in addition to this, copious literal translations from the Eddas and
Sagas show the reader something of the literary form in which the system found
permanent record. Occasionally entire songs or poems are presented, and, at
every point where they could be of service, illustrative extracts accompany the
elucidations of the text."—*Appleton's Journal.*

ANDERSON—VIKING TALES OF THE NORTH. The
Sagas of Thorstein, Viking's son, and Fridthjof the Bold. Trans-
lated from the Icelandic by Prof. R. B. ANDERSON; also TEG-
NER'S FRIDTHJOF'S SAGA, translated by GEORGE STE-
PHENS. In one volume, 12mo, cloth, $2.

" Prof. Anderson's book is a very valuable and important one."—*The Nation.*

" A charming book it is. Your work is in every way cleverly done. These
quaintly delightful sagas ought to charm many thousands of readers, and your
translation is of the best."—*Prof. Willard Fiske, Cornell University.*

BURRIS—THE TRINITY. By Rev. F. H. BURRIS. With an
Introduction by JOSEPH HAVEN, D.D., LL.D. 12mo, clo., $1.50.

" One of the most unique, sincere and thorough discussions of the subject of
the Trinity which we have ever seen."—*American Wesleyan*, New York.

CAREW—TANGLED. A Novel. By RACHEL CAREW. Square
16mo, cloth, $1.

A beautiful and sparkling tale of an Alpine watering place.

" The flirtation which gives its title to this very bright little novel is one of
the oddest, funniest and most original affairs we ever read of. We have enjoyed a very hearty laugh over the situation."—*Inter-Ocean.*

☞ *Books will be mailed postpaid on receipt of price.*

CONE—TWO YEARS IN CALIFORNIA. By M. CONE. With fifteen fine Illustrations, a map of California, and a plan of the Yosemite Valley. 12mo, cloth, $1.50.

> A thoroughly reliable book for tourists and settlers.
>
> "It abounds in information practical in character, and is stored with facts which will be new to the vast majority of our people. . . . No romance is more interesting, and no description of the book can do justice to it. Every page deserves to be read and studied."—*Albany Evening Journal.*

DEMENT—INGERSOLL, BEECHER AND DOGMA; or a Few Simple Truths and their Logical Deductions, in which the Positions of Mr. Ingersoll and Mr. Beecher are Considered. By R. S. DEMENT. 12mo, cloth, $1.

> "Mr. Dement's trenchant diction is well matched by his potent logic. He has written an earnest, honest, hearty and healthy book for the times."—*The Standard,* Chicago.

FAWCETT—GOLD AND DEBT. An American Hand-Book of Finance, with over Eighty Tables and Diagrams. By W. L. FAWCETT. 12mo, cloth, $1.75.

> "Of interest to the general reader, and quite invaluable to the banker and man of public life. . . . To those who want a handy volume of reference upon these important subjects, we can recommend this work."—*The Banker and Tradesman,* Boston.
>
> "As a full and very complete collection of monetary statistics this work has never been equaled or even approached. It is a storehouse of facts."—*The Philadelphia Press.*

FOSTER—PRE-HISTORIC RACES OF THE UNITED STATES. By J. W. FOSTER, LL.D. Crown 8vo. Illustrated. Cloth, $3; half-calf, gilt top, $5; full calf, gilt edges, $6.50.

> "It is full of interest from beginning to end."—*Popular Science Monthly.*
>
> "This book is literally crowded with astonishing and valuable facts."—*Boston Post.*
>
> "One of the best and clearest accounts we have seen of those grand monuments of a forgotten race."—*The Saturday Review,* London.

FORESTIER—ECHOES FROM MIST-LAND; or, The Nibelungen Lay revealed to Lovers of Romance and Chivalry. By AUBER FORESTIER. 12mo, cloth, $1.50.

> "The simplicity and directness of the ancient chronicle are admirably preserved in the version, and the work forms a unique addition to our store of sterling fiction."—*New York Home Journal.*
>
> "The Introduction traces the history of the legend, and its connection with the Indian myths and Norse legends, besides giving a large amount of information with respect to the Pagan mythology of our Teutonic ancestors."—*Boston Evening Traveller.*
>
> "The great epic poem of those early days of chivalry and knightly valor, the Nibelungen Lay, is opened to us in a rehearsal of the weird and fascinating story in clear and flowing English."—*Lutheran Quarterly Review.*

HOLCOMB—FRIDTHJOF'S SAGA. A Norse Romance. By ESAIAS TEGNÉR, Bishop of Wexio. Translated from the Swedish by THOMAS A. E. and MARTHA A. LYON HOLCOMB. 12mo, cloth, $1.50.

> "The translation is exceedingly well done. . . . This is not the first attempt to reproduce Tegnér's famous work in English, but we believe it to be quite the most successful."—*Harper's Magazine.*

> "No one can peruse this noble poem without arising therefrom with a loftier idea of human bravery and a better conception of human love."—*Inter-Ocean*, Chicago.

> "Wherever one opens the poem he is sure to light upon passages of exquisite beauty. Longfellow styles it the noblest poetic contribution which Sweden has yet made to the literary history of the world."—*Church Journal*, New York.

HUDSON—LAW FOR THE CLERGY. A compilation of the Statutes of the States of Illinois, Indiana, Iowa, Michigan, Minnesota, Ohio and Wisconsin, relating to the duties of Clergymen in the solemnization of Marriage, the organization of Churches and Religious Societies, and the protection of Religious Meetings and Assemblies; with notes and practical forms, embracing a collation of the Common Law of Marriage. By SANFORD A. HUDSON. 16mo, cloth, $1.

> "It contains what every preacher should have. It is a safe guide in securing deeds and titles to property, to churches, etc."—*Religious Telescope*, Dayton.

> "Every Western minister should have it. Its value to those for whom it is especially designed must be apparent at a glance."—*The Standard*, Chicago.

JONES—THE MYTH OF STONE IDOL. An Indian Love Legend of Dakota. By WILLIAM P. JONES, A.M. 1 vol. small 4to, handsomely bound, $1.

> "We read it through, beguiled by its melodious lines and the pathos of its simple tale. Its descriptions are fine pictures."—*Zion's Herald*, Boston.

KIPPAX—CHURCHYARD LITERATURE. A choice collection of American Epitaphs, with remarks on Monumental Inscriptions and the Obsequies of various nations. By JOHN R. KIPPAX, LL.D. 12mo, cloth, $1.50.

> "A collection remarkable for quaintness and eccentricity."—*N. Y. Daily Tribune.*

> "A volume both instructive and amusing, which will amply repay perusal."—*N. Y. Graphic.*

LIE—THE PILOT AND HIS WIFE. A Norse Love Story. By JONAS LIE. Translated by MRS. OLE BULL. cloth, $1.50.

> "Most absorbingly interesting. . . . In realism, picturesqueness and psychological insight, 'The Pilot and His Wife' leaves very little to be desired. Every one of the dramatis personæ is boldly conceived and elaborated with great skill. We have none of the stale repetitions of the usual well-worn characters of fiction, which is indeed no mean praise. . . . A delightful and entertaining book."—*Scribner's Monthly.*

MATHEWS—GETTING ON IN THE WORLD; or, Hints on Success in Life. By WILLIAM MATHEWS, LL.D. 1 vol. 12mo, cloth, $2; the same, gilt edges, $2.50; half calf, gilt top, $3.50; full calf, gilt edges, $5.

"As a work of art, it is a gem. As a counselor, it speaks the wisdom of the ages. As a teacher, it illustrates the true philosophy of life by the experience of eminent men of every class and calling. It warns by the story of signal failures, and encourages by the record of triumphs that seemed impossible. It is a book of facts and not of theories. The men who have succeeded in life are laid under tribute and made to divulge the secret of their success. They give vastly more than ' hints '—they make a revelation."—*Christian Era*, Boston.

MATHEWS—THE GREAT CONVERSERS, and Other Essays. By WILLIAM MATHEWS, LL.D. 12mo, cloth, $1.75.

"These pages are crammed with interesting facts about literary men and literary work."—*New York Evening Mail.*

"One will make the acquaintance of more authors in the course of a single one of his essays than are probably to be met with in the same limited space anywhere else in the whole realm of our literature."—*Chicago Tribune.*

MATHEWS—WORDS, THEIR USE AND ABUSE. By WILLIAM MATHEWS, LL.D. 12mo, cloth, $2.

"We heartily recommend the work as rich in valuable suggestions to those who desire to cultivate accuracy in speaking and writing."—*The Lutheran Quarterly Review.*

"It can be read with profit by every intelligent student of the English language."—*The International Review*, New York.

MATHEWS—HOURS WITH MEN AND BOOKS. By WILLIAM MATHEWS, LL.D. 1 vol. 12mo, cloth, $2.

"The elder Disraeli has certainly found a worthy successor in the present writer."—*New York Tribune.*

"A rare *entrepot* of information conveyed in a style at once easy, lucid and elegant. Any one desirous of cultivating an acquaintance with the leading thinkers and actors of all ages, and to have in a compendious form intelligent opinions on their lives and works, will find herein the result of deep research and sound reflection."—*Sheffield Post*, England.

MATHEWS—MONDAY-CHATS. By C. A. SAINTE-BEUVE. With an Introductory Essay on his life and writings by the translator, WILLIAM MATHEWS, LL.D. 12mo, cloth, $2.

"The translation is excellent throughout."—*New York Evening Post.*

"No essays of the kind in modern literature are superior, if equal, to these masterly portraitures, in which philosophy and elegance are happily combined."—*Boston Daily Globe.*

"It is not too much to say that the ' Introductory Essay ' is one of the best pieces of literary criticism in American literature."—*Utica Morning Herald.*

"To the man of letters this book will be a delight; to the general reader a charming recreation; to the student a model of taste and culture."—*Boston Christian Register.*

MATHEWS—ORATORY AND ORATORS. By WILLIAM
MATHEWS, LL.D. 1 vol. 12mo, cloth, $2.

MILLER—WHAT TOMMY DID. By EMILY HUNTINGTON
MILLER. Illustrated. 16mo, paper covers, 50 cents; cloth, $1.

"If there is any other way in which fifty cents will purchase as much sus-
tained and healthful amusement as is offered by this little book we should be
glad to know it."—*John Habberton, in the Christian Union.*

"We laughed all the evening over the many funny things Tommy said and
did. . . . We will warrant that no one, young or old, will lay it down until
read through."—*Northern Christian Advocate.*

MISHAPS OF MR. EZEKIEL PELTER. Illustrated. $1.50.

"Immensely amusing."—*Boston Commonwealth.*

"If it be your desire 'to laugh and grow fat,' you will find The Mishaps of
Ezekiel Pelter a great help."—*American Christian Review*, Cincinnati.

**ROBERT—RULES OF ORDER, for Deliberative Assem-
blies.** By MAJOR HENRY M. ROBERT, Corps of Engineers,
U. S. A. Pocket size. Cloth, 75 cents.

"Robert's Rules of Order is a capital little book. I have given it a very
critical examination. . . . For general use and application, I regard it the
best book extant."—*Hon. James W. Husted, Speaker of the New York State
Legislature.*

"It is just such a guide as is needed by all presiding officers. . . . The table
of rules relating to motions, and the cross references, which enable any one to
find almost instantly anything in the book, give it almost inestimable value."—
New York Christian Advocate.

SMITH—PATMOS; or, The Kingdom and the Patience.
By J. A. SMITH, D.D., Editor of *The Standard.* Cloth, $1.25.

"No one can read the nine chapters which this volume contains without
receiving a new inspiration to faithful service in the cause of Christ."—*Zion's
Advocate.*

TAYLOR—BETWEEN THE GATES. By BENJ. F. TAYLOR,
Author of "The World on Wheels," etc. etc. 12mo, cloth. Illustrated. $1.50.

"The light, feathery sketches in this volume glitter with all the colors of the
rainbow and sparkle with the reflection of the morning dew. The reader of
imagination and taste will delight in the subtle alchemy which transmutes gold
into beauty, and changes the facts of common life into ideal visions. Mr.
Taylor detects the enchantments of poetry in the most prosaic experiences, and
the dusty highways of life are refreshed with the waters of Siloam, and bloom
with the flowers of paradise."—*New York Tribune.*

"A series of verbal photographs of California characters and scenery that are
exceedingly graphic, poetic and entertaining. . . . Picturesque and romantic
in style, yet altogether accurate in fact."—*Episcopal Register*, Philadelphia.

"Lively as a novel and accurate as a guide book."—*Philadelphia Press.*

TAYLOR—IN CAMP AND FIELD. By BENJ. F. TAYLOR. 12mo, cloth, $1.50.

"Each of these sketches is a gem in itself. One may search the annals of war from Tacitus to Kinglake and not find anything finer."—*Inter-Ocean.*

"The description of Hooker's battle 'above the clouds' is one of the grandest pieces of word-painting in the English language."—*Peoria Transcript.*

TAYLOR—OLD-TIME PICTURES AND SHEAVES OF RHYME. By BENJ. F. TAYLOR. Illustrated, small quarto, silk cloth, price $1.50; the same, full gilt edges and side, $1.75.

"I do not know of any one who so well reproduces the home scenes of long ago."—*John G. Whittier.*

TAYLOR—THE WORLD ON WHEELS, and Other Sketches. By BENJ. F. TAYLOR. Illustrated. 12mo, clo., $1.50.

"One of the most elegant, as well as pungent and rich, specimens of wit and humor extant."—*New York Illustrated Weekly.*

"Brings you very near to nature and life in their pleasantest moods wherever you may happen to be."—*E. P. Whipple, Esq., in the Boston Globe.*

"Few equal Mr. Taylor as a word painter. He fascinates with his artistic touches, and exhilarates with his sparkling humor, and subdues with his sweet pathos. His sentences glisten like gems in the sunlight."—*Albany Journal.*

TAYLOR—SONGS OF YESTERDAY. By BENJ. F. TAYLOR. Beautifully illustrated. Octavo, with handsomely ornamented cover in black and gold. Full gilt edges, $3; morocco, $6.

"The volume is magnificently gotten up. . . . There is a simplicity, a tenderness and a pathos, intermingled always with a quiet humor, about his writings which is inexpressibly charming. Some of his earlier poems have become classic, and many of those in the present volume are destined to as wide a popularity as Longfellow's 'Village Blacksmith' or Whittier's 'Maud Müller.'"—*Boston Transcript.*

WALKER—PHILOSOPHY OF THE PLAN OF SALVATION. By J. B. WALKER, D.D. With an Introductory Essay by CALVIN E. STOWE, D.D. 12mo, cloth, $1.50.

"We think it more likely to lodge an impression in the human conscience in favor of the divine authority of Christianity than any other work of the modern press."—*London Evangelical Magazine,* England.

WALKER—THE DOCTRINE OF THE HOLY SPIRIT; or, Philosophy of the Divine Operation In the Redemption of Man, being volume second of "Philosophy of the Plan of Salvation." By Rev. JAMES B. WALKER, D.D. 12mo, cloth, $1.50.

"*Every minister and teacher should arm himself with strong weapons by* perusing the arguments of this book."—*Methodist Recorder,* Pittsburg.

"Of unanswerable force and extraordinary interest."—*New York Evangelist.*

TEXT-BOOKS — RETAIL PRICES.

BACON — A MANUAL OF GESTURE. With 100 Figures, embracing a complete System of Notation, with the Principles of Interpretation, and Selections for Practice. By Prof. A. M. BACON. 12mo, cloth, $1.50.

"The work comprehends all that is valuable upon the subject of gesture."— *R. L. Cumnock, Professor of Elocution, Northwestern University.*

BOISE — FIRST LESSONS IN GREEK. Adapted to Goodwin's, to Hadley's Larger and Smaller Greek Grammars, and intended as an Introduction to Xenophon's Anabasis. By JAMES R. BOISE, Ph.D. 12mo, half leather, $1.25.

"It is an admirable guide to the learner, and will teach the inexperienced teacher how to teach in the best way. I like the book better than any other manual for beginners I have seen, and I have seen most, and used several different ones in teaching."—*Prof. H. F. Fisk, Northwestern University, Ill.*

BOISE — HOMER'S ILIAD. The First Six Books of Homer's Iliad; with Explanatory Notes, intended for beginners in the Epic dialect; accompanied with numerous References to Goodwin's, to Hadley's Greek Grammar, to Kühner's Larger Greek Grammar and Goodwin's Moods and Tenses. By J. R. BOISE, Ph.D. 12mo, cloth, $1.50.

"Incomparably superior to any other edition of Homer ever published in this country."—*M. L. D'Ooge, Ph.D., Professor of Greek, University of Michigan.*

BOISE — EXERCISES IN GREEK SYNTAX. Being Exercises in some of the more difficult Principles of Greek Syntax; with References to the Grammars of Crosby, Curtius, Goodwin, Hadley, Koch and Kühner. A Sequel to "Jones's Exercises in Greek Prose Composition," and intended for the First Year in College. By JAMES R. BOISE, Ph.D. 12mo, half leather, $1.50.

"'Prof. Jones's Exercises' and 'Dr. Boise's Exercises in Greek Syntax' are a vast improvement upon ....'s books on Prose Composition. I like much the principles upon which they are constructed. . . . The two works taken together constitute an apparatus which is unsurpassed, or rather, if I mistake not, unequaled, for the acquisition of a thorough and familiar acquaintance with Greek forms."—*Henry M. Baird, Ph.D., Prof. of Greek Language and Literature, University of the City of New York.*

BOISE & FREEMAN — SELECTIONS FROM VARIOUS GREEK AUTHORS. For the First Year in College; with Explanatory Notes and References to Goodwin's Greek Grammar, and to Hadley's Larger and Smaller Grammars. By JAMES R. BOISE, Ph.D., and J. C. FREEMAN, M.A. 12mo, cloth, $2.

"I found the book so admirable in the matter selected, in the soundness and accuracy of the annotations, and in the unusual excellence of the press-work, that I could not do otherwise than urge its adoption, and my high opinion of the book has been corroborated by daily use."—*A. H. Buck, A.M., Prof. of Greek, Boston University.*

D'OOGE—DEMOSTHENES ON THE CROWN. With Extracts from the Oration of Æschines against Ctesiphon, and Explanatory Notes. By M. L. D'OOGE, Ph.D., Professor of Greek, University of Michigan. 12mo, cloth, $1.75.

"I have examined it again and again, and am better satisfied with it than any other text-book on The Crown I have seen. I shall therefore use it in preference to all others."—*Prof. R. B. Youngman, LaFayette College.*

JONES—EXERCISES IN GREEK PROSE COMPOSITION. With References to Hadley's, Goodwin's and Taylor's-Kühner's Greek Grammars, and a full English-Greek Vocabulary. By Prof. ELISHA JONES, Univ. of Michigan. 12mo, $1.

"No better exercises can be found for classes in Greek Prose Composition, whether in college or the preparatory school."—*From Edward North, L.H.D., Professor of Greek, Hamilton College, N.Y.*

JONES—FIRST LESSONS IN LATIN. Adapted to the Latin Grammars of Allen & Greenough, Andrews & Stoddard, Bartholomew, Bullions & Morris, Gildersleeve and Harkness, and prepared as an Introduction to Cæsar's Commentaries on the Gallic War. By ELISHA JONES, Professor in the University of Michigan. 12mo, cloth, $1.50.

"I do not know of a better drill book for classical schools to prepare the way for the reading of Cæsar and to lay the foundation of a very thorough and accurate scholarship in Latin."—*Prof. E. P. Crowell, Amherst College.*

PETERSON—NORWEGIAN-DANISH GRAMMAR AND READER. With a Vocabulary, designed for American Students of the Norwegian-Danish language. By Prof. C. I. P. PETERSON, 12mo, cloth, $1.25.

"I rejoice to see the door opened to American students to the treasures of Norwegian letters, and in so attractive a manner as in Mr. Peterson's book."—*F. Sewell, President of Urbana University.*

STEVENS—SELECT ORATIONS OF LYSIAS. With Introductions and Explanatory Notes. By W. A. STEVENS, Professor of Greek, Denison University, Ohio. 12mo, cloth, $1.50.

"A valuable contribution to our college text-books and ought to be most cordially welcomed."—*W. W. Goodwin, Ph.D., Prof. of Greek, Harvard College.*

THOMPSON—FIRST LATIN BOOK. Introductory to Cæsar's Commentaries. By D. G. THOMPSON, A.M. 12mo, $1.50.

"The plan is thoroughly excellent, the execution of it in all points admirable."—*Thomas Chase, Professor of Philology, Haverford College.*

ZUR BRUCKE—GERMAN WITHOUT GRAMMAR OR DICTIONARY; According to the Pestalozzian method of teaching by Object Lessons. 12mo, cloth back, 50 cents.

"By far the best method to enable pupils to acquire familiarity with a language and readiness in speaking it."—*Boston Commonwealth.*